"You okay, princess?"

Jonah threw the words over his shoulder as he set a swift pace through the trees that lined the creek.

"I've been better," she mumbled against his back. "I'm sorry I'm responsible for getting you shot at during your vacation."

She shivered as the remnants of icy fear spiraled through her body.

To her stunned amazement, Jonah leaned toward her to kiss her squarely on the mouth. His scorching kiss caused an explosion of her senses and sent hot sensations sizzling through her body. Maddie was still savoring the taste of his full, sensuous lips—and the delicious feelings he aroused—when he withdrew abruptly. Bewildered, she licked her lips and stared goggle-eyed at him.

Then, in a gruff voice that was a direct contradiction to the passionate kiss he'd just bestowed on her, he asked, "Do I have your attention now, princess?"

* * *

Texas Bride
Harlequin Historical #711—July 2004

Praise for Carol Finch

"Carol Finch is known for her lightning-fast,
roller-coaster-ride adventure romances
that are brimming over with a large cast of characters
and dozens of perilous escapades."
—*Romantic Times*

Praise for previous titles

Bounty Hunter's Bride
"Longtime Carol Finch fans…
will be more than satisfied."
—*Romantic Times*

Call of the White Wolf
"The wholesome goodness of the characters…
will touch your heart and soul."
—*Rendezvous*

"A love story that aims straight for the heart
and never misses."
—*Romantic Times*

CAROL
FINCH

TEXAS
BRIDE

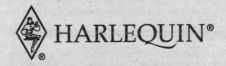

TORONTO • NEW YORK • LONDON
AMSTERDAM • PARIS • SYDNEY • HAMBURG
STOCKHOLM • ATHENS • TOKYO • MILAN • MADRID
PRAGUE • WARSAW • BUDAPEST • AUCKLAND

ISBN 0-373-29311-9

TEXAS BRIDE

Copyright © 2004 by Connie Feddersen

This edition published by arrangement with Harlequin Books S.A.

® and TM are trademarks of the publisher. Trademarks indicated with ® are registered in the United States Patent and Trademark Office, the Canadian Trade Marks Office and in other countries.

www.eHarlequin.com

Printed in U.S.A.

Please address questions and book requests to:
Harlequin Reader Service
U.S.: 3010 Walden Ave., P.O. Box 1325, Buffalo, NY 14269
Canadian: P.O. Box 609, Fort Erie, Ont. L2A 5X3

This book is dedicated to my husband, Ed,
and our children—Jill, Christie, Kurt, Jeff, Jon
and Shawnna. And to our grandchildren, Kennedy,
Blake, Brooklynn and Livia. Hugs and kisses!

Chapter One

Coyote Springs, Texas, 1880

Jonah Danhill eased his injured left shoulder against the edge of the bathtub and sighed heavily. After spending eight grueling months with his company of Texas Rangers battling Mexican cattle thieves near the Rio Grande, he was more than ready for this hiatus. The gunshot wound he'd sustained had earned him a month of rest and relaxation. Jonah couldn't remember the last time he didn't have somewhere he needed to be—immediately. It felt good to have time to himself instead of spending night and day tracking criminals and remaining on constant guard to ensure he didn't get his head blown off.

He glanced at the mending wound on his arm and smiled wryly. Could've been his head—the bullet had come damn close.

Jonah surveyed his bare torso to note the scars that were souvenirs of his death-defying battles against the worst elements of society. He definitely needed to associate with a better class of people. The ones he dealt with on a daily basis kept trying to kill him. But then, he reminded himself as he reached out to grab a cheroot, even regular folks were twitchy about associating with half-breeds.

Arms and legs draped over the rim of a bathtub way too small to accommodate his six-feet-two-inch frame, Jonah lit the cheroot, then took a drink of whiskey. While blowing lopsided smoke rings in the air he assessed his lot in life and decided he was probably destined to ride with the Rangers until a well-aimed bullet caught up with him. There was nothing to do but enjoy and appreciate his recuperation before riding back to the Rio Grande to track down another gang of desperadoes.

This was his life, he mused cynically. He was stuck with it so he might as well accept the fact that his worth was measured by how well he served and defended folks who were incapable of protecting themselves from murderers, rustlers and thieves.

Lifting the whiskey bottle, Jonah took another drink. "To life," he mumbled sardonically. "Fool that I am, I expect more from it. If the Hereafter isn't an improvement I'm sure as hell gonna be disappointed."

Jonah set aside the whiskey, clamped the smoking cigar between his teeth and grabbed the bar of soap. He'd just gotten himself all lathered up when the door flew open and a woman barged in unexpectedly. A wild tangle of curly golden-brown hair billowed around the woman's face—a bewitching face that flamed with embarrassment when she noticed Jonah's naked form sprawled in the tub. The private parts of his anatomy were concealed in sudsy water, but everything else was there for her to see. And she looked her fill, he noted.

Although her face blazed like a torch, she shook her finger at him. "Don't you dare tell the two men chasing after me that I'm here," she ordered hurriedly.

And then, to Jonah's amazement, the woman dived under his bed and curled up in a tight ball in the shadowy corner.

"What in the hell—?" Jonah grumbled around the cheroot that was still clamped between his teeth.

An abrupt knock rattled his door. Without awaiting an invitation, two men filled the entrance.

"Shut the damn door!" Jonah barked gruffly. "I'm bathing!"

The two men—cowboys, Jonah presumed—closed the door behind them. Colorful bandannas encircled their necks and rawhide vests covered their faded shirts. Holsters, equipped with well-used six-shooters, rode low on the men's hips.

"We're looking for a woman," one of them announced. "She stole money from us in Fort Worth and we followed her to Coyote Springs."

"We thought we saw her come in here," the other added as his assessing gaze panned the crudely furnished room.

"There's no one here but me, and I plan to keep it that way." Cautious by nature and by habit, Jonah reached down with his left hand to grab the Colt revolver that was concealed behind the bathtub. During his thirty years of existence he'd learned never to go anywhere or do anything without keeping his pistol within easy reach. "You're intruding," he snapped ominously. "Now get out. If I'd wanted an audience while I bathed I'd have sold tickets."

"Are you sure you haven't seen…?" The cowboy's gravelly voice trailed off when Jonah's pistol suddenly appeared. The deadly click of the trigger filled the silence.

"Out!" Jonah thundered in his most intimidating voice.

He continued to give the cowboys the evil eye until they'd backed from the room and shut the door. When the woman tried to wriggle out from under the bed Jonah made a slashing gesture with his good arm, demanding that she stay put until the two sets of footsteps faded into the distance.

When the coast was clear Maddie Garret came to her feet and willfully battled down the blush that left her face throbbing in rhythm with her pulse. Although her admiring gaze kept drifting up and down Jonah's brawny body, she jerked her attention to the shaggy black hair that framed his rugged face. His bronzed skin, high cheekbones and chiseled features indicated Indian heritage, but his eyes were a startling shade of green and they showed curiosity and mistrust. It was difficult to maintain her composure while he kept his six-shooter pointed directly at her chest.

Six months earlier Maddie would have turned tail and run from such an awkward situation, and likely burst into tears after such a harrowing day. But she'd been tested repeatedly and forced to face one difficult situation after another. In addition, she was in need of immediate assistance and this man was the only person she could come remotely close to trusting.

"I'm dreadfully sorry about this interruption," she blurted out. "But I need your help."

He snorted and narrowed those intense green eyes at her. The smoke from his cigar drooped around his dark head like a fallen halo. This hard-edged law officer didn't seem the least bit receptive or interested in her problems. She wasn't sure what she'd expected from a member of the legendary Texas Rangers, but Jonah Danhill wasn't it. Even unclothed he looked invincible, intimidating and unapproachable. Yet he was the most magnificent study of masculinity that she'd ever laid eyes on and she couldn't help but be fascinated by him.

"My name is Maddie Garret," she said, introducing herself nervously. "And I most certainly did *not* steal money from those two men. *They* are trying to steal money from *me!*"

Her comment drew very little reaction from the powerfully built man sprawled in the tub. When Maddie's betraying gaze darted to the sudsy water that concealed his hips, her face went up in flames—again. Damnation, it was humiliating enough to plead her cause, but pleading to a naked man whose physical attributes kept distracting her—to the extreme—was even worse. She couldn't help but admire the rippling muscles, sleek contours and dark skin that glistened with water droplets.

Maddie gave herself a mental slap for gawking, grabbed a quick breath and hurried on. "I heard you were a Texas Ranger so I came to find you, hoping for your protection." She shifted uneasily from one foot to the other and stared over his head—anywhere except at that incredibly masculine body. "The hotel proprietor refused to give me your room number because he knew that you didn't want to be disturbed.'' Her gaze darted to Jonah momentarily, then skittered away once more. ''With those two men hot on my heels I was frantic to find a safe haven—and I needed to find one fast. I told the proprietor that I was your wife and if anyone was allowed to disturb you then it definitely should be me.''

Jonah's dark brows nearly rocketed off his forehead. He sucked in his breath so abruptly that he choked on cigar smoke. *''My wife?''* he wheezed incredulously.

''I was desperate,'' she said righteously. ''I made a hasty trip from my West Texas ranch to Fort Worth to request a loan against my trust fund. My inheritance won't be available until my twenty-first birthday. I can't wait another three months to gain control of the money, because my younger sister has been kidnapped and she's being held for ransom.''

''Kidnapped?'' Jonah parroted as he surveyed the attractive female standing before him.

She reminded him of a pagan goddess in living flesh. Her pale yellow gown accentuated her feminine curves and swells. Golden highlights glinted in her hair. Amber shimmered in her thick-lashed eyes. The texture of her skin reminded him of honey. Jonah had seen a few strikingly attractive women in his time, but this female *radiated* beauty, spirit and determination, and his body involuntarily responded to the appealing sight of her. Jonah was damn glad the sudsy water concealed his stirring arousal.

Although it was obvious that Maddie was uncomfortable carrying on a conversation with a naked man, she seemed to be on an unswerving mission to present her side of the story.

"Yes, kidnapped," Maddie confirmed as she began to pace restlessly. "Christina is fifteen years old and I'm sure she must be terrified by this ordeal. Worse, she is uncommonly attractive and I fear she will be set upon by the band of cattle thieves who spirited her away."

Maddie halted abruptly and glanced in his direction. "Evidence indicates that renegade Comanches have escaped from their reservation and have returned to their former homeland to raid, rustle and terrorize ranchers. If I don't pay the ransom within a week I might never see Christina again. I'm in urgent need of your help."

Jonah inwardly winced when she mentioned the Comanche. Fifteen years earlier he had lived with his father's people in West Texas—before the land was taken from the Indians and opened for settlement. Because of his bitter past Jonah had refused to take arms against his people in that part of the state. Aware of his mixed heritage, Jonah's commander had not forced him to patrol the area. Instead, Jonah had been sent to subdue white outlaws and Mexican desperadoes who stole Texas cattle and drove them south of the border.

The very last thing Jonah wanted was to revisit his old stomping grounds and stir up bittersweet memories.

"Not interested," he said abruptly. "I'm in town to recuperate from an injury." He directed her attention to his mending shoulder. "I'm taking a long-awaited furlough. You need to speak with the sheriff who has jurisdiction in the county where your ranch is located.''

Her luminous eyes threw off molten sparks. ''I have to cross a wild frontier, carrying a considerable amount of money, to even *get* the opportunity to *ask* for the sheriff's assistance,'' she countered irritably. ''Reaching Fort Worth unscathed was difficult enough. Returning home will be worse because I'll have those two thieves breathing down my neck.''

''If they *are* actually thieves.'' Jonah smirked skeptically. ''I've been around long enough to know better than to be taken in by a pretty face and a wild tale of kidnapping, rustling and robbery.'' He rinsed the soap from his arms and chest, then puffed on his cheroot. ''Now, make yourself scarce, Miz Garret. I'd like to get dressed.''

She tilted her chin to a defiant angle, braced her fists on her shapely hips and said, ''I am *not* leaving this room until you promise to help me rescue my sister from death—or worse. You have an obligation as a ranger to aid and protect citizens in need.''

She was stubborn and determined, he'd give her that. But who was to say *which* side of the law she was really on?

''Lady,'' he retaliated gruffly, ''I don't get paid enough to go haring off to West Texas with a mending arm. Besides, I've learned to take nothing at face value. Why should I protect a woman who has been accused of theft? And why should I believe a female who is probably feeding me a wild tale to prey on my sympathy?''

''Because I'm an innocent victim! I will *pay* you

to escort me home and deliver the ransom,'' she insisted sharply.

His bathwater was getting cold, but her temper was getting hot, he noticed as she glowered, trying to scare him into submission. Before he could reject her request again—and he certainly intended to—she flounced on his bed, jerked up her skirt and tugged at the hem.

Jonah gaped at her well-shaped bare legs and silky skin for a long, appreciative moment before he forced his attention to the bundles of paper currency she had stitched into her skirt. He nearly swallowed his cigar when she stamped over to the tub, grabbed his hand and slapped a bundle of money onto his palm.

''It appears that the only way to gain your trust is to pay you up front,'' she muttered angrily. She dropped the remainder of the bundles atop the stack in his hand. ''I am entrusting my inheritance to you, as well. If I wind up dead—and with two thieves on my trail that is certainly a possibility—I expect you to rescue my sister. Surely even the meager amount of sympathy and conscience you possess won't allow you to ignore the welfare and safety of a terrified girl!''

When Maddie whirled toward the door, Jonah reflexively came to his feet. ''Wait just a damn minute, lady. I've been saving lives left and right for a decade—''

She whipped her head around—to fling a sassy retort, no doubt—and saw Jonah standing there in all his splendor and glory. Her face exploded with color as she gasped for breath, shrieked, then lunged for the door.

Her departure was as spectacular as her grand entrance had been. She was gone as quickly as she had intruded into his room and into his life. Thank goodness.

Jonah chuckled in amusement. If he'd known that unintentionally exposing himself would have gotten rid of her so quickly he would have stood up earlier.

Dripping wet, he stared down at the small fortune curled in his fist. If handing him money was supposed to be a gesture of faith, he still wasn't buying it. He was a man who did not trust easily. Those who did usually wound up dead and buried. For all he knew Maddie Garret was one hell of an actress, willing to do and say anything to ensure *her* protection and *his* cooperation. Even if it meant giving a melodramatic performance and leaving him holding what could very well be stolen money.

"Damn." Jonah scowled. "And all I had asked of the first day of my recuperation was a nap, a bath and a meal that didn't resemble trail rations."

While it was true that finding sexual gratification was also on his agenda, he hadn't expected to have a supposed *wife* barrel into his room. Not that he would mind a tumble with that disturbingly attractive female, but he'd be damned if he'd pay for it by being manipulated, betrayed and maybe murdered in his sleep. Maddie Garret, he predicted, would bring him nothing but trouble. Jonah had endured more than his fair share of it, thank you very much.

He hurriedly dried off, then pulled a clean set of clothes from his saddlebag. He rolled his dirty laundry around the bundles of money, crammed them in his leather pouch and stuffed it under the mattress.

For a few moments he contemplated the impulsive urge to turn his back on his profession, ride off to buy himself a few acres in an isolated area of Texas and avoid the complications of so-called civilization.

It was a tempting thought.

After a decade of battling cutthroats and inclement weather he was burned out and fed up with being a guardian angel for folks who wouldn't give him the time of day if he weren't saving their incompetent necks.

Jonah had volunteered to join the Texas Rangers for two reasons—one idealistic and one realistic. Given his mixed heritage, it wasn't easy to find work, and the Rangers were anxious to recruit sharpshooting survivalists who had few obligations that tied them down. In addition, Jonah had been taught to respect the fearless battalions of Rangers who had become the epitome of law enforcement on the frontier.

It was said that Rangers could ride like Mexicans, track like Indians, shoot like mountain men and fight like the very devil. The Mexicans referred to them as *Tejanos Diablos*—Texas devils—and the Comanches held a grudging respect for them.

When Jonah was a young warrior of twelve his father had led him through some rugged terrain and told him to observe the impressive tactics of the Rangers. Jonah had watched and learned that day when outnumbered Rangers had pitted themselves against ruthless outlaws that preyed on Indians and whites alike. To his amazement, the courageous Rangers had won a decisive battle. The small battalion of hard-bitten, eagle-eyed crack shots had stared death in the face with fearless defiance and charged full steam ahead.

''Rangers don't fight like white men,'' Jonah's father had said. ''More like Comanches. They make dangerous enemies. Never forget that.''

The incident had made a strong and lasting impression on Jonah.

Jonah strapped on his holster, tucked a dagger in his boot—and one in his shirtsleeve—and wondered as he had before if his departed father would be pleased to know his son had become a Texas devil. For certain, his father would be relieved to know that Jonah had not been confined to the hated reservation, forced to depend on the army to feed and clothe him, and left with his pride in tatters.

Guilt slammed into him, as it did on too many occasions. He was free to choose his profession, while his oppressed people were left to the mercy of the government and the army.

Frustration and resentment put him in a sour mood. Jonah strode over to chug a drink of whiskey. He couldn't help his vanquished people any more than he could change his mixed heritage. Life, he'd discovered, wasn't a damn bit fair. But a man had to play the hand fate dealt him. Jonah had cheated death several times and counted himself lucky to be in one piece—more or less.

He stepped into the hall and locked the door behind him. If he'd thought to do that before he'd trudged wearily up the steps and collapsed in exhaustion, he could have avoided Maddie Garret's unwanted intrusion. Now he was stuck with her money. He was certain he hadn't seen the last of that animated and highly articulate female.

The answer was still no, he decided. Maddie could find herself another guardian and protector. Jonah inhaled a deep breath and exhaled slowly as he ambled down the hall. Maybe a decent meal would relieve his black mood. He'd be damned if he'd spend this hiatus sulking, wishing there was more to life than what he'd gotten. For sure, he was going to find a willing female who cared more about a few moments of pleasure than she did about the color of his skin. As long as the room was dark it didn't matter who appeased a man or woman's needs. Only that both walked away satisfied.

He set his mind on forgetting that the feisty Maddie Garret existed, but even as he crossed the street to enter the barbershop, a beguiling vision loomed large in his mind. He wondered where she was, wondered if she was concocting another fantastic tale of woe to feed some unsuspecting pigeon that might be lured in by her arresting beauty and her sharp intelligence.

She was probably devising a scheme to steal more money to add to the stash of cash she'd thrust at Jonah for safekeeping. If Maddie Garret turned out to be a shyster and con artist, he would derive tremendous pleasure in herding her to jail.

Furthermore, he didn't approve of the way his body reacted to her, didn't appreciate the immediate physical attraction. It made him feel vulnerable and defensive. She was a distraction of the worst sort. Jonah refused to get involved because he doubted she was telling him the whole truth—and nothing but.

The sooner she left town the happier Jonah would be.

* * *

Maddie crawled beneath the loose boards near the foundation of the livery stable, then sank down beside her satchel. Legs drawn up, she rested her elbows on her knees and covered her flushed face with her hands. Seeing Jonah Danhill rise from the tub like a mystical Greek god had shattered her composure completely. She was certain the sight of his muscular body would be emblazoned on her mind for all eternity.

How could she ever gaze at him again without remembering the way he looked naked? But she *had* to confront him again, because she had left the ransom money in his care.

Inhaling a bracing breath, Maddie glanced around the shadowy confines of the livery. She suspected she wasn't the first unfortunate soul who had taken refuge here.

Her stomach growled, reminding her that she hadn't eaten since she had stepped down from the coach and dined at the crude stage station west of Fort Worth the previous afternoon. The meal had been inedible and the companionship lousy. The threat of those two men hovering around like vultures, waiting to separate her from her money, had kept her in a nervous state of constant alert.

Maddie marshaled her resolve by reminding herself that her fear and frustration were nothing compared to the frightening nightmare Christina was enduring. Her sister was all the family she had left in this world, and despite the disheartening obstacles in her path, Maddie vowed to stand strong.

Even while the noble thought blazed through her mind, she felt her body slump in exhaustion. She had been operating on raw nerves for days on end. It would have been so easy to throw up her hands in defeat and fall apart, right where she sat. But her concern for Christina refused to allow her to give up this crusade. Her sister was counting on her.

Hold your head up high, daughter, her father used to say. *Garrets don't mope around with their chins scraping their chests. No one promised life would be easy. You just keep placing one foot in front of the other and don't let the troubles that come your way get you down.*

The quiet voice that whispered in her heart usually provided inspiration, but today it brought only tears and a lost, empty feeling that tugged at her soul. Maddie sniffled, wiped the tears from her cheeks, then curled up in the straw. Sighing heavily, she closed her eyes and forced herself to unwind emotionally and allow her tense body to relax.

After giving herself an hour to rest, and ensuring that gathering darkness would work to her advantage, Maddie eased between the dangling boards and slithered from the livery. Clinging to the shadows, she stepped onto the boardwalk to return to the hotel to confront Jonah again. She intended to leave town at daybreak, and that bullheaded Texas Ranger was going to be riding horseback beside her, she vowed resolutely. He could come willingly—or not. His choice. But he was *definitely* accompanying her to West Texas to save Christina.

Maddie recoiled in alarm when an unseen hand snaked out to clamp over the lower portion of her face. She was jerked roughly back against a foul-smelling body.

"Gotcha," one of the scoundrels sniggered in her ear.

Helpless frustration hammered through Maddie when her captor hooked his free arm around her waist, left her feet dangling in midair and carted her into the alley. She battled for all she was worth to escape imminent disaster, quickly discovering that it wasn't fear that ruled her chaotic emotions, it was fury. She struck her heels against the man's shins and bit a chunk out of his hand, forcing him to release her.

Once she was free to snatch a quick breath, Maddie screamed bloody murder, ducked her head and plowed into the second man, who stood directly in her escape route to the boardwalk. She was not going down without a fight, she promised herself as the top of her head collided with the man's soft underbelly.

Maddie darted sideways when he swore foully and stumbled over his feet. She thought she was home free as she sprinted toward the street, but his partner tackled her from behind and sent her pitching forward in the dirt. Arms flailing wildly, Maddie kicked like a mule and screamed again at the top of her lungs. Expecting to be clubbed on the head with the butt end of a pistol any moment now, she flopped this way and that, hoping someone would hear her shouts of alarm and come to her rescue.

And sure enough, a hard thump connected with her

skull, causing a starburst of color to explode around her. Maddie wilted in the dirt.

The world spun out of focus and swallowed her in silence.

Chapter Two

Jonah was in the restaurant, savoring a bite of juicy steak that had been cooked to his specifications, when he heard a feminine shriek in the distance. Although the other customers merely glanced curiously toward the door, Jonah drew his Colt and was on his feet in a single bound.

The second shriek put Jonah in a dead run, and he followed the sound to an alley that was two doors down from the restaurant. The instant he spotted the downed female being dragged deeper into the shadows by two men, Jonah charged like a one-man army. He sent one of the men to his knees with a well-aimed kick to the groin. A doubled fist to the jaw left the other spinning like a top before he collapsed in the dirt.

Jonah reached down to grab a handful of Maddie's soiled gown and hoisted her up beside him. When her legs folded up like a tent, he curled his injured arm around her waist to lend support. Despite the pain that was throbbing like a son of a bitch in his shoulder he gave her a shake to rouse her to consciousness.

Big mistake, Jonah realized. She came to, fighting to escape. "Hold still, damn it," he growled. "It's just me."

"About time you showed up," she muttered as she sagged heavily against him.

"You're welcome," he snapped sarcastically.

The feel of her full breasts meshed to his chest and her lower abdomen pressing against his hip were vivid reminders of his unwanted response to this troublesome woman. Hell and damnation, she affected him worse than a rattlesnake bite.

Despite the ache in his left arm, he didn't nudge Maddie away as he should have, just steadied her against him. He vented his frustration on the two men, who were staring warily at the speaking end of his Colt.

"If you boys lay your hands on *my wife* again I'll blow them off at the wrists," he snarled—and wondered why he had claimed she was his wife. Dealing with Maddie had obviously made him crazy. It was the only explanation.

"Your wife?" the men echoed in unison.

"That's right," Jonah confirmed. "If you go near her there *will* be hell to pay. Do we understand each other?"

Both men nodded, then one of them said, "But Maddie is still a thief and she has our money. We'll let the town marshal deal with her if she doesn't give it back!"

The familiar use of her name and the challenging remark triggered another round of uncertainties in Jonah. Maybe Maddie *was* the world's biggest con artist and she *had* stolen their money, but these two rascals

weren't going to drag her off by her heels, search her
person and spitefully use her to appease their lust. No
matter who or what she really was Jonah refused to
stand aside and see her mauled.

"It is *not* their money," Maddie muttered as Jonah
drew her backward toward the street. "I don't know
who they are. I swear it. They are nothing but
clever—"

When her voice evaporated and she slumped
against him, Jonah grimaced at the excessive pressure
on his injured arm. He glanced down to see Maddie's
head loll against his chest and her uncoiled hair cas-
cade over his wrist. She'd fainted, he realized. And
most likely at *her* convenience.

Muttering at the constant *inconvenience* this female
caused him, he scooped her up in his arms and pivoted toward the hotel. The bystanders who had con-
gregated in the alley parted like a curtain as he carried
her across the street.

Jonah made the mistake of glancing down into
Maddie's ashen face when he stepped into the lighted
hotel lobby. She reminded him of a fairy princess who
only needed a prince's kiss to revive her. Well, *she*
might be akin to a princess—who knew for sure?—
but he sure as hell was no Prince Charming. He was
not going to yield to the temptation of kissing her
because he didn't want to know how she tasted. He
was afraid he'd like it too much.

"My God, what happened to your wife?" Charley
Halbert, the hotel proprietor, asked in concern.

"Too much excitement. She fainted." Jonah inclined his head toward the door. "Would you trot
across the street to pick up my unfinished dinner?"

He stared pensively at Maddie, wondering if she'd taken time to eat while she was on the run. As an afterthought he added, "And order a steak for my wife, if you don't mind."

"Sure thing, Mr. Danhill. Always glad to help a Ranger, ever since a Ranger helped me out of a scrape once." Charley darted off while Jonah ascended the steps.

He resituated Maddie in his good arm and retrieved the key from his pocket. She roused with a wobbly moan as he carried her into the room to deposit her on his bed. He watched her blink a couple of times to get her bearings before those mesmerizing, tawny-colored eyes settled on him. She appraised his faded black shirt, breeches and scuffed boots before she gazed at his face.

"You got your hair cut," she said sluggishly.

"Thanks for noticing. You fainted. When was the last time you ate?" Jonah didn't trust himself to sit beside her on the bed, so he propped himself against the wall.

Maddie levered herself onto an elbow, raked the disheveled tendrils of golden hair away from her face and said, "Yesterday. And thank you for coming to my rescue. I didn't mean to sound ungrateful earlier. Being mauled, tackled and pounded on the head made me testy."

Jonah was on the move in one second flat to determine if she did indeed have a knot on her head or if she was using the ploy to gain his sympathy. Sure enough, his fingertips skimmed over a noticeable swelling. Switching directions, he grabbed the pitcher from the commode, dribbled water onto a towel and placed the compress against her head. She winced slightly at the contact, then brushed his hand away to hold the wet cloth against her injury.

She stared him squarely in the eye again. "Why did you tell those men that I was your wife?"

"Damned if I know," Jonah replied flippantly. "It just sort of popped out of my mouth. It seemed a legitimate reason to demand that they keep their distance from you."

She cocked her head and studied him for another long, contemplative moment. "You don't like me very much, do you, Mr. Danhill?"

"It's Jonah. And no, I don't," he said candidly. "But don't take it personally. I don't like anyone very much."

His plainspoken comment caused the corners of her Cupid's bow mouth to curve upward, and Jonah felt another unwanted jolt of attraction sizzling through his unruly body.

"I'm not particularly fond of men in general," she admitted. "Most of them seem to harbor ulterior motives. It has been my experience not to trust what they *say* until I see what they are willing to *do,* and determine how far they are willing to *go* to get what they want."

Jonah decided Maddie's insight was right on the mark. But natural suspicion made him wonder if this quick-thinking female was simply trying to get on his good side by agreeing with his wary approach to life.

"Half of the men I know try to flatter me while they court me for my inheritance. The other half seem intent on stealing it outright," she added, then frowned curiously at him. "My money *is* in a safe place, I hope?"

"You're lying on top of it," Jonah informed her. "Whether it's yours or not, I stuffed it under the mattress."

She got that determined look on her face again as she leaned toward him. "I am telling you the truth. Didn't I own up to the fact right off that I lied to the hotel proprietor in order to enter your room?"

Jonah scoffed. "An honest liar. That's a new one." He flashed her a sardonic glance. "My faith in your integrity and sincerity is growing by leaps and bounds."

She jerked up her delicate chin and thrust back her shoulders in offended dignity. Jonah's attention immediately dropped to the full swells of her breasts and he cursed himself inventively for becoming distracted.

"Fibbing to the hotel manager is the *only* thing I have lied to you about. And that is the truth," she declared. "I *am* the innocent victim here!"

"I've heard the same claim of innocence from every lying, cheating criminal I've hauled to jail," he said cynically.

"I am *not* a criminal," Maddie maintained. "How many times do I have to tell you that my sister and I are victims before you believe it?" She huffed out a frustrated breath. "If you weren't so pigheaded you might be able to figure that out…!"

Her voice trailed off as she grabbed her aching head. She continued in a softer tone. "Name your price for escorting me home, Jonah. In addition to paying you in cold hard cash I'll even promise to be nice to you during the journey.''

He crossed his arms over his broad chest and stared her down. ''Given that decent folks are rarely nice to me—except when they want something—and the scoundrels I encounter curse me to hell and back, that *might* serve as incentive. But I'm not inclined to tramp through West Texas.''

Her perfectly arched brows lifted quizzically and she smiled impishly at him. ''Why not? Don't you like the scenery?''

''I like it fine. It's just that—''

An abrupt knock rattled the door. Jonah strode over to retrieve the tray of food Charley provided.

''I'll settle up with you later,'' Jonah promised as the man craned his neck around the door to check on Maddie's condition.

''Glad to see you're feeling better,'' Charley said compassionately. ''I know Mr. Danhill was dreadfully worried about you.''

Jonah rolled his eyes in annoyance while Charley poured on the fatherly charm and Maddie left him basking in a radiant smile. Hard-hearted though he was, even Jonah felt himself responding to Maddie's dazzling expression.

Definitely trouble, he reminded himself. If a man wasn't careful and vigilant he could become intoxicated by those whiskey-colored eyes and bewitched by that smile.

Jonah planned to be *damn* careful and vigilant.

When Charley exited, Maddie levered herself upright to dive into her meal like a woman who had been on prison rations for days on end. She was half-way through her steak before she remembered Jonah had been about to tell her why he found West Texas distasteful.

"Why don't you like my part of the country?" she asked curiously.

He shrugged impossibly broad shoulders, swallowed a bite of fried potatoes and said, "Long story."

Exasperated, Maddie tossed him a withering glance. "I realize you are a man of few words, but you'll have to do better than that."

"Why do you care?" he asked between bites.

"Because I'll be traveling with you," she said matter-of-factly.

He glared at her. "I have not agreed to go."

Maddie smiled confidently. "But you will. You didn't want to rescue me from those thieves, either, but you did because that's simply the kind of man you are."

Jonah set aside his fork and glared flaming arrows at her. "Look, lady—"

"Maddie," she corrected, flashing another charming smile.

He ignored that. "I'm no do-gooder. I do what I'm paid to do, which is fight outlaws and renegades. I have personal reasons for avoiding your part of the country. I don't want to discuss them, I'm *not* going and that's that."

Maddie finished her meal, set aside her plate and surged to her feet. The room careened around her momentarily, but she inhaled a steadying breath, then reached beneath the mattress to locate the money. She felt Jonah's intense gaze drilling into her, but he said not one word as she sorted the banknotes from his clothing. She noticed the moccasins among his belongings. A reminder of the past he'd been forced to leave behind, no doubt.

She stuffed the money inside the bodice of her soiled dress—save a few dollars to compensate Jonah for the meal and his assistance. Resolved to the inevitable, she pivoted toward the door. "Goodbye, Jonah. I hope your shoulder heals without complication."

"Where are you going?" he demanded gruffly as she clamped her hand around the doorknob.

"Out of your life." She tilted her head at a dignified angle. "I have obviously misjudged you. My mistake. The past six months have taught me to cut my losses and get on with life. I have learned that I have no one to depend on but myself. Dealing with you has reinforced what I already knew and simply allowed myself to forget while facing all this emotional turmoil." She drew herself up, inhaled a determined breath and said, "I will handle this myself, *as usual.* Rest assured that I won't inconvenience you again."

And then she walked from the room and left him sitting on his bed with his plate on his lap.

Maddie had finally accepted the fact that she was wasting precious time trying to elicit Jonah's cooperation. She had pleaded, demanded and even tried to charm him. Nothing had worked on that stubborn, ill-mannered, suspicious Ranger.

Time was of the essence and she had no choice but to gather her carpetbag, buy a horse from the livery and race home. If she departed during the night she might even gain a head start on those two ruffians.

For certain, she wasn't waiting for the afternoon stage, knowing those two riders would follow closely behind it, awaiting the chance to attack and divest her of the money. Furthermore, Maddie was not going to risk involving other innocent victims in her problems. There was no telling how many stage passengers might be accidentally injured because of her. She couldn't bear the thought of carrying more guilt on her conscience. She had plenty of emotional burdens trying to drag her down as it was.

Maddie made a quick transaction with the owner of the livery, who kept sleeping quarters near the front door of the barn. Within a few minutes she had a horse, saddle and tack at her disposal. Leading the mount around the barn, she wiggled between the dangling boards to fetch her satchel. She nearly leaped out of her skin when she emerged to see a looming shadow off to her left. She shrank back so quickly that she conked her tender head on the board.

"Ouch!" She hissed in pain.

"Nice accommodations." Jonah smirked as he reached down to assist her to her feet. "You do travel in style, princess."

She could have sworn she heard a hint of amusement in that deep baritone voice. Mr. Hard-hearted Texas Ranger had a sense of humor? She wouldn't have believed it if she hadn't heard it with her own ears.

"Kinda makes a man wonder if you're the wealthy heiress you've implied that you are."

Ah, the sarcasm was back. Now *that* she recognized.

Gathering her dignity around her like a fur cloak,

Maddie tied her satchel behind the saddle and pulled herself astride the horse. She deeply regretted that Jonah wouldn't be accompanying her, but that adage stating that you couldn't lead a jackass where it didn't want to go certainly applied. Mule-headed Danhill had only followed her this far so he could harass her one last time for good measure.

Nudging the mare, Maddie veered around the barn and circled through the small residential area behind Main Street to reach the trodden path west. Behind her she heard the clip-clop of hooves and she twisted in the saddle to see Jonah sitting atop a horse that looked as black as the devil's heart. Of course, it was dark, so she couldn't be positively certain the horse was solid black, but that's just the way she would have pictured Jonah's mount—coal-black in color, irascible in disposition and as independent as a polecat.

"I thought you weren't coming," she commented when she reached the open road.

"I'm not. Just checking to see if this is another of your spectacular exits to milk my sympathy," he said as he eased his mount up beside her. "Did you pack trail rations?"

"No, I'll chew on my fingernails if I get hungry," she said smartly.

"No canteen of water?"

"I'll suck on a pebble if I get thirsty," she assured him aloofly.

"Are you armed?" Jonah asked as she urged her mount into an easy canter.

"Yes, I can shoot off my mouth with lightning speed," she insisted. "Now go away. I'm sure that soft mattress at the hotel is calling to you. You've made it abundantly clear that you don't like me and don't believe me.''

Maddie was inordinately pleased and enormously relieved that he continued to ride beside her rather than reversing direction. She felt as if the heavy yoke of responsibility and desperation that had been bearing down on her shoulders had eased slightly.

Two miles later she glanced at Jonah and asked, ''What made you change your mind?''

''I'm still trying to figure that out,'' he said sourly.

She smiled in the darkness as a sense of comfort and satisfaction stole over her, easing her nervous apprehension somewhat. Jonah hadn't turned his back on her, after all. Despite his surly disposition, he had a good heart.

''Don't get cocky,'' he warned darkly. ''I'm not here because I'm starting to like you or because I believe your story. I'm only here to see that you complete the first leg of your journey without mishap.''

''So...'' she said, biting back a pleased grin ''...you are going no farther than Fort Griffin?''

''That's right. After that you're on your own. I'm only doing this for the money. So don't think you can gallop off without paying for my escort service.''

''Wouldn't dream of it.''

Maddie frowned, bemused, when she realized her manner of speech had become as condensed as his. She would have preferred that something else about him might rub off on her. Such as his impressive fighting and survivalist skills. Fortunately, she was no slouch when it came to riding. Her father had taught both of his daughters to be accomplished equestrians.

The thought of her father melted the smile from her lips and caused the empty ache to expand in her chest. Six months ago Maddie hadn't been over-whelmed with responsibility and hadn't had a care in the world, except for dodging marriage proposals that didn't interest her.

Now her father was gone, cattle rustlers were de-pleting ranch profits and Christina had been snatched up while she'd been taking an afternoon ride on her favorite mount. The world had caved in on Maddie, testing her spirit, her emotions and her strength of character. She was almost afraid to ask herself what else could possibly go wrong, for fear that it would sound like a defiant challenge and more tormenting blows she'd be dealt would send her reeling.

The prospect that her life might get even worse before it got better was a depressing thought that caused Maddie to slump in the saddle. In addition, the dull throb in her skull tempted her to close her eyes and catch a catnap. Willfully, she thrust back her shoulders and tilted her chin. She was not stopping to rest until she'd placed several miles between herself and those scoundrels.

A few miles later Maddie felt her eyelids drooping and her rigid posture sagging. She was exhausted, and the adrenaline high that had sustained her the past two days was fizzling out. Despite her firm resolve, her chin bobbed against her chest and she fell asleep in the saddle.

Jonah grabbed Maddie's arm the split second be-fore she cartwheeled to the ground. Although this headstrong female annoyed him to no end, he reluc-tantly admired her determination—misguided though it probably was. With more gentleness than he realized he possessed, he eased Maddie's limp body forward until she was draped over the saddle, her cheek resting against the horse's neck. Keeping a watchful eye on her, Jonah led her horse off the beaten path toward a creek lined with cottonwood and willow trees.

Leaving Maddie where she slept, he unrolled his pallet. When he pulled her from the saddle she didn't wake up, just cuddled against him and sighed against his neck. The whisper of her breath was like a lover's caress, and Jonah inwardly cursed when his contrary body responded and his imagination tried to run away with him.

Thoroughly aggravated at himself, Jonah laid Maddie on the pallet and covered her with the quilt. If he had been a gentleman he would have bedded down on the ground a respectable distance away. But he was a practical kind of man who saw no need to freeze his tail off for the sake of propriety. Just because he intended to share the makeshift bed with Little Miss I'll-Go-It-Alone-If-You-Won't-Help-Me Garret didn't mean they were going to gain intimate knowledge of one another.

No, Jonah promised himself. He was *not* going to become physically or emotionally involved with this woman, even if his male anatomy was cursing his vow of abstinence.

At Fort Griffin, he planned to hire a guide to take her deeper into what had once been the Comanchería. If she got herself in trouble on the far side of the fort, then she was someone else's problem. Jonah was going to head back to Coyote Springs, check into the hotel and hibernate like a grizzly until he was functioning at full capacity once again.

After unsaddling the horses and canvassing the campsite Jonah eased beneath the quilt. It occurred to him a few minutes later that he had never officially spent the night with a woman. Yes, he had shared a bed for an hour or two, but never actually slept beside a temporary lover. That implied a commitment Jonah was not willing to make.

He cast a quick glance at Maddie's shadowed face and told himself that the only commitment he felt toward his pretend wife was to get her out of his hair—for good.

Wife? Jonah smirked caustically as he made the very practical and sensible decision to cuddle closer to Maddie to share warmth. *Mrs. Jonah Danhill?* That'd be the day, Jonah thought as he drifted off to sleep.

Serenaded by chirping birds, Maddie came awake the next morning to see the first colorful rays of dawn spearing through the overhanging trees. Propping herself on her elbow, she glanced sideways to see her mare tethered to a tree. The dark horse and its rider were nowhere to be seen.

Disappointed but hardly surprised, Maddie presumed Jonah had changed his mind about escorting her. His reluctance had been obvious in the way he behaved and spoke to her. And he had made no bones about the fact that he didn't like her or trust her. Jonah Danhill was nothing if not plainspoken and straightforward.

Pushing herself upright, Maddie raked her tangled

hair from her face, then stared longingly toward the stream. She needed a refreshing bath to wash the fuzzy cobwebs from her brain and a clean set of clothes to restore her sense of self.

The instant she sank into the stream a sigh of relief tumbled from her lips. She immersed herself completely, allowing the water to work its magic on her stiff neck and sore muscles. She allowed herself a few precious moments of pleasure by swimming in midstream before she brushed the matting of wet hair from her eyes and headed to shore.

Maddie gasped in shock when she noticed the towering figure on the creek bank. She instinctively sank down until nothing but her head appeared above the surface of the water. Wiping her eyes, she recognized Jonah—and *not*, thank goodness, one of the two men who were anxious to part her from her money.

"I thought you went back to town," she said awkwardly.

He frowned curiously. "Why would you think that?"

His gaze was so intense that Maddie squirmed, wondering if the clear water made it as easy for him to appraise her as she had assessed him when he'd stood up in his bathtub. Modesty might not be a problem for him, but it was for her. She didn't gad about unclothed in front of anyone.

"Why would you think I left for good?" he prompted impatiently. "Answer the question."

"First off," she said, reeling in her wandering thoughts, "you don't like me. Secondly, I'm interfering with your vacation. I simply presumed that you'd changed your mind."

"No, I went to fetch breakfast." He gestured toward the small campfire, where a rabbit roasted on a spit. "I don't have all day, princess. Come eat so we can hit the road."

Maddie raised her arm and flicked her wrist in a shooing motion. "If you're in a hurry, then turn your back so I can come ashore."

One thick black brow arched and he grinned scampishly. "No. You've seen me naked. Turnabout is fair play."

"Very amusing," she muttered. "If I thought for one minute that I could shock you as speechless as you shocked me, I'd do it in a heartbeat. But I'm willing to bet the ransom money that nothing shocks or surprises you. And if this is some kind of test to determine my integrity or my habit of prancing around naked in front of men, you might as well know that I don't. Ever. You aren't going to be the first, either."

Maddie was pretty sure that it *had* been a test of some sort, because Jonah stared at her for a long, pensive moment before he turned and walked uphill to the campfire. She glided sideways to come ashore near the bush where she had draped her clean clothes. Dressed in the riding breeches, boots and linen blouse that she'd hurriedly purchased in town—when it had become apparent that she'd have to make a hasty ride on horseback to outrun the two men—she hiked up to join Jonah.

When his assessing gaze flooded slowly and attentively over her Maddie's breath jammed in her throat. This man had a unique and unsettling way of looking at her that provoked unfamiliar stirrings inside her.

For reasons she couldn't begin to explain she was attracted to this abrupt-mannered, distrustful Ranger.

It would have done wonders for her self-confidence if she thought he was the least bit attracted to her. But with Jonah it was difficult to tell, because he wore an unreadable expression. He could be coldly furious or uproariously amused and she doubted she'd ever know which.

"You gonna stand there woolgathering or are you gonna eat?" Jonah waved a skewer of meat at her. "By the way, those skintight clothes are not a good idea," he added grouchily.

"Why am I not surprised that you object to my wardrobe?" she mumbled before tasting the tender meat. "There is very little about me that you do approve of or appreciate."

"I would have *appreciated* seeing you naked," he replied, the barest hint of a smile on his chiseled mouth.

With a bite of meat poised a few inches from her lips, Maddie glanced bewilderedly at Jonah. It seemed that he was teasing and flirting with her. He wasn't very good at it, but it pleased her to realize that he wasn't an accomplished womanizer whose goal in life was to charm every female out of her petticoats.

It also made her wonder about his background and upbringing. Given his heritage she imagined his life had not been easy. Maddie decided to overlook his lack of social skills, because the simple truth was that Jonah Danhill intrigued her and she wanted to get to know him better.

"So you like seeing women naked," she said belatedly. "What else do you like, Danhill?"

"Being left alone, for the most part," he said dismissively. "Enough chitchat, Garret. Let's hear it."

Completely bemused, she gaped at him. "Let's hear *what?*"

"Your story." He chewed and swallowed another bite of meat. "That whole abduction, cattle rustling, thieves hot on your heels thing."

"You said you weren't interested in my problems."

He shrugged indifferently. "Not interested, just curious. If I'm aiding and abetting a fugitive I want to know. So, get on with it, Garret," he demanded in an impatient voice.

Chapter Three

Maddie quickly organized her thoughts and began her explanation. "Since my father mysteriously disappeared six months ago, I've been responsible for running our ranch and caring for my sister. Until then I admit that I was a pampered rancher's daughter whose only challenge was to avoid the marriage proposals that were aimed at acquiring control of my property and dowry. Suddenly I was overwhelmed with responsibilities and decision-making, and left to face the alarming realization that my father might *never* return, because he might have encountered the rustlers who have been stealing our livestock."

Maddie drew in a shuddering breath, blinked back tears and picked at her food. "I formed search parties and contacted the sheriff, but to no avail. I have tried to hold on to the hope that Papa is still alive, but so much time has passed that I have had to accept the fact that I might never discover what happened to him.…"

When her voice disintegrated she ducked her head and clenched her fists in an attempt to gather her crumbling composure. It was a long moment before she felt confident to speak without her voice failing her again. "Rustling has been on the rise the past few months, depleting ranch profits. A few days ago Christina vanished, very much like Papa had. But this time a ransom note was left hanging from a tree limb, demanding money for her return. I was given a week."

Jonah assessed her carefully, trying very hard not to notice those trim-fitting clothes that accentuated her shapely physique. He could ignore her effect on him better, he decided, if she'd dress in a shapeless feed sack.

Muttering at the distraction she presented, he willfully concentrated on the tale she was pouring out to him. If her family truly had been taken from her, then he could identify and sympathize. He wanted to believe her because, despite his strong-willed resistance, he was getting attached to her. She amused, annoyed and aroused him—simultaneously. She made him feel sensations and experience emotions that he'd kept in cold storage for years. In his profession, emotion was a dangerous distraction. Jonah had to rely on sharpened instincts, hard facts and unerring logic.

And then along came Maddie....

"Two of the men who have been pressuring me into marriage offered to loan me money to pay ranch expenses and the ransom," she continued as she stared off into space. "I refused to be beholden to either of them. My only option was to consult our family lawyer in Fort Worth and request a loan that I can repay when I gain control of my trust fund."

Jonah wondered how much money they were discussing—or whether this was a fictitious fund that she kept harping about—but he didn't ask. He preferred to hear her out.

"When I left the bank with the money in my satchel, I saw the same two cowboys that I had encountered twice while I was in Fort Worth," she explained. "I had even convinced myself that I was being followed long before I arrived by stage." She shrugged helplessly. "Wild imagination and too much stress, perhaps. In any event, the men approached me a few minutes before I caught the stage to Coyote Springs, and I managed to elude them because there were dozens of passersby on the busy streets.

"When we stopped at a stage station for lunch the men appeared on horseback, and I realized that they intended to steal my money the first chance they got." She glanced somberly at Jonah. "And you know the rest, since I came knocking at your door."

Jonah knew that Maddie could easily have twisted the truth, that she could have been in cahoots with the two men and tried to double-cross them. This entire tale of woe, with the addition of a few tears and a crackling voice, could have been a melodramatic performance to prey on his sympathy and gain his cooperation.

It wouldn't be the first time, he reminded himself. He'd seen several clever scams in his day. He had also heard such convoluted and conflicting testimonies in previous cases that it was damn near impossible to sort out the truth. He had no intention of taking Maddie Garret strictly at her word, even if she did fascinate him and tug at his emotions. He did, however, intend to hear her version of the story before he confronted her two attackers.

Jonah knew for a fact that the men were still following like shadows because he had seen them in the distance this morning. Without his protection Maddie wouldn't be allowed safe passage to Fort Griffin. Her ex-partners in crime—or would-be thieves—weren't backing off.

"Now what's *your* story, Jonah Danhill?" Maddie asked, jostling him from his suspicious thoughts. "I'd really like to know."

Jonah came to his feet, kicked dirt on the fire and headed toward his horse. He wasn't in the mood—or in the habit—of discussing his past with anyone, and he wasn't about to start now.

"Let's go, Garret. We're wasting daylight and your two friends are following us."

He hoped that would be the end of the conversation about his past, but knowing how relentless and determined Maddie Garret could be when she was on one of her crusades, he doubted it.

Maddie strode toward the horses, then reflexively ducked when she heard the crack of a rifle and felt a whizzing bullet rush past her ear to plug into the tree beside her. Wild-eyed, she tried to scramble onto the mare, which was prancing in a nervous circle.

"Give me your hand," Jonah ordered.

Maddie flung up her hand and then winced when Jonah nearly jerked her arm out of its socket in his haste to hoist her behind him on the saddle. When another bullet whistled past them she pressed herself against the solid wall of Jonah's back. Maddie wrapped her arms around his waist and prayed for all she was worth.

Being shot at was a new, unnerving experience for her, but it didn't seem to faze Jonah. He leaned sideways to grab the mare's trailing reins, then took off like a cannonball. While they rode hell-for-leather, Maddie wondered how many consecutive days of dodging flying bullets she would have to endure before she could remain as unflinching and focused as Jonah.

My God, how did he deal with this kind of fear without having the living daylights scared out of him on a regular basis?

"You okay, princess?" Jonah called over his shoulder as he set a swift pace through the trees that lined the creek.

"I've been better," she mumbled against his back. "I'm sorry I'm responsible for getting you shot at during your vacation."

When they encountered the dense underbrush that grew along the creek bank, Jonah reined the gelding to a walk, then drew the mare up beside them. Using his good arm, he grabbed Maddie around the waist and deposited her on her own horse. Her feeling of security vanished when she was no longer wrapped around Jonah's sinewy form. She shivered as remnants of icy fear spiraled through her body.

To her stunned amazement Jonah leaned toward her to kiss her squarely on the mouth. His scorching kiss caused an explosion of her senses and sent hot sensations sizzling through her body. Maddie was still savoring the taste of his full, sensuous lips—and the delicious feelings he aroused—when he withdrew abruptly. Bewildered, she licked her lips and stared goggle-eyed at him.

"Do I have your attention now, princess?" he asked in a gruff voice that was a direct contradiction to the passionate kiss he'd just bestowed on her. When she nodded mutely, he said, "Good. I don't care how scared you think you are, you're still going to be fine." He moved his horse in front of hers, zigzagging through the maze of trees and brush. "Your friends—"

"I keep telling you that they are not my friends," she interrupted emphatically.

"—will have a hard time taking potshots at us if we use the trees as shields," he said implacably. "They might decide to follow the road so they can be ready and waiting to confront us. But we're going to avoid the road entirely. It will take longer to reach Fort Griffin, but at least we won't be sitting ducks."

Jonah picked his way northwestward and silently cursed himself for yielding to the need to kiss Maddie. She'd looked so shaken and terrified that he'd wanted to comfort and console her. He *should* have given her a consoling pat on the back instead. Now the sweet taste of her was on his lips and her clean scent invaded his senses—feeding his forbidden desires, tormenting him until hell wouldn't have it.

Jonah had sworn he was about to suffer heart seizure when bullets started flying earlier and Maddie had almost been shot. He was accustomed to facing personal danger, but it had unnerved him when her safety was threatened. Jonah had accepted the inevitability of his own death years ago, but he hadn't been prepared for the possibility of watching Maddie die while she was under his protection.

She had a lot of living left to do. She had a life and family to return to, would-be fiancés waiting in the wings—if her story was to be believed. All Jonah had to his name was a well-trained horse and an arsenal of weapons. His only connection was to a company of Rangers who were careful about getting too attached to each other for fear of losing a dear friend when a gun battle broke out.

"You'll have to find yourself an experienced guide at Fort Griffin," Jonah said a few miles later. "A novice won't do you a damn bit of good. Your two pistol-packing friends mean business."

"Would you please stop referring to those bushwhackers as my friends?" She scowled at him. "And for your information, I am not going to hire another guide or take the stage. I refuse to involve anyone else in my problems or become personally responsible for causing someone else's injury or death."

Jonah swiveled in the saddle to stare disapprovingly at her. He wasn't surprised to see her chin elevate a stubborn notch when she met his gaze head-on. The woman had cornered the market on stubborn and defiant.

"And furthermore, you are fired," Maddie decreed. "You have an injured arm already. I have to get used to taking care of myself and I'm sorry I made the selfish mistake of involving you in this affair."

"One kiss does not make an affair," he said dryly.

Maddie flung him another irritated glance. "Don't practice your rarely used sense of humor on me, Danhill. I am not a simpleton whose attention is easily diverted. I will *not* be listed as *the cause* on your death certificate.'' To make her point she drew the mare to a halt, then hitched her thumb over her shoulder. ''You're off the hook. Go back to Coyote Springs. You didn't want to come in the first place.''

He had expected her to stick to him like a sand burr after the ambush, but he'd forgotten to take into account her independent nature. Every mishap she had encountered since he'd met her served to stiffen her resolve about confronting her problems alone. He admired that—in a frustrated sort of way—but he'd made a promise he intended to honor.

''Damn it, Jonah,'' she railed at him when he nudged his steed forward. ''What does it take to get rid of you?''

''I would have left if you had walked naked from the water. That would've evened the score between us,'' he teased, straight-faced. ''Now that's what it'll take to get rid of me. Go ahead, strip naked and I'll backtrack to town.''

Maddie's disbelieving snort transformed into a chuckle. ''You are, without a doubt, the most outrageous, perplexing, disagreeable and impossible man I have ever met. I swear, it seems you have made it your mission to deliberately shock and provoke me.''

''Sticks and stones, Garret,'' he said with a careless shrug. ''But regardless, I'm going to take the roundabout route to Fort Griffin so we can avoid your cohorts.''

''How is it that you know this area so well when you claimed you never trekked across it?''

Her question convinced Jonah that she had finally given up her objections to his friends-and-cohorts comments. "I didn't say I wasn't familiar with the area," he corrected grimly. "I said that I preferred to avoid it." He stared stonily at her. "I'm half Comanche. The half that counts. This is where I grew up. This was the Comanchería, until the army descended like hornets to slaughter Comanche warriors, old men, women and children, and march the survivors to Indian Territory."

Maddie flinched when she noticed the hard expression that settled on his rugged features. She had unintentionally hit an exposed nerve. Quite frankly, she was surprised that he had opened up to her, since he had refused to do so earlier. Jonah was a prickly man who had built walls around himself and rarely let others close enough to know and understand him.

"I was fourteen when I watched my father die," he muttered as he stared into the distance. "I was fifteen when I was herded onto a train with the rest of the Comanche children and shipped to Pennsylvania to a boarding school designed to train us to think and behave like whites. I was seventeen when I sneaked away, took a new name and made my way back to Texas to work any job I could get in order to survive."

His gaze swung back to her and she could see bitter emotion shimmering in those emerald depths. "When I look across this frontier I see ghosts of the past and hear the anguished cries of a people who were forced off their sacred land. It's like walking over graves, princess. There are too many painful memories, too much resentment."

"All the more reason for you to turn back," Maddie murmured as tears of compassion clouded her vision. "If this ordeal with Christina ends badly, I'll be tempted to walk away from a host of bad memories, too."

Maddie curled her arm around Jonah's neck and pulled him forward to press her lips gently to his. She kissed him because her heart went out to him, because the swift taste she'd had of him earlier hadn't lasted long enough to appease her. In addition, this rapidly developing craving to make emotional and physical contact with him overwhelmed her.

Her senses filled to overflowing as his mouth moved upon hers. Sensual lightning flickered through her as she breathed him in, tasted him, savored the tantalizing sensations she had never experienced in her limited encounters with men. His darting tongue delved deeper, stealing her breath, then returning it to her in the most arousing manner imaginable. Desire intensified until her mind was reeling and her body was burning with unfamiliar need and simmering with erotic pleasure.

Suddenly he jerked away and retreated into his own space—long before she was ready to give him up. Maddie was so unprepared for his abrupt withdrawal that she nearly dived off her horse before she could regain her balance. She clutched at the pommel of the saddle and dragged herself upright.

Sweet mercy, when Jonah Danhill decided to let loose and kiss a woman senseless he could knock her world completely off-kilter!

"Why'd you do that?" he demanded in a strangled voice.

"Why'd you kiss me earlier?" she retorted promptly.

"To snap you out of your fear-induced trance and get you moving," he said reasonably. "So why'd *you* do it?"

She smiled mischievously as she took the lead, though she had no idea where in the devil she was going. "Because I *have* seen you naked already."

"What the hell is that supposed to mean?"

"Maybe it means that, having seen all there is to see of you, I find you irresistible."

"I doubt it. And for the record, two kisses is two too many. From now on, this is strictly a business arrangement. You're paying me to escort you on the first leg of your journey. Simple and as temporary as that."

"I thought you said you were tagging along, just for the chance of seeing me in the altogether." She tossed a cheeky grin over her shoulder, finding that she enjoyed saucy flirtation—with Jonah, specifically. "I've got news for you, Danhill. I'm not going to bare my body and soul until long past Fort Griffin."

"My loss, Garret. I'll be long gone by then."

And he would, too, Jonah promised himself as he trotted past Maddie to ensure she didn't lead them in the wrong direction. He was not tramping deeper into Comanche territory to revisit sacred ground that might stir up another caldron of bubbling resentment.

He would convince Maddie to hire an experienced guide—or at the very least, take the stage—because she was *not* going to go it alone, no matter what she said to the contrary.

On that determined thought Jonah picked up the pace and headed due west. He didn't slow down until they had galloped across a wide-open meadow and took cover in the thicket of cottonwoods and oaks that lined the meandering river. He knew of one place in particular that provided a natural fortress where they could bed down without worrying about being set upon by the bushwhacking duo.

Jonah kept a close eye on Maddie, bewildered by his sudden sensitivity and consideration of her needs. Each time her face became flushed and she squirmed uncomfortably in the saddle, he halted to let her rest and sip from his canteen. She held up well, all things considered, and she matched his relentless pace without complaining, not even once.

Her only near brush with disaster in eight hours came when her mare, spooked by a coiled bull snake, bolted and tried to run away with her. Being an experienced rider, she managed to rein in her horse before it tried to leap the creek and head for higher ground.

Maddie sent Jonah a questioning glance when he veered toward an oversize briar patch. It stood in the shadows of a rugged stone cliff beside the stream they had been following.

"As a boy, we camped here many times while hunting buffalo," Jonah explained as he dismounted. "It doesn't look like much—"

"I'll say it doesn't." Maddie stared dubiously at the outcropping of rock on the cliff. "Looks like the perfect place to meet up with rattlers, mountain lions or wolves."

Jonah tethered the horses, grabbed his gear and gestured for Maddie to follow him up. He climbed a winding trail that was camouflaged by the briar patch and led upward to an inconspicuous spring tucked into a deep crevice of the ridge. Setting aside his rifle, pallet and saddlebags, he waited for Maddie to make her way up the steep incline.

"You have to know where this secluded spring is or you'd never find it." He directed her attention to the inviting pool when she stepped onto the flat stone cliff top.

Maddie sighed appreciatively as she assessed the hollowed-out basin of rock tucked beneath a jagged sandstone bluff. It resembled a gigantic bathtub. She pivoted beside him to admire the panoramic view of the lush valley below, alive with colorful wildflowers and spring grasses.

"Spectacular," she commented as she sank down cross-legged to rest. "You could see a herd of buffalo coming from five miles away."

Jonah stared out over the land—and remembered too much. "Yeah, if the buffalo weren't practically extinct after the army ordered their slaughter to starve out the Comanche, Kiowa and Apache."

Maddie could tell that this trek down memory lane was taking its toll on Jonah. Had she known what she was asking of him she never would have gone to him for assistance. Impulsively she came to her feet and walked up behind him to glide her arms around his waist, then glanced around his broad shoulder, wondering what he saw that she didn't.

She wasn't sure she wanted to know.

To her surprise, he tugged her in front of him and rested his chin on the crown of her head while he stared through time and space. "It was a different way of life," he murmured. "A peaceful coexistence with nature. Never taking from Earth Mother without giving something back. The problem was we stood in the way of white expansion. Our people paid the sacrifice so that you, and others like you, could lay claim to this land.''

''Jonah, I'm sorry,'' she whispered as she rubbed her shoulder consolingly against his chest. ''Fifteen years ago I was just a child in East Texas who thought her parents were being terribly unfair by uprooting her and dragging her away from the only home she'd known. I can't even begin to imagine the violence, resentment and confusion you endured.''

''What happened to your mother?'' he asked after a moment.

''She died giving birth to Chrissy. And your mother? How did she come to be with the Comanche?''

''A captive from childhood. She taught me to speak English, but she had no wish to return to her abusive father. She became Comanche, lived as a Comanche and died from complications of the bullet wound she sustained when our clan was captured and taken to the reservation.''

For the life of him Jonah couldn't fathom why he was confiding in Maddie. Even his commander didn't know the details of his life before he'd joined the Rangers. Jonah had kept his own counsel for half a lifetime.

And this certainly was not the time to become sentimental and talkative, he chided himself. He and Maddie were merely strangers who had crossed paths temporarily. By this time tomorrow she'd go her way and he would go his. That would be the end of it.

Clinging to that sensible thought, Jonah released

her—and wondered what in the hell he'd been thinking by holding her possessively to him in the first place. That kind of physical contact was tempting and dangerous. It was as if he had needed her warmth and her gentle touch while he faced the onslaught of memories triggered by stopping at this old Comanche campsite.

She pivoted toward him, then flicked a glance at the rolled pallet on the stone ledge. He could practically see her mind churning with curiosity when her gaze returned to him.

"If you have only one bedroll, and I slept on it, then where did *you* sleep last night?"

He'd wondered when she would ask that question. He'd expected it earlier, but he supposed getting shot at had dominated her thoughts.

"I slept beside you, under the same quilt," he said, expecting her to start ranting about propriety. But she surprised him by staring inquisitively at him.

"I was so exhausted last night that you could easily have taken advantage of the situation." Those amber eyes drilled into him. "Why didn't you?"

"Good question. Maybe because I was plumb worn-out, too."

"Or maybe because you don't like me and you don't find me desirable."

"Yeah, that's it."

That was *not* it, but he'd be damned if he'd let her know she was getting under his skin and that getting naked with her was a fantasy that was occupying too much of his thought processes.

Jonah scooped up his rifle. "You can enjoy a leisurely bath while I hunt down supper."

"No rattlesnake steak. Tried it once. Didn't like it."

"You'd be surprised what you can eat when left with no choice, princess," he assured her, more gruffly than he intended. "Believe me, I've had worse."

Jonah descended the trail and vowed he was going to be his old self again when he returned. Sharing his thoughts and emotions made him feel uncomfortable and exposed. He related better to Maddie when he relied on taunts and sarcasm. If he kept this up she might come to mean too much in the short span of a few days. He planned to leave her without regret, because he had regrets aplenty already and revisiting the outer boundaries of the Comanchería was getting him stirred up.

She was getting him stirred up, too.

It was amazing how quickly he had reached the point where just staring at those clingy clothes that accentuated her curvaceous figure made him want her—badly.

He just needed *a* woman. Any woman would do, he tried to convince himself. He could relieve that problem at the bustling town that had sprung up beside Fort Griffin. The Flat, as the raucous community was called, was known for its saloons, dance halls and harlots. Simple sexual pleasure was what he craved.

Maddie Garret was to be cautiously avoided because she came with all sorts of complications. Hell, he couldn't even guarantee that she wasn't feeding him some fantastic lie.

Oh, certainly, he wanted to believe her, wanted to think that he wasn't *that* bad a judge of character. But he'd heard too many nightmarish tales of men who were enticed and betrayed by a beautiful woman. Maddie, with her hypnotic golden eyes, sun-kissed hair and honeyed lips could lead him into disaster like a sea siren luring a doomed ship into the eye of a hurricane.

"Well damn," Jonah muttered as he stalked off to hunt. He was getting allegorical and philosophical all of a sudden, wasn't he? If this wasn't an indication that a tempting woman could tie a man up in knots and leave him waxing poetic, he didn't know what was.

Right there and then, Jonah promised himself that he would be back on solid mental footing by the time he returned to the campsite. He was not going to let Maddie Garret get to him worse than she already had.

As soon as he dumped her off at Fort Griffin he was as good as gone. And you could write that down in stone because he was not going to change his mind. Fort Griffin was the end of the line for him.

Chapter Four

Maddie sensed the change in Jonah the instant he returned to camp, carrying three quail that he'd cleaned for cooking, and an armload of firewood. His gaze skipped past her and he smirked when he noticed her recently washed clothes, and his, draped over bushes and outcroppings of rock. Maddie was pretty certain that Jonah felt uncomfortable about sharing a part of himself with her earlier, and had decided that wasn't going to happen again.

"You didn't have to do my laundry," he said curtly.

"No, and you didn't have to fetch *my* supper." She walked over to retrieve the quail. "One good turn deserves another. Maybe next time I'll fetch supper and you can do the laundry."

He scoffed at that, as she figured he would. "You can hunt your own game?"

She nodded. "I am not entirely helpless." She took pride in telling him that.

Jonah stacked the firewood, then grabbed a matchbox from his saddlebag to ignite the campfire. Then he slid his pistol from the holster and handed it to her. "Prove it," he challenged.

Lips twitching, Maddie focused on a scraggly weed that protruded from a crack in the rock and fired away. She glanced sideways to note Jonah's stunned reaction after she hit the weed dead center.

His narrowed gaze swung to her. "Where did you learn to do that?"

Maddie blew on the smoking barrel of the gun, then returned it to Jonah butt first. "Our ranch foreman, Carlos Perez, taught me. At my insistence. After my father disappeared and rustling escalated, I decided I needed to be able to defend myself." Her smile faded. "I should have encouraged Chrissy to take lessons, as well. Perhaps she could have escaped capture if she had been armed."

Jonah handed the pistol back to her. "Take this with you while you lead the horses to the river to drink. I'll bathe while dinner is cooking."

Maddie grinned impishly into his expressionless face. "What's wrong, Danhill? Afraid I'll sneak peeks at you?"

He cast her a withering glance as he peeled off his shirt, exposing the rippling muscles that had captured her rapt attention the previous day. "Go away, Garret. And watch what the hell you're doing down there. I scouted the area, but that doesn't mean someone won't sneak up on your blindside while you're dawdling."

Maddie tucked the pistol in the band of her breeches, then snatched up the empty canteen. Leaving Jonah to his bath, she followed the path to retrieve the horses. She smiled to herself, thinking what a refreshing change Jonah was from the other men of her acquaintance. They fawned over her, flattered her incessantly. But Maddie was no one's fool. She knew her suitors saw her as a means to an end. They lusted after her prize property. But not Jonah. He resented the fact that she owned land that had once belonged to his people. In addition, he didn't trust her. She had to earn *his* trust and prove her worth.

She had likely made him more cautious of her by assuring him that she could handle firearms. Maddie suspected he wouldn't turn his back on her, for fear she'd shoot him. She wondered what it was going to take to convince him that she was telling him the truth.

Ah well, what did it matter? she asked herself. Jonah wasn't going to stick around.

A rumble of thunder caught Maddie's attention as she waited for the horses to drink their fill. She glanced southwest, noting that the bank of gray clouds she'd seen earlier was rapidly approaching. She knew spring thunderstorms could wreak havoc in this part of Texas, because she'd endured her share of sandstorms and windblown rains that transformed gullies into roaring rivers. She wasn't sure she wanted to be perched on that cliff when lightning bolts speared from the threatening clouds.

Maddie tethered the horses on a patch of spring grass so they could graze, filled the canteen, then made the strenuous climb to the cliff. By the time she returned, Jonah had changed into the clean clothes—another black ensemble—that she'd draped over the scrub. He flicked her a glance while he was hunkered over the fire.

"Storm's coming," she said. "We may have wasted our time bathing because we'll probably get drenched."

Jonah gestured a brawny arm to the east. Frowning, she wandered around the jutting boulders, then halted in surprise when she noticed a wide-mouthed cavern tucked beneath the overhanging rock ledge. It wasn't an enclosed space, which would have left her with that hemmed-in feeling and made her uneasy—thank goodness.

She noticed that Jonah had unrolled the pallet, and she was relieved that they could bed down without dodging lightning bolts during the night.

When she rejoined him and made an attempt at casual conversation, he wasn't the least bit responsive. Since he didn't seem to be in the mood for idle chatter Maddie decided to explore the foot trail that led to higher elevations.

The grumble of thunder overrode a low warning growl, and Maddie recoiled in alarm when she finally noticed a sleek mountain lion crouched on a ledge ten feet above her head. The big cat snarled and swiped the air with its paw.

Heart in her throat, her pulse pounding like hailstones, Maddie retreated several steps. She realized too late that she had only provided a better angle for the mountain lion to pounce—if that was its wont. Wild-eyed, Maddie watched the great cat gather itself, and she frantically grabbed the pistol tucked in her waistband. With a screeching snarl the tawny mountain lion lunged from its perch.

Maddie screamed her head off as the two-hundred pound beast plunged directly at her.

* * *

Jonah was on his feet the split second he heard the wild, inhuman screech and recognized it for what it was. When Maddie's terrified shriek erupted, his heart nearly beat him to death. Fear for her safety sizzled through him as he raced up the winding path. Jonah sprinted around the outcropping of rock, then instinctively leaped sideways when a gunshot exploded. The sound echoed down the rugged peak, then died in a rumble of thunder.

Rounding the bend, Jonah braced his arm on the wall of rock and glanced up to see Maddie sprawled, half on, half off, a chair-size boulder. Panting for breath, Jonah stared at the unmoving mountain lion that lay across her knees.

"Maddie?" he called softly.

Her goggle-eyed gaze leaped from the cat to him, but she didn't move, just sat there gasping for breath. Jonah approached her, then reached down to grab the mountain lion by the scruff of the neck and dragged it off Maddie's legs. She was in his arms, tucking her head against his shoulder, before he could react. The pistol she had clutched in her hand swerved toward his ear, and Jonah pushed it away before the damn thing could go off accidentally and take his head with it.

"Oh, God!" Maddie wheezed, her body shuddering against his. "I thought I was a goner. All I could think about was that if I got eaten alive my sister wouldn't stand a chance of survival unless I left everything up to you. But then I remembered that you don't like me and you might not—"

"Shh-shh, calm down," Jonah interrupted. "You're okay and everything is going to be fine." He nuzzled his cheek against her forehead and felt her shivering against him with the aftereffects of fear. "It's over, princess. Just take a deep breath and try to relax."

She clung to him, meshing her lush body against his overly sensitive male contours, and Jonah steeled himself against the sensations that rippled through him. Well hell, he thought. He'd vowed not to get this close to Maddie again and here he was, cuddling her protectively against him. Events beyond his control kept sabotaging his attempt to keep a physical and emotional distance. He should have set her away from him and told her to toughen up because danger was an everyday occurrence in the wilds. Instead he held her close while her seesawing breath fanned his neck and she struggled to regain her composure.

"I didn't realize the cat was above me until it was too late," she jabbered nervously. "The poor thing might have been trying to protect a den of young cubs, and I unintentionally intruded on its territory."

"The poor thing?" Jonah repeated incredulously. "The *poor thing* nearly had you for dinner." He glanced down to note that Maddie had shot the great cat in the neck. It was probably all that had saved her from mauling and death.

"Carlos taught me to aim for the neck," she mumbled, following his gaze. "He said that would bring an animal down immediately. Anything less wouldn't ensure that the beast couldn't keep coming at you."

"Carlos is right. It's the only way to stop an animal in its tracks." Jonah eased Maddie away and turned her back in the direction she'd come. "Dinner should be ready."

"I'm not hungry," she mumbled as she made the descent on wobbly legs.

Jonah reached out to lend support before she stumbled downhill. "You're eating, regardless."

Bracing shaking hands against the boulders, Maddie made her way back to camp. Even after inhaling several cathartic breaths she was still rattled by the incident.

"That was a careless mistake," she grumbled to herself.

"You got that right. Next time pay attention to your surroundings."

"Right. Eagle-eyed Danhill would never have made that error. But then, you probably have eyes in the back of your head."

"I've seen too many men die with surprised looks on their faces, Garret. If you wanna stay alive you take nothing for granted and you keep your eyes and ears peeled."

Thunder exploded above them, as if to punctuate his comments. Maddie instinctively shrank back and lost her footing. Her arms flailed wildly before Jonah jerked her upright and tightened his grasp on her.

"Take a couple of deep breaths and get yourself together," he demanded.

"Tried that. Didn't help. I noticed that bottle of whiskey in your saddlebags. Mind if I have a drink of it? I'll replace your supply when we reach the Flat."

"Help yourself."

Maddie rounded the bend of the trail and made a

beeline for the saddlebag. She fished out the bottle and took a swig. Fire burned her throat and left her choking for breath. Jonah whacked her between the shoulder blades, then snatched the bottle from her trembling hand.

"Take it easy with that stuff. *Sip* it. Don't *gulp* it."

Nodding mutely, Maddie pried the bottle from his fingertips, took a sip and then said, "How do you do it?"

His dark brows bunched over his thick-lashed eyes. "How do I do what?"

"Face outlaws and wild beasts daily without letting it get to you?" She wheezed, then helped herself to another sip.

"Practice," he replied, then jerked the bottle from her hand once more. "You've had more than enough. The way you're going at it you'll be stumbling drunk and pitch yourself off the edge of the cliff."

"I'm sure you'd prefer that," she mumbled as she wilted bonelessly to the ground. "Then you'd be rid of me for good."

It was more than obvious that Maddie wasn't a connoisseur of liquor. The stuff went straight to her head in nothing flat. "Better eat something," he advised as he strode over to lift the burned quail from the fire.

Reluctantly she accepted the food he extended to her.

"Hell's going to break loose soon," he predicted as he glanced at the threatening sky. "We'll call it a night and get an early start in the morning. We should reach Fort Griffin by noon."

"And *then* you will be rid of me," she said between bites.

Yes, he would. In less than a day he could put Maddie Garret out of his mind and enjoy his vacation.

Jonah hurriedly finished his meal, then doused the fire. The wind was swirling around the bluff with increasing speed and a shaft of rain hung over the valley. He estimated that they were going to be drenched in less than five minutes. He strode off to tuck his gear in a dry place before the storm unleashed its fury.

Jonah scowled when he exited the cave and saw Maddie tipping the whiskey bottle again. In four long strides he was at her side, snatching the bottle away. "Damn it, gimme that."

"You're no fun a-tall."

"I'm alive and kicking. That's fun enough," he muttered, noting her goofy smile.

"Wha'd it take fo' you to like me better? You might fin' this har' to believe, but some men act'lly do like me."

"Do tell. Garret, you're wasted," Jonah stated. Then he frowned disapprovingly. "Rule number two, if you can't handle liquor, don't drink."

She looked at him, eyelids drooping noticeably. "What's rule number one? I forget."

"Pay attention to your surroundings," he prompted as he reached down to hoist her to her feet. "If you weren't soused you'd recall that we're about to get wet." He directed her attention to the sheet of rain that was sweeping over the valley, heading directly toward them.

He curled his arm around her waist and shepherded her toward the cave as raindrops splattered the sandstone ledge beneath his feet. Maddie didn't object, thank goodness, just allowed him to guide her into the cavern to wait out the storm. Sighing heavily, she sprawled on the pallet while he tucked away the whiskey—what was left of it.

Jonah stood there watching her stretch like a cat before she pulled the quilt over her. Damn, she looked so incredibly tempting lying there with that droopy smile on her dewy lips. The curtain of rain that tumbled past the mouth of the cave gave the impression that he and Maddie were all alone in the world. There was nothing he wanted more than to stretch out beside her and create a storm of passion that rivaled the one that Earth Mother had unleashed outside.

But that erotic fantasy was *not* going to collide with reality, Jonah promised himself resolutely.

"Come to bed, Jonah," Maddie murmured as she drew back the quilt and patted the empty place beside her. "I promise not to throw myself at you."

Jonah looked around, trying to figure out where he was going to sleep. It couldn't be with her. He trusted himself less tonight than he had last night.

"Please," she whispered.

The self-discipline and restraint he'd spent three decades cultivating failed him completely. He was moving toward the inviting pallet and the alluring woman upon it before he realized it. The moment he eased down beside her Maddie snuggled up against his hip and rested her head on his shoulder. Forbidden sensations hammered at him as the scent and feel of her bombarded his senses. Jonah held himself perfectly still, afraid to move, for fear he'd moved toward her. Because if he did he was pretty sure his willpower would abandon him in one second flat.

"You're a nice man, Jonah Danhill," she murmured against his chest.

A *nice man* wouldn't be thinking the kind of impure thoughts that were chasing around in his head at the moment. The feel of her full breasts pressed against his rib cage was arousing him to the extreme. The feel of her arm draped over his chest reminded him of being wrapped in a cocoon of living flesh. He wanted her in the worst way, wanted to be *inside* her, sharing the same flesh, the same breath.

The erotic thought played havoc with his self-restraint, especially when her enticing feminine scent kept wrapping itself around his senses and practically drowned him. Gritting his teeth against the onslaught of tormenting temptation, Jonah shifted sideways and turned his back on her. Which was just as bad, because Maddie cuddled spoon-fashion against his back and looped her arm around his waist.

Her breath stirred against his neck, causing gooseflesh to pebble his skin. Desire clenched inside him and one arousing fantasy after another flooded his mind and left him hard and aching. Damn it, even if he'd been made of stone he couldn't guarantee that he wouldn't crack under the intense pressure of wanting her like hell blazing.

After what seemed forever he heard her methodic breathing and felt her slump in slumber. Jonah thanked Indian and white men's deities equally for granting him relief.

One more day, he chanted silently. Surely he could endure one more day of nearly impossible temptation before she found another guide to lead her back to familiar territory.

Jonah winced when an odd sensation nipped at him. He didn't want to visualize another man cuddling up with Maddie. He'd buy her a bedroll, Jonah decided immediately. And he'd make double damn certain that her next guide had the restraint and integrity to keep his hands off her.

Hell! Where in the blazes was he going to find a saint on such short notice?

Maddie awoke the following morning with a queasy feeling in the pit of her stomach and a dull throb thudding against her skull. The whiskey, she recalled. Though drinking had taken the edge off her nerves, there seemed the devil to pay later.

Raising heavy-lidded eyes, she glanced sideways, not surprised to note that Jonah was up and gone. She smiled slightly, remembering that she'd practically had to twist his arm to get him to share the bedroll with her.

Drowsily Maddie pushed upright and scrubbed her hands over her face. She needed to get up and get moving. She predicted Jonah had the horses saddled already and was champing at the bit, eager to be on the way to the fort so he could drop her off.

Maddie stepped from the cave to draw in a deep breath and revel in the lingering scent of rain that hung in the early morning air. Her gaze drifted across the valley and she admired the spectacular view for a long moment. With her senses cleared—partially— she ambled over to the pool to wash her face, then reversed direction to gather the bedroll and gear.

* * *

Jonah glanced up to see Maddie, the saddlebags, satchel and bedroll slung over her shoulder, making her way down the trail. Her face was pale—the aftereffects of her bout with whiskey, he diagnosed. Nonetheless, she had gathered up the gear and climbed down from their elevated campsite to join him.

"How's your head?" he asked without preamble.

"And good morning to you, too," she replied. Maddie walked over to tie the gear behind the saddle. "Sleep well, Jonah?"

The casual tone of her voice provoked him to frown. She was laboring under the erroneous notion that resisting the temptation she presented wasn't driving him crazy. Well, she was dead wrong about that, but he'd shoot himself in the foot a couple of times before he admitted it.

Jonah suspected that most men drooled over this fetching female, and he wasn't about to join the ranks of her hopeless admirers. And for all he knew she could be a cunning crook who was using him to protect her stash of money during her getaway. Hell, there could be wanted posters out on Maddie Garret and he wouldn't know for sure unless he visited the nearest sheriff's office to check.

"Jonah?"

He corraled his rambling thoughts and shot her a quick glance. "I slept just fine, thanks for asking," he replied in a clipped voice. "We'll forgo breakfast since we'll be at Fort Griffin by noon. Ready to ride, Garret?"

When Maddie swung into the saddle Jonah's betraying gaze riveted on the shapely curve of her derriere. He swore ripely and mounted his horse.

Jonah circled the sandstone bluff and headed north. Although Maddie commented on the rugged beauty of the hills that were dotted with juniper and mesquite, Jonah kept a sharp lookout for unwanted company. Two hours into the journey they encountered a supply wagon. The ogling stares that the two bearded men directed toward Maddie didn't escape him. Although she waved and smiled cordially, Jonah nodded curtly.

"Are you always this grumpy or are you having a bad day?" Maddie questioned belatedly.

"I've found that if you treat every stranger like a potential enemy you're never surprised if trouble comes your way."

When she shook her head in dismay sunlight blazed like fire in that mass of curly hair. Jonah did his damnedest not to notice how utterly appealing she was to him.

"You've spent entirely too much time associating with murderers and thieves. They are poisoning your outlook on life."

Jonah didn't reply, just headed north at a fast clip. When he spotted the flag flying on Government Hill, where the fort was located, he veered west to approach the community from the opposite direction than the two bushwhackers might have anticipated.

"Our first order of business is to find a guide," Jonah said as they trotted into the Flat that sat at the base of the hill overlooking the river.

"I told you I'm going alone."

"Not acceptable." Jonah grabbed the mare's rein,

just in case Maddie decided to be contrary and tried to take off in the wrong direction.

"I am not your responsibility," she muttered in annoyance. She reached into the pocket of her breeches for the money to pay Jonah for his services. "Here. Take this and go."

Jonah ignored her as he weaved around the horses and wagons that filled the streets of the community. He made a beeline for the fort and rode right past the soldiers who tried to waylay him. Jonah wasn't wasting his time with peons. He was going to speak to the highest-ranking officer at the fort.

"What's your commander's name?" Jonah asked the young soldier who was standing guard outside headquarters.

"Major Thorton," the soldier informed him, though his eyes kept straying appreciatively to Maddie and the trim-fitting garments that advertised every shapely curve and swell she possessed.

"Jonah Danhill, Texas Ranger," Jonah announced authoritatively, then flashed the badge he kept tucked in his pocket.

The soldier snapped to attention. "Yes, sir." Turning an about-face, he preceded Jonah and Maddie through the door. After quick introductions, the soldier exited and Jonah got right down to business.

"I'm looking for an experienced scout and guide to escort my wife west while I return to Coyote Springs," Jonah declared.

Major Thorton thoughtfully stroked his goatee and frowned. "Why can't she take the stage? That would eliminate the need for a guide."

"She prefers to ride horseback," Jonah replied,

then flashed the major a wry smile. "My life is much easier if I give my wife what she wants."

Major Thorton chuckled as his gaze darted around Jonah's shoulder to appraise Maddie. "I usually follow the same policy for the same reason," he agreed. He propped his fingertips together, contemplated for a long moment, then said, "I would recommend three men. One of them is a civilian scout we employ on occasion. You can probably find Kiowa Boone at Wild Card Gaming Hall down at the Flat. He usually prefers to trail north, not west, but he might be convinced to help you if the price is right.

"Henry Selmon is a buffalo hunter who has been all over these parts," the major continued. "When he's in town he frequents the Crested Butte Saloon. Your last prospect is Yancy Clark, who rides shotgun for freight wagons headed up the cattle trail to Dodge City. You can probably find him at the mercantile shop that he and his brother own."

Jonah nodded gratefully. "I appreciate your help, Major."

Thorton came to his feet behind his desk and extended his hand. "Good luck finding a guide, Mr. Danhill. With a pretty wife like yours, I can understand why you want to be selective."

Maddie silently fumed when Jonah turned around and shoveled her from the office, as if she was too stupid to find the door by herself. The way he was lording over her made it seem as if they truly were married.

Maddie made up her mind there and then that if she did marry eventually she was not going to be dominated and ordered around. She'd spent the past months making decisions for herself, and she was not going to depend on any man the way she had allowed herself to blithely do with her father.

"Don't give me that mutinous look," Jonah said as they descended Government Hill.

Maddie jerked up her chin and glared at him good and hard. Not that it fazed him. Going up against Jonah Danhill was like banging her head against a stone wall. Nonetheless, she was not going to be walked over and treated as if her opinion counted for nothing.

"I do not want a guide," she told him firmly and decisively.

"Tough. You aren't leaving town without one," he retorted. He halted in front of a shabby saloon and dismounted. "Stay here. I'll be right back."

Maddie glared meat cleavers at his departing back as he strode off. When she eased her horse away from the hitching post, impulsively deciding to turn tail and ride away, hell-for-leather, Jonah wheeled on her and his eyes narrowed dangerously. "Do not make me track you down. It's what I do and I'm damn good at it."

"All this and conceited, too."

"No, *confident*. I've been tested repeatedly. And if you leave while I'm inside the gaming hall I'll be mad as hell *when* I track you down, so stay put!"

Although everything inside Maddie rebelled, she sensibly reminded herself that outrunning Jonah would be a waste of time and effort. Besides, she could dismiss her unwanted guide the moment Jonah rode east, and he would never know the difference.

She gave him a mocking bow from atop her mare. "Yes, master. Anything else?"

"Just stay put." Muttering, Jonah spun on his heels and disappeared inside the saloon.

Maddie glanced longingly at the restaurant down the street. Despite Jonah's agenda of locating a suitable guide, Maddie decided their next stop was going to be the café because her stomach was growling to beat the band. After that, she intended to rent a hotel room and relax before she began the next leg of her journey in the morning.

Though she hated to admit it, she was going to miss having Jonah underfoot. He hadn't gotten attached to her, but she had definitely become attached to him. The simple, undeniable fact was that she was attracted to him, fascinated with him, no matter how much she wished otherwise.

Maddie sighed heavily and shifted restlessly in the saddle. There was something to be said for having a pretend husband, she mused. You could lose one as quickly as you acquired one. It was a pity that Jonah was in more of a rush to get her off his hands than she was to part company from him. She was starting to like the man—a lot. It would have soothed her feminine pride considerably if Jonah felt the same way about her.

No such luck, she mused dejectedly. At this very moment he was scouring the saloon, looking for someone to take her off his hands so he could hightail it out of town—pronto.

Chapter Five

Without asking around, Jonah singled out Kiowa Boone at a single glance. The man looked to be three or four years younger than Jonah and exactly what he'd expected—a half-breed who offered his scouting services to the army, to freight companies and wagon trains. For a price, Kiowa Boone led the way through the frontier—and avoided confinement on the reservation. Boone was a kindred spirit with whom Jonah could easily identify.

Boone glanced up from the table where he sat with his back to the wall—a technique Jonah always observed so he could see trouble coming before it pounced on him. Unspoken recognition and connection passed between Jonah and the scout, who tossed down his poker hand and came agilely to his feet.

"You're looking for me." It wasn't a question but rather a statement of fact.

Jonah sized up the rugged-looking scout, who stood a few inches shorter than himself. Other than a difference in height, Jonah saw the same dark, angular features that he encountered when he looked in the mirror. Two of a kind, he mused as a faint smile pursed his lips.

"Got a problem," Jonah declared.

"Our kind usually do," Boone remarked as he glanced around the gaming hall. "We have to deal with palefaces."

Jonah chuckled as he led the way to the door. It had been a while since he'd had the chance to associate with someone who understood what he felt. He liked the dark-eyed, raven-haired half-breed immediately.

Pausing outside the gaming hall, Jonah gestured toward Maddie, who waited impatiently. "My wife," he announced. Strange how that lie tumbled so easily from his lips these days.

Boone's brow shot up like exclamation marks as his appraising gaze bounced from Maddie to Jonah. "You, my brother, are one very lucky man."

Jonah didn't bother to debate that issue. "She is heading west and I have to return to Coyote Springs. The name's Jonah Danhill. I'm a Texas Ranger," he added.

The scout nodded pensively. "I considered that option myself, but I'd want a guarantee that I wouldn't have to go up against one of my own kind."

"I asked for the same guarantee. My commander respects my wishes. I can make the necessary contacts if you're interested."

"Might be," he murmured as he stared appraisingly at Maddie.

"What is taking so long?" Maddie asked as she gave Kiowa Boone a quick once-over. "He'll suit me just fine. Now let's go eat. I'm starved."

"Your woman has a sassy mouth." Boone smiled wryly. "I like that in a woman."

"You wouldn't if you had to deal with it repeatedly," Jonah countered as Maddie stared irritably at him. "Regardless, I will pay you to escort her to the ranch located northwest of Yellow House Canyon."

The light evaporated from Boone's dark eyes and his expression hardened. Jonah realized that the man experienced the same resentment that tormented him. "Not interested," the scout said with absolute finality.

Jonah nodded in understanding. "Figured you'd feel that way. Not that I blame you. I'll find someone else," he said as motioned to Maddie.

After Jonah mounted his gelding, he met Boone's penetrating stare, then reined away from the hitching post. He could feel the scout's gaze on him as he and Maddie headed down the street.

"Well? Is it settled?" Maddie asked curiously.

"Kiowa Boone declined the offer," Jonah said as Maddie bounded from her horse and made a beeline for the restaurant.

"I intend to eat and rent a room for the night. You can scour the town for a guide, if you're so inclined, but I plan to be refreshed and ready to ride at dawn."

Jonah glanced around to locate Crested Butte Saloon and Clark's Mercantile. Although he wanted the matter settled and out of the way, he followed Maddie inside the restaurant and took a seat. The café was bustling with patrons, several of whom darted speculative glances at Maddie, then at Jonah. He had the unshakable feeling that no one in attendance thought the attractive female belonged in his company. It was a prejudice he'd encountered for half his life.

Since the crowd seemed harmless, Jonah ordered his meal, then stood up. "I'll check out one of the other possible scouts before lunch arrives."

"Fine," Maddie said stiffly. "Heaven forbid that you have to spend another few minutes with me when you could be locating someone to pawn me off on."

"Look, princess—" he tried to object, but she cut him off with a slashing gesture of her hand.

"Just go."

And off he went. Jonah walked across the street to request that the barkeeper at Crested Butte Saloon point out the potential scout. Jonah frowned disapprovingly when his attention was directed to a scraggly haired buffalo hunter half sprawled across a table, his hat askew on his head. An empty glass sat a few inches away from the man's grimy hands, which were tipped with filthy fingernails. Flies buzzed around him.

It was high noon and Henry Selmon, the sorry son of a bitch, had already passed out.

No way in hell was Jonah going to entrust Maddie's safekeeping to this pathetic drunkard. Without shaking the snoring buffalo hunter awake, Jonah wheeled around and exited the saloon. Two down and one to go, he mused as he strode toward the mercantile store to locate Yancy Clark.

Jonah introduced himself to the short, stocky Clark brothers, who were carrying supplies to the back of the store to load in the wagon waiting in the alley. When he explained his request, Yancy shook his frizzy red head.

"Too busy," he said as he shoved the wooden crate across the wagon bed. "I'm heading out to Dodge City with supplies in the morning."

Frustrated, Jonah returned to the restaurant and plopped into his chair to devour the meal that awaited him.

"That was fast.... Well?" Maddie prompted.

"Selmon is a drunk and Clark is taking a shipment of supplies north first thing in the morning," he reported between bites.

"Then the matter is settled," Maddie declared. "Since you refuse to accompany me, then I will use your tactic of avoiding the open road and following tree-lined creeks. I'll ride west tomorrow and you can head east." She dropped money on the table to pay for her meal, then rose to her feet. "If you feel inclined to say goodbye, you can find me at Horning's Hotel."

Exasperated, Jonah watched her walk away—and noticed that at least a dozen admiring male gazes followed her until she disappeared from sight. Jonah sighed heavily. That woman drew entirely too much attention, just by living and breathing. It would be impossible for her to make an unescorted jaunt across the frontier without getting herself in trouble.

Maddie paid for her hotel room and carted her satchel upstairs to find meager but tolerable accommodations. All she wanted was an afternoon nap on a real bed. Then she would gather a few supplies before she enjoyed a hearty supper and settled in for a good night's sleep. She also wanted to forget that Jonah Danhill had stomped on her feminine pride and hurt her feelings by racing around town, trying to foist her off on someone else so he could be rid of her.

She supposed this was her comeuppance for rejecting several suitors who didn't interest her in the least. Suddenly she had stumbled onto a man who intrigued her and inspired a host of feminine yearning. Unfortunately, Jonah viewed her as a nuisance and inconvenience, and he didn't trust her.

Being rejected was hard on her pride, but she would learn to deal with that, just as she'd learned to deal with all the obligations and difficulties she'd encountered after her father disappeared. For sure and certain, her personal disappointments were no match for the terror Christina was enduring. Maddie resolved, there and then, to focus all of her thoughts and efforts on blazing a path toward home to deliver the ransom money.

Sprawled faceup on the lumpy bed, Maddie closed her eyes and ignored the image of coal-black hair and intense green eyes that floated across her mind's eye. Jonah Danhill was just a footnote in the annals of her life, she reminded herself sensibly. She had survived without him before she met him and she would manage just fine without him now.

On that determined thought Maddie fell asleep.

A century later—or maybe it was only a few minutes; she couldn't say for sure—Maddie was jolted awake to see that the same two cowboys who had been chasing her were hovering over the bed. She felt the spitting end of a six-shooter jammed against her throat.

"Give us that money and you can be on your

way,'' one of them growled ominously. ''We're damn tired of chasing you all over creation. Now hand it over.''

Maddie had no weapon with which to defend herself, and the money that might save Christina's life was stuffed in her satchel at the end of the bed. Although she didn't want to involve Jonah, she said the first thing that popped into her head in order to buy herself precious time.

''My husband is carrying the money,'' she wheezed.

The other man's eyes narrowed on her as he stuffed his pistol a little deeper into the side of her neck. ''Where'd you find a husband so fast? Nobody told us about him.''

Rattled though Maddie was, she realized that these two men weren't working alone. The only other individuals in Fort Worth who knew she was carrying a hefty stack of money were the family attorney and the bank teller.

''My husband should be here soon,'' Maddie insisted nervously.

When her assailants glanced expectantly at the door, Maddie bolted into action. Her hand shot upward to shove the pistol away from her neck as she rolled off the side of the bed. Amid snarls and foul curses the pistol discharged—sending feathers flying from the pillow where her head had been. Heart pounding like a tom-tom, she slithered beneath the bed and screamed down the walls. All the while she kicked at the protruding arms that reached beneath the bed to grab hold of her.

''Better get the hell out of here while the getting

is still good,'' one of them muttered when the sound
of doors opening and closing and the thump of footsteps indicated that Maddie's wild screams and the
gunshot had drawn attention.

Maddie poked her head out from under the bed as
the two cowboys slipped between the dingy panels of
the curtain and escaped through the window. Bound-
ing to her feet, Maddie darted across the room to
watch the would-be thieves drop down onto the
wooden crates they had stacked up in the alley to
form a makeshift staircase. Although the crates top-
pled as the men clambered hastily downward, they
reached the ground, split up and sprinted off in different directions at a dead run.

Maddie sagged heavily against the windowsill and
dragged in a shaky breath. Her gaze swung back to
the bed to focus on the pillow and scattered feathers.

That could have been her head, she thought with a
gulp.

She was still trying to collect her wits when the
door crashed open and Jonah dived inside. With both
pistols drawn, and looking as formidable as the devil
himself, he rolled across the floor.

When he bounded to his feet, her first reaction was
to fly into his arms like a homing pigeon coming to
roost. But Maddie clamped her fingers on the windowsill and willfully stayed where she was. She had
to remain independent and rely on no one but herself.
And by damned, she was going to teach herself to be
as unflinching and unruffled as Jonah!

Ignoring the curious bystanders in the hall, Jonah
kicked the door shut with his boot heel, then shoved
his six-shooters into the holsters. When his assessing

gaze landed on the defeathered pillow, he snatched it up to note that the bullet had gone clean through the mattress.

He spit out a succinct curse and focused his absolute attention on Maddie. ''What the hell happened?''

''When?'' she asked smartly. ''Before or after *my two friends* jabbed a pistol in my throat and demanded the money?''

He stalked to the window and stared down at the disheveled stair steps of crates. He spouted a string of profanities that apparently offended Maddie's ears because she stared disapprovingly at him.

''*That* will help the situation,'' she said sarcastically. ''Wish I'd thought to do it.''

''Sorry,'' he muttered, then looked her over carefully to determine how much damage her assailants had done. She seemed fine—a little peaked, but still in one piece.

Jonah felt an uncharacteristic shudder riddle him as he slumped in relief. He'd been on his way up the steps when he heard the shot and the screams. He'd knocked bodies out of his way to reach Maddie's room and he nearly suffered apoplexy when he spied the bullet hole in the pillow and mattress. He considered it an incredible stroke of luck that she hadn't been shot full of holes.

Maddie pushed away from the window and half collapsed on the end of the bed. She grabbed the satchel containing the money and hugged it protectively. ''I was taking a nap and awoke to find those same two scroungy-looking men looming over me, demanding the money,'' she elaborated. ''I told them that you had the bills stashed away and that you'd be

here any minute. When they glanced toward the door
I knocked aside the gun and rolled under the bed.''

"You knocked the gun…" His voice disintegrated
into a horrified gasp. "Damn it, woman!" He erupted
in bad temper. "You could be the deadest woman
who ever lived!"

Maddie bolted up to confront him, toe-to-toe and
eye-to-eye. "What was I supposed to do? Lie there
submissively, waiting for you to show up when I
didn't know if you would? I *can* take care of myself.
I *will* take care of myself!"

"Yeah, that's what worries me," he grumbled as
his gaze returned to the brutalized pillow. "I don't
like your daredevil techniques."

"They don't seem to bother you when you're the
one performing them. And what purpose was that
drop-and-roll tactic supposed to serve?"

"Most men aim for the chest. I prefer to come in
low and fast. Loaded for bear."

"I'll add that to my self-defense repertoire," she
said, then frowned pensively. "One of those men demanded to know how I'd acquired a husband so
quickly."

Jonah's attention zeroed in on Maddie's waxen
face. He didn't like the sound of that. Of course, he
only had her word for it. She could have made it up
to reinforce her claim that she had no idea who the
two assailants were. Now she implied there was a
conspiracy working against her.

Silently he watched Maddie retrieve the money
from her satchel, dump the water from the pitcher out
the window and replace it with several bundles of

cash. After tucking part of the money in the pocket of her riding breeches, she strode toward the door.

"Where are you going?" he demanded. "Haven't you invited enough trouble for one afternoon?"

"I need to gather supplies for my trip," she called over her shoulder. "Unlike you, I can't live off the land so easily. I'm also going to buy a pistol because I'm probably going to need it."

"No, you won't," he insisted as he followed her into the hall. "I'm going with you."

She halted in the process of locking the door then narrowed her amber eyes at him. "No, you aren't." She drew out several bills and crammed them into his shirt pocket. "You've been paid for your trouble. Now kindly get out of my way. I have places to go and things to do."

"I said that I've decided to escort you on the next leg of your journey and that's what I'm going to do," Jonah said in no uncertain terms. "I'll turn back when you reach familiar territory."

"If memory serves," she said as she walked off, "you swore up and down that you were going no farther than Fort Griffin. You said this was the end of the line for you—or something to that effect."

He fell into step beside her. "Well, I changed my mind."

Maddie and Jonah halted in their tracks when they rounded the corner to see Kiowa Boone propped negligently against the wall, arms folded over his thick chest.

"Heard you had trouble," Boone remarked as his acute gaze made a slow, assessing sweep of Maddie's arresting figure.

"Minor incident," she said as she thrust out her hand. "I'm Maddie...Danhill. Nice to make your acquaintance, Kiowa Boone."

The rugged, bronze-skimmed scout stared at her tapered fingertips, as if he didn't quite know what to do with them, then shook hands. "Just plain *Boone* will do fine," he requested. "It's a pleasure to meet you, ma'am."

When Maddie descended the steps, the scout's curious gaze riveted on Jonah. "What happened?"

Jonah offered an abbreviated version of the encounter. "The two unidentified men who have been following us overtook Maddie, but she managed to frighten them away."

Boone's dark gaze monitored Maddie's departure from the hotel. "She must be tougher than she looks. Maybe the two of you aren't such a mismatch, after all."

"Of course, we are. You know it. I know it. The whole world knows it. But Maddie has toughened up. That's what scares the hell out of me," Jonah added as he pivoted on the landing and headed down the steps.

"Decided to go with her," Boone said from behind him. "She obviously needs a protector. But just so you know, I'm doing this as a favor to one of my own kind."

Although Jonah had finally found a willing, competent scout to take Maddie west, he was reluctant to send her off, knowing her two assailants were still determined to relieve her of the money—even if it meant riddling her with bullet holes. "Thanks, but

I've decided to take another two days and escort her into familiar territory,'' he told Boone.

The scout's wide shoulders lifted in a casual shrug. "Your wife, your choice.'' Then he asked abruptly, "Which tribe raised you?''

"The Comanche,'' Jonah replied as he stepped onto the boardwalk.

"So you are going to walk over the graves of our people.''

"Looks like. I'm asked to face danger every damn day on the job. Might as well learn to face the bitter disappointments and resentments of the past, too. Why should I expect *you* to do what I don't particularly want to do myself?''

"You do the Comanche proud, my brother,'' Boone murmured as he veered toward Wild Card Gaming Hall. "I do not envy you facing the ghosts of our lost clans.''

Jonah hiked across the street and stood as posted lookout while Maddie purchased canned beans and fruit, a canteen and a tin of coffee. She pretty much ignored him as she strode to the mercantile to buy a bedroll and an extra change of riding breeches. He allowed her to have her own space as she wandered down the boardwalk, pausing occasionally to peer into the windows of various stores before she entered the gunshop. Although she didn't seem to want his company, he never let her out of his sight and kept a constant vigil, hoping to spot the cowardly hombres who kept harassing Maddie.

There was nothing Jonah would like better than to corner those two rascals and twist their arms a dozen different ways until they told him the truth about their association with Maddie. Unfortunately, the men seemed to have gone into hiding again. They reminded Jonah of a couple of snakes that kept slithering under rocks to avoid detection.

Jonah frowned thoughtfully when he recalled that Maddie had informed the men that *he* was carrying the money. A wry smile pursed his lips as he ambled toward the saloon. Maybe it was time he posed as bait. He'd let those pistol-packing rascals come to him and maybe he would finally get the truth.

An hour later Maddie returned to her room with her purchases, then checked to ensure the money was where she'd left it. Sure enough, it was. She did notice, however, that someone had rummaged through her satchel without replacing the items exactly as she had packed them.

Muttering, she stalked over to the window to note that the wooden crates had been restacked. Since the lock on the window had been damaged Maddie moved the dressing screen in front of it, then piled up the cans of beans and fruit to form an obstacle path. If the intruders decided to make another surprise visit they would knock over the pyramid of cans and unintentionally give her advanced warning.

Satisfied with her improvised booby trap, Maddie strode down the hall to refill the pitcher with water, and then freshened up for supper. She donned the green gown she'd brought along with her and took time to twist her hair into a fashionable coiffeur.

Locking the door behind her, Maddie descended to the hotel lobby to see Jonah parked nonchalantly in a chair, puffing on a cheroot. The instant his gaze drifted over her in thorough appraisal heat coiled inside her. Damn the man! He was the only one who had ever been able to draw a tingling reaction from her with just a look. She was entirely too sensitive to him, too attuned to him.

That was going to stop, she promised herself as she swept regally out the door. Starting now, she was going to ignore him completely and see how well that worked.

Jonah smiled in amusement as he watched Maddie sashay outside and pretend he wasn't there. The woman had sass and spunk, even if she was too stubborn to rely on common sense. No matter what else happened she was *not* going to continue her journey alone, not when she had to cross some of the most unforgiving and demanding terrain Texas had to offer. There were miles of craggy stone escarpments and winding ravines inhabited by wild animals and dangerous outlaws.

Dust storms blew up without warning. Anyone who wasn't familiar with the area could become hopelessly lost in the time it took to blink. Although Jonah had no inclination to revisit the Llano Estacado—the Staked Plains, where his people had once roamed freely—he was not going to allow Maddie to make that perilous journey alone.

But he was definitely turning back after two days of hard riding, he promised himself. And you could write that down in stone.

Levering himself from his chair, Jonah followed Maddie to the café and noticed that another round of admiring gazes came her way. Too damn pretty for her own good, Jonah thought, not for the first time.

Taking a seat in the corner of the restaurant, Jonah put his back to the wall so he would have a clear view of the door—and of Maddie. He scowled when a string of men ventured toward her, but she turned them all away with a gracious smile and gentle rejection.

If it were true that Maddie was an heiress and had would-be fiancés lining up to vie for her attention, he wouldn't be surprised. She attracted men as easily as she attracted trouble.

Jonah polished off his meal and pushed his plate aside. He held his seat until Maddie got to her feet and exited. A moment later, Jonah followed her outside and watched her stroll up and down Main Street before she returned to her room.

Veering into the alley, Jonah strode behind the hotel, then swore foully when he noticed the crates had been restacked to form steps leading to Maddie's room. He made quick work of tossing them aside. Damned if he was going to make it easy for those ruffians to enter Maddie's room via the window again.

And where the hell were they hiding out? he wondered irritably. He'd frequented every saloon in town earlier, expecting them to show up to steal the money he was supposedly carrying.

Or was that a manipulative fib Maddie had fed him to reassure him that she was the innocent victim in all this? No, he reminded himself. He had heard the gunshot and seen her mutilated pillow. Those cowboys were definitely threatening her. But that didn't necessarily mean that she hadn't double-crossed them earlier.

Jonah sighed in frustration. He was damn tired of wavering back and forth between Maddie's innocence and guilt. Those two men held the answers and he had seen neither hide nor hair of them. His only other option was to put faith in Maddie's story, but he was too much the cynic to take anyone's word as gospel. Especially a woman who attracted and intrigued him against his will.

To be deceived was unacceptable, but to deceive *himself* was unpardonable, Jonah reminded himself.

Pensively, he stared up at the window, drawn toward Maddie against his ironclad will. Damnation! That woman was sure enough making him crazy. He couldn't trust his instincts when it came to her. Wanting her kept getting in the way of calculated logic. She monopolized his thoughts and preyed on his forbidden desires until hell wouldn't have it.

Two more days, Jonah chanted silently.

Maddie might not want his company, but she was getting it, nonetheless. He'd make a pallet on the floor to guard the window and the door.

And that was the way it was going to be, he told himself resolutely as he headed up to her room.

Jonah tapped lightly on the door and said, "It's me." He expected to meet with resistance, or to be ignored completely.

She surprised him by saying, "Come in."

He stepped into the room and smiled approvingly when he noted the blockade at the window, then he glanced at the bed to see Maddie tucking herself beneath the covers.

"First I couldn't convince you to come west with me. Now I can't get rid of you. I even tried ignoring you, but that didn't work, either. You're like a rash that won't go away."

"Glad you've accepted the inevitable," he said as he dropped his gear on the floor and unfastened his holsters.

She leaned out to extinguish the lantern, plunging the room into darkness. "Come to bed, Jonah. If I've learned nothing else I know that your only interest is sharing a soft mattress for the night."

A lot she knew, he thought as he walked around to the other side of the bed. He slid beneath the quilt and immediately picked up her enticing scent. His body hardened in three seconds flat. It was all he could do not to pull her into his arms and demonstrate to her that sleeping was the very last thing on his mind when he lay down beside her.

When she rolled sideways to buss a kiss over his cheek he bit back a tormented moan.

"You aren't going to try to sneak off without me in the morning, are you?" he asked in a gravelly voice.

She just turned her back to him and settled in for the night. Jonah wasn't sure if that implied a yes or a no.

Chapter Six

Although Maddie had contemplated sneaking away from Jonah at dawn, common sense assured her that she had a better chance of surviving the trek across unfamiliar territory with him as her guide. She and Jonah set a relentless pace through the broad river valley that was flanked by rolling hills covered with thickets of mesquite and oak.

According to Jonah, the area was once part of the Comanches' and Kiowas' favorite hunting ground because of the abundance of water, wild game and wooded retreats. Daisies, yellow buttercups and reddish-brown gaillardias added splashes of color to the fertile valley, which was now dotted with small farms.

As the day wore on Jonah became more withdrawn and less talkative. Maddie presumed his bittersweet memories were tormenting him. But by late afternoon she realized they were zigzagging the area rather than taking a due west route.

When Jonah halted to rest the horses and fished his field glasses from his saddlebag, Maddie frowned warily. "What's wrong?"

"We're being followed." He scanned the copse of thick oaks and cottonwoods on the south side of the river.

Maddie glanced around in alarm. "How could those cowboys have caught up with us so quickly?"

"It's not them," Jonah murmured as he made another thorough and deliberate sweep of the shadows in the thickets. "Looks like we've attracted some other kind of trouble." He tucked away the spyglass. "Mount up, Maddie. I want you to curl over the saddle so you don't make an easy target," he instructed.

Maddie did as she was told, then frowned curiously when Jonah led her mare, and his, into the thick underbrush.

"What are we…" Her voice trailed off when Jonah resituated his gear atop his saddle, and tied it in place to look as if he, too, were hunched over the saddle. He removed his boots and stuffed them in the stirrups.

"Follow the river, but cling to the protection of the underbrush so no one can get a clear look—or shot— at you." He grabbed the pistol she'd purchased in the Flat, then handed it to her. "You'll lead my horse behind you so it looks as if I'm still with you."

Maddie's apprehensive gaze darted across the river, then back to Jonah, who removed his holsters and six-shooters and draped them over the pommel of her saddle.

"Just in case…" he said grimly.

"Just in case what?" she demanded anxiously. "Where are you going to be while I'm creating the impression that we are forging through the bushes?"

"I'm going to introduce myself to our unwanted

guests." He pulled a lethal-looking dagger from his shirtsleeve. "Watch your back, princess, and don't hesitate to start shooting without bothering to ask questions first."

"Is that your policy?" she asked as she watched Jonah crouch down to make his way to the riverbank.

"Generally. The desperadoes I associate with aren't much on answering questions. They prefer to let their pistols and rifles do their talking for them."

And so did Jonah Danhill, Maddie mused as she watched him skulk from one clump of bushes to the next to reach the water. Everything inside Maddie rebelled against leaving Jonah to confront whoever—or whatever—was stalking them. She tried to remind herself that he was highly skilled, experienced and perfectly capable of dealing with trouble. But he had come to mean more to her than just an escort. The prospect of seeing him hurt—on her behalf—was difficult to accept.

"I'll signal you with the hoot of an owl when I return," he called back to her. "Now go, princess."

With the pistol clutched in her fist, her body hunkered over the back of her mare, she picked her way through the bushes and prayed fervently that this would not be the last time she saw Jonah alive. She'd developed a fond attachment to her pretend husband, even if he only saw her as an unwanted assignment.

With the dagger clutched in his hand, Jonah slithered into the water. He came up for a quick breath in midstream, then submerged again. When he reached the south side of the river, he crawled on hands and knees to avoid detection. Jonah scooped up a fistful of stones along the bank, then stuffed them in his pocket.

In the near distance he heard a horse snort and stamp impatiently. That indicated that it was a man, not a beast, that was stalking them. Obviously the rider had dismounted. At least one of them had. Jonah couldn't say for certain how many men had been following them, without taking time he didn't really have at the moment to study tracks.

He crouched behind a bush, then raised his head to see the shadowy images of Maddie and the horses moving in and out of the bushes on the north side of the river. He did not, however, spot the unidentified man who had left his horse tethered to a tree.

Jonah frowned pensively, aware that he wasn't dealing with an inexperienced tracker. Whoever was following them was damn good at concealing himself. Which was all the more reason to dispose of the elusive shadow that had been trailing them for more than ten hours.

Relying upon the stealth and cunning he'd learned from the Comanche, Jonah crept slowly through the trees, pausing at irregular intervals to listen for sounds that might give his adversary away.

He saw and heard nothing.

Damn, he's good, Jonah mused as he quietly shifted position to scan the area from a different angle. His Comanche training had taught him to outwait his nemesis, but minutes passed before he heard a muffled noise near the riverbank. Jonah fished a pebble from his pocket and tossed it in the direction the sound had come from. He expected to hear a shot ring out, pinpointing the man's position.

Nothing. Damn. If he and his adversary were destined to play cat-and-mouse for an hour, Maddie might find herself lost or in trouble. Jonah couldn't guarantee that there weren't at least two men on their trail. One might well be keeping surveillance on Maddie while the other hung back.

The instant Jonah felt himself growing impatient he inhaled a steadying breath and focused on outlasting the clever rascal who had staked out his horse for bait. Jonah grabbed another pebble, tossing it sideways as he crept off in the opposite direction. Again he heard a muffled sound, but no one rose from the bush to take a wild shot.

After a quarter of an hour of playing hide and seek, Jonah sprawled in the grass and inched soundlessly toward the horse. He swore he heard the soft rustling of underbrush, but when he raised his head he saw nothing but a roan gelding grazing on a clump of grama grass.

As he'd been taught as a young warrior, Jonah eased onto his back, clamped the dagger between his teeth and speared his arms and legs outward so that most of his body was covered by the blades of grass, making detection difficult.

He waited.

Then he waited some more.

Eventually he decided to launch a stone at the horse's rump. When the horse bolted sideways, Jonah lifted his head and finally caught a glimpse of movement off to the right. Now he was finally making progress. His adversary had exposed his position in the underbrush.

This time Jonah tossed a pebble toward the far side

of the bush where the man had crouched, then he sprang up to launch himself directly as his adversary. Arm cocked, dagger clutched in his fist, Jonah landed directly on top of the man, who had a dagger clutched in *his* fist.

"Damn it to hell!" Jonah hissed as he stared down into the familiar face. "If those sons-a-bitches hired you to track us you're a dead man!"

"What the hell are you doing on this side of the river?" Kiowa Boone questioned sourly. "I thought someone was after *me!* You must've put a decoy on your horse. Where'd you learn that deceptive trick?"

"From a white man, believe it or not," Jonah growled while he and Boone held each other in stalemate—two nasty-looking daggers aimed at each other's throats.

A wry smile quirked Boone's lips as he made the first move to withdraw his knife, then shoved it into the leather sheath strapped on his leg. "Those two sons-a-bitches *did* contact me and wanted me to help them track you," he reported, as Jonah eased down to sit cross-legged beside him. "But now there are *four* sons-a-bitches on your trail and they offered to split the money you're carrying five ways."

Jonah stared curiously at Boone. "Who are the other men?"

Boone rolled into a sitting position and brushed the leaves off his shirt. "Henry Selmon, for one," he replied.

Jonah snorted. "The drunken buffalo hunter?"

Boone nodded his dark head. "The other one is Selmon's sidekick. Since the hide trade has dropped off, Selmon and Rance Lewis have taken whatever work they can get. Legal or not.''

Jonah rose to his feet and pulled Boone up beside him. ''Did you catch the names of the two men who have been chasing us?''

''Jesse Gibbs and Beau Newton,'' Boone reported. ''I figured you might need someone to watch your back, so I followed you from the Flat this morning.''

Jonah arched an amused brow. ''I thought you weren't too thrilled with the idea of encountering the lost spirits of the Comanchería.''

''I'm not,'' Boone acknowledged as he ambled over to fetch his horse. ''But I got to thinking that I'd probably have to face the past sooner or later.'' He swung gracefully onto the saddle. ''Figured I might as well face it with someone who feels the same way I do.'' He extended his hand to Jonah. ''Climb aboard, Danhill. Better find your wife before she gets herself lost.''

Jonah settled himself on the roan gelding. ''I wondered why I had such a hard time flushing you out,'' he said, chuckling. ''Damn Kiowas always did steal the Comanches best tricks.''

''Steal? Hell!'' Boone scoffed in mock offense. ''The Comanche learned stealth and cunning from the Kiowa.''

''Glad to have you along,'' Jonah said after a moment. ''I've met some tough and capable men among the battalions of Rangers, but they aren't—''

''*Breeds,*'' Boone finished for him. ''I know. And you're damn good, too, Danhill. Took me a long time to figure out that you'd put a decoy on that devil horse of yours. At first I thought one of those four men on your trail had caught up with me while I was guarding your back.''

Jonah smiled curiously as they trekked through the trees. "How'd you figure out that it was me?"

"Didn't know until you jumped me," Boone admitted. "I figured it was Selmon or Lewis, and I decided I might as well lessen the odds against us while I had the chance. But I can tell you it is damn hard on my pride to have you get the best of me. I don't usually find myself outsmarted. But at least a damn paleface didn't do it. That would've been the ultimate insult.''

Jonah was mighty relieved to have Boone on his side. Two-to-four odds were acceptable. Plus, the Kiowa would serve as a buffer between Jonah and Maddie. With Boone along for the ride maybe Jonah could avoid the temptation that was always within arm's reach.

Maddie jerked upright when she heard the faint hoot of an owl behind her. But just to be on the safe side, she shifted sideways in the saddle so she could point her pistol west, then grabbed one of Jonah's Colts to aim in the direction she'd come. Relief washed over her when Jonah, his clothes clinging to his muscular body like wet paint, emerged from the underbrush near the river.

"Did you find out who was following us?" she asked.

"Yup, and don't shoot him," Jonah cautioned before he motioned for Boone to lead his horse from the brush.

Maddie blinked in surprise when Kiowa Boone

stepped into view. "What are you doing here? I thought you didn't want to tramp through this area any more than Jonah did."

Boone smiled slightly. "Don't. But I decided my Comanche cousin might need help, since the number of men following you has doubled."

"*Four* men?" she chirped incredulously.

"'Fraid so." Jonah strode over to resituate his gear behind the saddle, then retrieved his boots. "Ever heard of Jesse Gibbs and Beau Newton?" he asked.

Maddie frowned pensively, trying to place the names. She noticed that Jonah was watching her astutely. He still didn't trust her completely, she realized, disappointed. He was waiting to see if recognition registered on her face.

"I don't know anyone by those names. Who are the other two riders?"

Jonah filled her in as he mounted his black gelding.

"I don't understand any of this," Maddie muttered. "You'd think I was carrying a grand fortune that attracts unwanted interest."

"How much money are you packing?" Boone questioned as he nudged his horse forward.

Maddie glanced uncertainly at Jonah, who nodded, indicating his acceptance of Boone's integrity and trustworthiness. Jonah trusted Boone without question, but he was leery of *her,* she noted. That really hurt.

"Eight thousand dollars," Maddie told Boone. "Five thousand in ransom to rescue my sister and three to cover the losses from cattle rustling."

Boone whistled softly. "That's more than enough money to attract a crowd, ma'am. Your friends—"

"They are not my friends!" she shouted at him.

Jonah snickered as he took the lead. "Forgot to tell you that she's mighty sensitive about referring to our shadows as friends."

"So I noticed," Boone said dryly.

Before Jonah could interject his usual skepticism, Maddie offered Boone an abbreviated version of Christina's disappearance and the ransom demand.

Boone glanced quizzically at Maddie, then at Jonah. She suspected that Boone was trying to figure out why Jonah had never been to the Bar G Ranch if they were supposedly married. She decided it was time for Boone to know exactly what was going on.

"The fact is, Jonah and I aren't really married," she stated as they trotted across a rolling hill.

"You're not?" Boone's surprised gaze darted to Jonah. "Since when do Comanches speak with forked tongues? You must have more white man's blood in you than I first thought."

"I forced him into it," Maddie said in Jonah's defense. "I needed help and the only way to get past the hotel clerk who had instructions not to disturb Jonah was to claim to be his wife."

"Ah, now this makes sense," Boone said thoughtfully.

"What makes sense?" Maddie questioned, bemused.

Boone smiled as he hitched his thumb toward Jonah. "You and the Comanche. Couldn't quite picture the two of you together, right from the start."

Maddie narrowed her gaze on Boone. "And why not? Don't you think I'm good enough for him, either?"

Boone flung up his hand and grinned in amusement. "Easy, wildcat. Save that fiery tone and sharp claws for your supposed husband."

"He thought it was the other' way around, princess," Jonah informed her. "*I'm* the one who should be taking offense here."

"Then why aren't you? The two of you are living testimony that it is possible to bridge the gap between different backgrounds and cultures. You grew up in one civilization and live in another. We're all the same. *Americans.*"

That shut them up, Maddie noted. As well it should have. They rode in silence for an hour before Jonah called a halt.

"We'll camp here for the night," he announced. "We can make use of the sheltering trees and the river before we face the rough terrain, formidable thorns and oversize patches of prickly pear cactus that lie to the west." He glanced quickly at Maddie as he retrieved his gear from behind the saddle. "You might as well take advantage of the river for bathing because waterholes will be few and far between tomorrow."

Nodding agreeably, she grabbed her satchel and headed to the river.

"I'll double back to see how close our shadows are following," Boone volunteered.

"No," Jonah countered. "You can hunt supper and set up camp. Your gear got wet when we had to swim your horse across the river. You have clothes to hang up to dry. I don't."

Assured that he was leaving Maddie in capable hands, Jonah mounted up and headed for higher ground. He was oddly pleased that Maddie had come to his defense earlier, even if anyone with eyes in his head could see that he and Maddie were hopelessly mismatched. But Boone understood perfectly, even if he hadn't debated the issue with Maddie.

In most of the places Jonah had been through, half-breeds were considered second-class citizens in white society. Freaks of nature. Boone could identify with that prejudice. It was as familiar to him as it was to Jonah.

Besides, if Maddie truly was an heiress and land baroness, as she claimed, Jonah had nothing to offer that she didn't have already. He didn't have a home to call his own. He didn't have a deed to acres of property. True, he had money in the bank at Coyote Springs that he didn't have time to spend because he lived and breathed his assignments with the Rangers. But no woman he'd ever met was interested in a no-madic half-breed. Why would Maddie be any different?

And why was he wasting time mulling over unpro-ductive thoughts in the first place? he asked himself irritably. There was nothing between him and Maddie Garret except a temporary business association. By tomorrow night he could deliver her to Mobeetie. From there she could return to her ranch with ease, because Jonah intended to waylay the four men who refused to give up their crusade to separate her from her money.

If Boone decided to guide Maddie all the way to her ranch, then that was his business. Johan winced uncomfortably at the thought of leaving Boone and

Maddie together. It was obvious to him that Boone
found Maddie attractive and intriguing. Being a man,
Jonah had no trouble interpreting the glances Boone
had sent Maddie's way after he'd discovered the marriage was a hoax.

Jonah's thoughts trailed off when he lifted his spyglass to scan the countryside. Sure enough, four riders
were following the same path Jonah had taken along
the river. Determined to throw the men off track and
buy some time, Jonah retraced the trail to a place
where he could cover their previous tracks and leave
the impression that he had turned due north toward
the stage road that connected Fort Griffin to Mobeetie.

When Jonah finished setting his decoy trail there
were three sets of hoofprints leading over the mes-
quite-covered hill and down into the narrow valley
that followed the river tributary.

Let that drunken buffalo hunter and his cohort assume Jonah had taken to the shallow creek to avoid
leaving a trail. When those scoundrels finally figured
out that they'd been duped they would have to waste
precious time backtracking. By then Jonah would be
deep into the winding ravines and rugged terrain that
he had once known like the back of his hand.

Unfortunately, he and Boone were going to be
forced to follow the trails and revisit sites that were
steeped with Indian history and legend. Jonah
frowned bleakly at the thought. He had spent half a
lifetime *avoiding* the only place that had ever felt like
home to him. He figured it was the same with Boone.
But come tomorrow, both of them were going to encounter the unresolved resentment of their past.

* * *

Maddie returned from her bath feeling revived and refreshed—and starved. Breakfast and lunch had entailed no more than chewing on the beef jerky and pemmican that Jonah carried in his saddlebags. Maddie was more than ready to sprawl out on a blanket to rest her aching backside and consume a meal that wasn't as tough and tasteless as leather.

To her surprise, she saw Boone rather than Jonah crouched by the small campfire set on a sandy knoll.

Boone glanced up as Maddie approached. "How's the water, princess?" he asked.

She pulled up short and stared him down. "It's wet. And the name is Maddie Garret. Don't call me *princess* unless you want me to refer to you as *heap big chief.*"

"You let Danhill get away with it."

"Yes, well, he's a tough nut to crack, but I intend to break him of that annoying habit if it's the last thing I do."

Boone chuckled as he laid the prairie chicken that he'd cleaned and dressed for supper over the fire. "You give as good as you get, Maddie. No wonder Danhill is having a difficult time adjusting to you."

Maddie spread out her bedroll, then plunked down upon it. "Jonah Danhill would have a difficult time adjusting to any woman. Male arrogance hampers him," she diagnosed as she opened a can of peaches to stave off her hunger pangs. She stared pointedly at Boone. "I'd say you suffer from the same malady."

"You're wrong, Maddie. I have a healthy respect for females." He grinned mischievously and added, "As long as they stay in their place."

His teasing remark prompted Maddie to smile. Unlike Jonah—Mr. Serious and Skeptical—this particular half-breed had a well-developed sense of humor and he wasn't so wary and suspicious of everything she said and did.

Maddie munched on a juicy peach and studied Boone consideringly. "If you and Jonah share similar backgrounds, I'm surprised that you don't hold the same grudge against me because my ranch sits in the heart of your former homeland."

"I hold a grudge, all right," Boone admitted candidly. "I just don't happen to suffer from the same complications that Danhill has encountered with you."

Maddie cocked her head and frowned curiously. "I'm afraid I don't follow you."

"Didn't figure you could," he said enigmatically. "You and Danhill are both wearing blinders. Noticed that right off."

On the wings of that baffling comment Boone rose from a crouch and ambled downstream. "You're in charge of cooking while I bathe.... And keep your pistol handy," he cautioned.

When he disappeared from sight, Maddie plunked back on the quilt to stare up at the vault of blue sky illuminated with the pastel rays of sunset. Maybe her first impression of Boone had been all wrong, she mused. The man was as perplexing as Jonah. The only difference was that Boone spoke in riddles while Jonah spoke bluntly and left little doubt as to what he really thought of her.

She was an aggravating inconvenience to Jonah,

Maddie reminded herself. If he didn't possess such a strong sense of duty he wouldn't be here right now.

Why hadn't he turned back? she asked herself. He still didn't believe her. And he certainly didn't find her as attractive as she found him, because he'd had ample opportunity to make amorous advances—and hadn't. When he *did* touch her he always pulled away long before she was ready to let go.

Maddie sighed in frustration. Her one-sided fascination for Jonah was a waste of time and emotion. She knew that. But it didn't stop her from wanting to explore those unprecedented sensations he aroused in her.

Judging by Jonah's standoffishness, Maddie was surprised any of her would-be suitors pursued her at all. But then she reminded herself that most men knew of her family's wealth and saw her as a convenient means to an end. None of them really cared about the person she was on the inside. They were only interested in her inheritance.

Given Jonah's indifferent behavior, Maddie wondered if she had a single endearing quality that might attract a man.

She was seriously beginning to doubt it.

Her self-deprecating thoughts scattered like buckshot when she heard rustling in the bushes behind her. She grabbed the pistol she had laid beside her and came to her knees in one swift motion. She watched a grin of approval spread across Jonah's ruggedly handsome face as she held him at gunpoint.

"Good. You're learning, princess," he praised as he ambled toward her. "Always keep your guard up."

"Stop calling me princess," she said as her admiring gaze flooded helplessly over his impressive physique.

"Whatever you say. You're the one holding the pistol."

Maddie set aside the weapon and rose to her feet. She couldn't say for certain what compelled her, but she walked impulsively to Jonah, slid her hands up his chest and pushed herself up on tiptoes to kiss him. Maybe she wanted to draw a reaction from him, just to prove to herself that she could. Her dealings with him constantly pummeled her feminine pride and compelled her to make a lasting impression on him because his indifference offended and challenged her.

The instant her lips found his the frustration that had been hounding her melted into a swirling vortex of desire. Maddie kissed Jonah for all she was worth, foolishly wishing he would return some of the hungry need that he constantly aroused in her.

When his arms fastened around her hips and he lifted her off the ground, her mind reeled with satisfaction and pleasure. The self-restraint she'd come to expect from him suddenly seemed nonexistent. His mouth moved demandingly, possessively upon hers, and she reveled in the taste of him, the feel of his masculine body pressed tightly to hers.

Wild, uninhibited sensations rippled through her body when Jonah's hands glided over her hips, then guided her legs around his waist. And all the while his lips devoured and his tongue thrust in and out again, setting an erotic rhythm that caused a coil of red-hot desire to burn into her very core.

Maddie had never fully understood what wanting

felt like—until now. When his hand drifted up from her hip to caress the side of her breast, sizzling pleasure shot through her. If she hadn't realized it before, she now understood the power Jonah held over her body. A power she *allowed* him to have because she wanted him in a way she had never dreamed it was possible to want and need a man.

"Damn it, Maddie, you make me crazy," Jonah growled against her kiss-swollen lips. "Tell me to stop this insanity."

"I can't because I want more of it," she whispered breathlessly. "*You* make *me* crazy."

Her body arched involuntarily against his as his fingertips brushed across the fabric that covered her aching nipples. She felt as if she had gone up in flames, felt her pulse pounding like the wings of a captive bird fighting for freedom. But she didn't want to be free of these ineffable sensations. She wanted to touch him as familiarly as he touched her, and let the passion he instilled in her intensify and expand until she was drowning in it.

Refusing to break the scorching kiss, Maddie fumbled with the buttons on his shirt, then sighed in pleasure when her palms splayed over the sleek, muscled flesh of his chest. When Jonah groaned, she felt empowered, fascinated that she could draw an answering response from him. She moved her hand experimentally over his washboard belly and was rewarded with another rumbling growl of need.

He wanted her, she realized. She could taste it in his hungry kiss, feel it in the hard arousal that pressed against her thigh. She had moved this unyielding rock of a man to something more than suspicion and skepticism. Even if he refused to let himself trust her completely, he was not immune to her. That revelation provided Maddie with an incredible sense of satisfaction.

"No one ever kissed my lips off when I returned to camp," Boone remarked as he stepped into plain view and shattered the haze of passion that had wrapped itself around Maddie and Jonah like a cocoon.

Chapter Seven

Jonah grimaced the instant he heard Boone's taunting voice. Swiftly he set Maddie away from him and stepped back. He cursed under his breath as he watched Boone amble over to hunker down by the campfire. A sly smile played on the Kiowa's lips as his gaze bounced between Jonah and Maddie.

"Prairie chicken is burned to a crisp," he said, then tossed Maddie and Jonah another teasing grin. "Not the only thing around here that's burning to a crisp, I see."

Jonah was so hard and aching that he wanted to drop to his knees and howl in unholy torment. For the life of him he didn't know why Maddie had approached him out of the blue. But the moment her dewy lips had melted against his he couldn't remember his own name or recall why it was necessary to keep his distance from her.

Hell, he wasn't sure he could have kept from savoring those honeyed lips or mapping the supple curves and swells of her body if someone held a gun to his head.

She had unleashed his restraint in one second flat and left him a slave to his forbidden desires. It was as if he had been plucked out of reality and dropped into an erotic fantasy. He'd become so needy and desperate so quickly that he'd wanted to fill his hands with her, consume her, possess her completely.

If those betraying thoughts weren't bad enough, Boone was on hand to observe just how little control Jonah possessed when he came within touching distance of this female who could turn him wrong side out and crumble his defenses in one fell swoop. She could transform him from a powerful mountain lion into a helpless pussycat in the time it took to blink.

Hell and damnation, Jonah silently fumed. He'd thought that having Boone underfoot would discourage and prevent him from acting on these obsessive cravings that he battled daily. Apparently not. The way this woman made him feel was downright scary. He simply could not trust himself to touch her without ardent desire boiling his good sense into mush.

"I need to unsaddle my horse and stake him out to graze before supper," Jonah said before he wheeled away from the other man's all-too-knowing stare.

"Yeah, that'll solve the problem," Boone mocked playfully. "Be sure to put that frisky demon on a short leash."

Jonah scowled sourly as he stalked off, knowing the frisky demon Boone referred to was *not* the horse. Although Jonah had liked the Kiowa since their first meeting, he wanted to wring the man's ornery neck for taunting him about his very obvious obsession with Maddie.

Well, at least tonight he wouldn't have to sleep

beside her and spend half the night trying to keep his hands to himself. She had her own sleeping bag, and Jonah had no excuse to cuddle up next to her. That was one less temptation he'd have to face. Thank goodness.

Jonah felt his mood rapidly deteriorate the following morning when they rode away from the lush river valley to encounter the craggy sandstone escarpments, dotted with junipers, mesquite and cedars, that stretched as far as the eye could see. He sensed the change overcome Boone, as well. They were heading straight into the heart of the Comanchería.

As a young brave Jonah had ventured off on vision quests to communicate with his guardian spirit. He, like Boone, had ridden through the deep ravines to visit the isolated haunts where the guiding spirits of the Comanche and Kiowa resided. Jonah could almost feel the eerie presences gathering around him as they trekked near, but not across, the gone-but-not-forgotten battlefields where The People had clashed with their white and Mexican enemies in years gone by.

At high noon they reached the canyon where Colonel Mackenzie had decided to crush the Indians once and for all by rounding up and slaughtering more than fourteen hundred of their prized horses. The army had burned the tipis and food supplies before marching the last band of Indians to the reservation.

"My God, what is that?" Maddie asked as she stared past the mirage that shimmered across the arid ground, studying the western slope of the basin, which glowed eerie white.

"Bleached bones," Jonah said as a wrenching ache knotted in his chest. "This is where the army destroyed our people's beloved horse herd and living quarters. The army left our people with nothing and drove them off their land, just as surely as they exterminated the buffalo."

"Damn them to hell," Boone muttered bitterly as he nudged his mount forward to stare across the gravesite of bones. "The army took our last stronghold and turned it into a bloodbath. And they call *us* savages and heathens!"

Boone's expression mirrored Jonah's boiling resentment. A holocaust of emotions crowded in on him. The whispering wind seemed to carry the haunted voices of his anguished people. He could almost hear the tortured cries of outrage and disbelief, hear the wild screams of horses pelted mercilessly by army rifles. With fanatical fascination Jonah rode closer to the site, knowing it was time to view the atrocity he'd heard about but had refused to visit, until he'd agreed to lead Maddie on her journey home.

The impact on his emotions was everything he'd heard it would be. Outrage, grief and fury blazed through him. The demons of his past rose up like ominous thunderclouds. He looked across the mouth of the rugged valley that seethed with death and despair, and felt bottled resentment, grown more bitter and intense with age, rising like a smothering fog.

His horse shifted uneasily beneath him, as if the gelding sensed the eerie presence that loomed over this tragic site. Jonah glanced sideways to see Boone's horse, as well as Maddie's, shying away from the bone-covered hill, where legend claimed a phantom herd of horses thundered across the valley beneath every full moon.

Jonah flinched when he felt Maddie's small hand slide over his. Shaking off the unnerving sensations that bombarded him, he noticed she had slipped her other hand consolingly over Boone's. Tears streamed down her cheeks as she stared at the skeletons that told the grisly tale of ruthless violence and cruel death.

"I'm so sorry I forced you to face the past," she said with a shaky breath. "*I didn't know.* Couldn't even imagine..." Her voice dried up as her watery gaze settled on Jonah. "Go back." She gave their hands a sympathetic squeeze. "I can't bear the thought of making you confront more hellish memories like this one."

Maddie swallowed convulsively as emotions, guilt and regret foremost among them, knotted in the pit of her stomach. She had hurt both men deeply by forcing them to pass through this area. She could tell by the stricken looks on their faces that it was like riding through the valley of doom.

"Go back," she repeated brokenly.

Abruptly she gouged her heels into the mare's flanks and thundered off, circling the gravesite and heading due north. Jonah and Boone didn't give chase. Couldn't. Not yet. They had to work through the tormented emotions that swirled around them and converged to strike with the force of a thunderbolt.

"The army knew they would devastate our people, who prided themselves in being experienced horse trainers and skilled riders when the herd fell beneath their firing squad." Jonah scowled angrily.

"I wonder how those bastards would feel if the
situation were reversed and the Indians had destroyed
their way of life and stole all that was vital and important to them?" Boone growled resentfully. "I
won't be able to offer my services to the army as a
guide after this." His stormy gaze swept over the de-
moralizing site again and again, as did Jonah's.
"Even though Major Thorton and his men aren't personally responsible for this violent atrocity I still hold
them accountable in my heart."

Jonah shared the same fierce feeling of contempt
for the army. "First the Trail of Tears to remove the
tribes from the fertile lands the whites coveted in the
East. Then the Sand Creek Massacre, which came on
the heels of a supposed peace treaty," he snarled in
disgust.

"And the Washita Massacre," Boone added ve-
hemently. "Not to mention the strychnine poisonings
and premeditated introduction of smallpox and chol-
era epidemics to annihilate our people."

Old hatreds seethed around Jonah like a host of
fire-breathing dragons. Hatreds that he had willfully
buried deep inside him and spent years avoiding now
rose, one by one, to haunt him.

He reminded himself that he had learned to face
the dangers of his occupation and that he had to con-
quer the demons of his past before they swallowed
him alive. But this was far more devastating than any
physical injury he'd ever suffered. This was a wound
that struck heart-and-soul deep.

Jonah forced himself to shift his attention to the
lone rider who scrabbled up the rock-strewn slope,
then vanished into another glimmering mirage on the

mesa. As much as he despised the coil of emotion that ate away at him, he would not allow Maddie to venture northwest without him. He would escort her safely to Mobeetie before he turned back. He couldn't bear the thought of her perishing out here among the other ghosts of his tormented past.

"Go back, Boone," Jonah murmured as he reined his steed in the direction Maddie had taken. "I'll contact you when I return to the Flat."

"Is she worth this, Danhill?" Boone asked pointedly.

Jonah brought his skittish horse to an abrupt halt and twisted in the saddle to meet the other man's dark, smoldering gaze. "You tell me, Boone. It suddenly seems as if our roles have been reversed and she was sent into our lives to guide *us* through our past because we refused to face it ourselves. Just what is the measure of a man who allows his fears and bitterness to dictate who he is and what he will become?"

Boone's quiet laughter held not one hint of amusement. "Damn, Danhill. I was thinking the same thing. Maybe visiting the boiling spring beneath Eagle's Ridge, where the spirits reside, will soothe this ache inside me. If you're going after her then I'm coming with you."

"For only one more day," Jonah told Boone.

"After that, I'm thinking I'll take you up on your offer to join your Ranger battalion."

Jonah nodded agreeably. "At least on the Rio Grande you're too damn busy dodging flying bullets and fighting to stay alive to let your mind wander back into the past to gruesome landmarks like this one, where phantoms call out for justice and revenge that can never come."

Side by side, Jonah and Boone circled the canyon to track down Maddie. Ironic, thought Jonah. Maddie Garret had become their guide, though she had no idea where she was going or what she would find. Jonah figured that he and Boone would be better men for this, but right now it felt as if they were trekking through hell to endure every torment of the damned.

Maddie reached a deep gully overgrown with juniper and mesquite, and couldn't stir another step. She couldn't forgive herself for forcing Jonah and Boone to revisit that grotesque site. She was thoroughly upset with herself for causing them to endure such outrage and grief.

She dismounted and sank defeatedly to the ground. Tears scalded her eyes and regret descended upon her with the impact of a rockslide when she imagined all Jonah and Boone had lost. As tough and invincible as Jonah was, she knew he was hurting in places that he refused to allow the world to see. Yet what wounded him cut deeply into herself like a razor-sharp sword. She was so attuned to him that watching him suffer tortured her beyond measure.

And if that wasn't enough to shatter her composure, she only had two days left before she was to deliver the ransom. *If* Christina was still alive or even cared if she were rescued. The thought provoked an outburst of tears and an eruption of emotion.

Amid wrenching sobs Maddie asked herself how it was possible to weather some kinds of adversity courageously and then fall completely apart when confronted with others. Seeing Jonah and Boone hurting, and speculating about her sister's terror crumbled Maddie's composure thoroughly.

You are such a fool, Maddie chastised herself as she wiped away the streams of tears with the back of her hands. *You've become so prideful and independent the past six months that you refused to become beholden to Ward Tipton or Avery Hanson. Imbecile that you are, you've made this situation worse, not better!*

She knew both Avery and Ward had been waiting for her to accept their marriage proposals, and she had refused to let them believe for one minute that any assistance with the ransom money would guarantee her willingness to wed. Maddie had raced off on the first stage bound for Fort Worth to acquire the necessary funds. It had cost her valuable time that Christina might not have, and it had caused Jonah and Boone unnecessary torment.

Dear God! If Maddie's own newfound independence hadn't gotten in her way, Christina might have been home by now. Damn it, what had Maddie been thinking? If she hadn't been such a stubborn, self-centered imbecile she would have agreed to marry Ward or Avery, just to ensure the ransom would be paid quickly.

"Damn, princess, I didn't know you had so much water in you," Jonah remarked.

Maddie blotted her eyes, then glanced up to see Jonah and Boone poised on the rocky escarpment above her. She thought she'd found the perfect, out-of-the-way place to fall apart. She should have known these two human bloodhounds would track her down.

Now she'd humiliated herself by allowing them to see and hear her bawl like an abandoned child.

She was responsible for dragging these two men through hell and for prolonging Christina's captivity and torment. No doubt, her father would have been bitterly disappointed in her inability to take command of her life and resolve the problems she'd encountered. She was an absolute failure and she was causing turmoil in every life she touched.

"I'm s-so s-sorry," she stuttered.

"You said that already," Jonah reminded her.

"I've p-put you and B-Boone through unnecessary misery and my sister is suffering needlessly because I'm an imbecile!" she finished on a shuddering breath.

Jonah glanced quickly at Boone. "Do me a favor and get lost for a few minutes."

"Fine," Boone said, and snorted. "I'll go see what other bad memories I can stir up."

Her wild-eyed gaze flew to Boone and more tears dribbled down her flushed cheeks.

"Thanks a lot, Boone," Jonah muttered sardonically. "You've been a tremendous help. Now go away."

Jonah sidestepped down the steep slope, starting an avalanche of sand and pebbles. "You about done crying?" he asked as he came to stand over her.

"No," she said, then hiccuped as she tried—in vain—to stem the flow of tears down her cheeks.

Jonah squatted in front of her, curled his forefinger beneath her quivering chin and forced her to meet his gaze. She could barely see him through the burning tears.

"Now tell me how you've made your sister suffer needlessly," he insisted softly.

"I could have married one of the two men who have asked for my hand. They offered to provide the ransom if I agreed to a wedding."

"And you're exceptionally fond of one or both of these men?" Jonah questioned as he rerouted the trail of tears on her cheeks.

"No, but I could have tolerated a marriage to one of them. *Should have,*" Maddie said on a seesaw breath. "But I wasn't thinking about my sister. I was thinking of *myself!* I might never see Christina again because I was too mule-headed to agree to a liaison I didn't want."

Maddie further disgraced herself by flinging herself at Jonah and holding on to him for dear life. Here was yet another of her weaknesses exposed, she realized too late. She had vowed not to depend on him for comfort or consolation when the going got tough. Yet here she was, clinging to him like ivy for physical and moral support. To her everlasting disgrace, she soaked the shoulder of Jonah's shirt with her tears and buried her head beneath his chin. Arms locked tightly around his neck, she succumbed to the tidal wave of emotion that crested within her.

"Shh-shh," Jonah whispered as he sank down on the ground to cradle Maddie in his lap. "You did nothing wrong, sweetheart."

"Yes, I did," she mumbled against his chest. "I defied a commitment that might have spared Chrissy several days of anguish!"

"You told me that you had a week to gather the ransom money," he reminded her as he gently stroked her back and her arms. "You'll return home in time. I promise."

"You don't even believe I have a sister," she sniffled. "You think I'm a conniving thief and you despise me for dragging you and Boone where you didn't want to go. I don't blame you. I hate myself more than you can possibly imagine!"

Jonah couldn't name another moment in his life when he'd felt so utterly useless. He was lousy at offering compassion. He had very little practice at it. Nor was he the kind of man people usually turned to for solace. But watching Maddie bleed tears and beat herself black-and-blue over what-ifs and should-haves tormented him to the extreme. She was questioning her decisions and actions. She was too emotionally distraught to give herself the slightest credit or cut herself any slack.

Feeling inadequate, Jonah simply held her to him until she finally cried herself out and there was nothing left but shuddering sobs of misery. He finally raised her blotchy, tear-stained face to his and placed a featherlight kiss on her quaking lips.

"Everything is going to be okay," he assured her softly.

"No, it isn't," she said, taking a ragged breath. "It's becoming apparent that I'm the curse of your's and Boone's lives. My sister's, too."

Jonah applied the same technique he'd used a few days earlier to snap Maddie back to her senses: he kissed her breathless. But this time she didn't respond to him the way she had previously. She just sat there on his lap, dispirited, defeated, devoid of emotion.

The Maddie he had come to know was suddenly

an empty shell who had cut herself off from the world that caused her pain and anguish. She reminded him so much of the man he had become the past few years that he wanted to shake her. *He* had forgotten how to hope, how to dream. But *she* was usually vital and animated and defiant. He wanted the old Maddie back and he wasn't sure how to retrieve her from the desolate place she'd withdrawn to.

"Enough of this," he said gruffly as he pushed her to her feet, then bounded up beside her. He scooped her up and set her atop her horse. "You've mewled and whined long enough, princess," he said, purposely goading her. "I've seen enough of your self-pity. The whole world, and everyone in it, has troubles galore. Just because you've led a pampered life until recently doesn't grant you special privileges. So what are you gonna do? Throw up your hands and give up on rescuing your sister? I never figured you for a quitter—until now."

Sure enough, the harsh criticism fueled her temper, as he'd hoped it would. Her chin snapped up and those amber eyes blazed down at him like molten fire. Her spine stiffened as she grabbed the reins in her fist.

"You can go straight to hell, Jonah Danhill," she snapped before she dug in her heels and sent the mare scrambling up the steep incline.

"Been there at least a dozen times. Don't recommend it," Jonah murmured as he climbed the ridge to retrieve his own horse.

Well, at least by inciting Maddie's indignation he had stiffened her resolve to get up and get moving. Whatever worked. He'd rather face her anger than deal with the tears that dribbled into the cracks and crevices of his shriveled heart and tugged at his emotions.

Every time he turned around she was getting to him, somehow or another, and he couldn't back away from her.

After witnessing that unsettling scene, Jonah was starting to believe that Maddie had been telling him the truth. No one was such an extraordinary actress that she could pull off the convincing performance Jonah had witnessed a few minutes earlier. But for the life of him he couldn't understand her connection to the two men who had called her by name in Coyote Springs. There was definitely something going on here that Jonah had yet to figure out.

"Feeling better?" Boone asked as Maddie trotted her horse past him.

She didn't glance in his direction, just galloped off as if the devil were nipping at her heels.

Boone glanced over his shoulder when he heard Jonah thundering toward him. "Charmed her into pulling herself together, I see. You *do* have a way with women, Danhill."

"Of course I do. That's why women have lined up to share my company all these years," Jonah said sardonically.

He watched Maddie ride ahead of them, following the narrow ledge that led to a higher plateau.

Boone chuckled as he trotted his roan gelding alongside Jonah. "Right. I've been fighting off women with a stick for years myself." He shifted awkwardly in the saddle. "Sorry about that thoughtless remark I made earlier. I didn't help the situation when you were trying to console Maddie.''

Jonah shrugged off the apology. "I think she was being too hard on herself to notice your comment. Now she's questioning all of the hard choices she's had to make and she feels enormously guilty for putting us back in touch with our past when she knows it's the last thing we wanted.''

They rode in silence for several hours, allowing Maddie her privacy. Jonah looked out across the rough terrain and felt hundreds of charged memories condense around him. Boone, it seemed, was fighting the same silent battle as his gaze drifted, then settled on one looming bluff and twisting gully after another.

Jonah noticed that Maddie had veered west to follow a winding ravine. She couldn't possibly know where she was going, which made him wonder again if a higher power was indeed guiding her. She was headed for an obscure spring nestled deep in the chasm. She had given her mare her head, and it had picked up the scent of fresh water, trotting eagerly forward.

Jonah and Boone urged their horses into a canter. Here was yet another favorite haunt that Jonah recalled from childhood. At least this one provoked pleasant, soothing memories. It was as if Maddie had led them from the jaws of hell into this piece of heaven on earth.

"It is here that the Great Spirit looked down and decided to create man." Jonah recited the legend passed down by his father. "The Spirit took the body from Mother Earth, the bones from the stones and his blood from the morning dew.''

"His eyes were born from the depths of clear water," Boone interjected as his gaze followed Jonah's uplifted eyes to the towering peak that jutted out like an eagle's beak. "He took the light from the sun for eyes and his thoughts from the endless waterfalls."

Jonah smiled as he continued where Boone left off. "Man's breath came from the stirring winds and his strength was born from powerful storms. The Great Spirit created man from all that was admirable and mighty in this world."

"And the Great Spirit ordered all the inhabitants of the spirit world to bow in recognition that man was the most superb creation on the earth," Boone recited.

"All obeyed the command except one," Jonah murmured as he drank in the welcome sight of the sacred landmark of his people. "The defiant demon was cast from the world of guardian spirits and took refuge in the fang of the serpent, the spider, the centipede and other poisonous creatures that sought to torment and harm man."

Maddie listened, fascinated by the Indian legend of creation. She stared at the sparkling spring that bubbled from the base of the towering precipice. A sense of peace and resolution stole over her as she dismounted, then walked into the shallow stream that spilled from the glittering silver pool.

Jonah was right, she decided as she immersed herself in the waters beneath Eagle's Peak. She could waste precious time regretting her decisions and cursing her selfish motivations, or she could take control of her life. Sulking and brooding wouldn't bring back her father and it wouldn't spare Christina. Maddie couldn't give up hope, not while she still had breath left in her and an unwavering will to fight.

She purged herself of her shortcomings and resolved to do whatever was humanly possible to save her sister and their ranch. This wild country was not the place for the faint of heart. If she had learned nothing else from the time spent with Jonah it was that it took courage and determination just to get from one day to the next. The obstacles she encountered were the building blocks of her character, and she would not permit her weaknesses to control her.

Maddie sank into the depths of the pool to cleanse her mind and body of doubts and misgivings. If there truly were guardian spirits that endowed man with omnipotent talents, then she eagerly awaited a vision and empowerment.

Drawing her feet beneath her, she surged from the water—and met Jonah's intense green eyes head-on. Realization hit her with such impact that she staggered backward, and tripped over an oversize rock in the pool. With a shriek she fell on her backside and took another dousing.

Sweet mercy, she thought as she scrambled back to her feet. If she hadn't been aware that Jonah Danhill was her guardian angel, and the man she tried to emulate, she knew it now. *He* was the one who gave her strength and encouragement when despair threatened to destroy her. If she had been too stubborn to admit it before, she couldn't deny now that she was falling in love with this remarkable, complicated man.

She had alternately idolized and despised him. She'd discovered that she craved him in ways she'd never wanted to share her entire being with another man.

Love might not be known for its perfect timing or sensible logic, but it seized control of the heart nonetheless. Love simply *happened,* and it was staring directly at her when she finally stood up again.

Jonah frowned warily when he dragged his lusty gaze off the clinging blouse that outlined the full swells of Maddie's breasts. There was an odd expression on her face, as if she had seen a supernatural vision, or experienced an epiphany. She looked stupefied, astonished. She stared at him as if he were some strange and curious creature that had materialized from the spirit world.

"Maddie!" he barked sharply, hoping to jostle her from her trance. "What's wrong with you?"

He was off his horse, striding hurriedly forward to snatch her from the pool. He looked down, wondering if she might have been bitten by a snake. But he saw nothing but the rock bed beneath his feet.

He carried her ashore and grabbed her by the arms to study her carefully. "Maddie?" he murmured, searching her face—and getting lost in the depths of those luminous eyes.

She threw back her head, and laughter bubbled unexpectedly from her lips, totally baffling Jonah.

"Not a good idea to let a paleface submerge in the spirit springs, I guess," Boone remarked as he walked cautiously toward Maddie. "She's gone crazy."

"I swear that even if I live to be one hundred I'll never figure out what makes a woman tick," Jonah said, exasperated. "First she gushes tears, then spouts in temper and now howls with laughter." He gave her a shake, hoping to bring her back to her senses. "Maddie, snap out of it!"

Maddie just kept giggling. She *had* gone a little crazy, she decided. She was in love with someone who was not going to be a part of her future. He would be gone by nightfall, and she would be left with the knowledge that the man she could have loved forever—the man who could be her soul mate—was going to turn his back and walk out of her life. If she ever decided to wed she'd have to settle for second best and spend the rest of her days comparing her husband to the mate she truly wanted.

She had seen Jonah at his best, his worst and every mood in between, and she still loved him. But she wouldn't be able to share his life and she would never have his love, respect or trust. Considering the various stages of hell Jonah had endured in his life, he might not even be capable of love, she reminded herself. He certainly wasn't *in love* with her. He didn't even want her in his life. He'd simply gotten stuck with her temporarily.

"Maddie?" Jonah's penetrating gaze bored into her, as if probing the secrets of her soul. "Are you okay or not?"

She dragged in a cathartic breath, then let it out slowly. "As good as can be expected, all things considered." She stretched out her hand, palm upward. "Loan me your field glasses and I'll keep watch while the two of you pay your respects without a *paleface* contaminating this sacred place."

Boone grinned guiltily. "I've developed a bad habit of shooting off my mouth without thinking first.'' He winked mischievously at her. "Spent too much time with you palefaces, is my guess.''

Jonah handed her the spyglass, then said, "Don't venture off too far, princess. We won't be long.''

She nodded mutely, then ambled back to her horse, leaving Jonah and Boone to whatever Indian ritual they might be compelled to observe. As for herself, she had encountered a shocking revelation and accepted the inevitable.

She was in love for the first and last time in her life, and the man who held her heart didn't even know it.

And probably wouldn't care if he did.

Chapter Eight

The sun glimmered in the vault of blue sky like a twenty-dollar gold piece as it made its final descent on the western horizon. Maddie stared toward the silhouette of the West Texas community with a mixture of relief and regret. She was only a three-hour ride from her ranch, but she was only minutes away from bidding Jonah a final farewell.

Her emotions had ebbed and flowed continuously during the day. So many warring feelings bubbling inside her that she couldn't possibly sort them all out and address them one at a time. But she had vowed to cling determinedly to her self-control, and refused to succumb to another bout of ungovernable emotion. Jonah's last memory of her was *not* going to be that of a cackling madwoman.

"If you have it in mind to race home after supper, you can forget it," Jonah declared as they reached the outskirts of town.

Maddie snapped her head around and opened her mouth to tell him what she thought of that idea. Jonah flung up his hand to forestall her and gave her a stony stare that she was sure had stopped many a man in his tracks. When it came to intimidation, Jonah Danhill was the best there was.

"You are too close to home to get yourself shot out of the saddle after dark," he told her.

"Listen to him," Boone chimed in. "You have a better chance of seeing trouble coming during daylight than you do after dark. Be sensible, Maddie."

She slumped in the saddle and told herself that Jonah and Boone were probably right. Being overanxious to return home might make her careless. She could wait until morning and still arrive home with plenty of time to deliver the ransom.

"I'll rent a room at Saxon's Hotel for the night," Maddie agreed as they rode into Mobeetie. "If I leave here at dawn I can be home by midmorning." She glanced at Jonah, then at Boone as she fished into her pocket for money. "I'm dreadfully sorry for what I've put you through, but I'm eternally grateful for your assistance."

When Jonah refused to take the money she leaned out to stash it in his shirt pocket, then did the same with Boone. Wearily, she dismounted and tied her horse to the hitching post in front of the hotel. Familiar places and recognizable faces surrounded her now. She could deal with the difficulties awaiting her at the ranch, she convinced herself.

Maddie pasted on a smile as she pivoted to glance up at Jonah and Boone. "I bid you a safe journey back to Fort Griffin…and beyond." Squaring her shoulders, she strode into the hotel.

"Well," Boone said. "Guess you're off the hook, Danhill."

"Yup." Jonah watched Maddie disappear from sight and felt an unfamiliar sensation riddle him. His temptation and torment were over, he reminded himself. He'd anticipated this moment for days. Yet now that it was upon him he felt oddly discontent. Go figure.

"Don't know about you, but I could use a stiff drink and a willing woman to make me forget that it's been one hell of a day." Boone shifted restlessly in the saddle, then glanced down the street. "Think I'll mosey over to Caprock Saloon and drink my supper. You coming?"

Although the prospect of drinking himself unconscious held considerable appeal, Jonah shook his head. "I want to make a few purchases before the stores close. Go on ahead and I'll catch up with you later."

Boone stared at the front door of the hotel, then at Jonah. A wry smiled kicked up one corner of his mouth. "Bet you're glad to have that troublesome female out of your hair."

"Definitely," Jonah felt compelled to say.

"I've been like an emotional train wreck most of the day," Boone confided.

"Same here," Jonah confirmed.

"The ladies of the night that we'll find at the saloons and gaming halls can help us forget our ordeal. Plus, they will be a welcome change from that sassy female we've been traveling with," Boone added.

"Right. No complications," Jonah agreed. "Can't think of anything I anticipate more."

Boone chuckled as he reined west. "Keep telling

yourself that, Danhill. By midnight you might start believing it.''

Jonah released his breath in a frustrated huff. He was glad to have Maddie off his hands and out of his life. Now he could get back to his long-awaited vacation before he headed south to rejoin his battalion.

His assessing gaze drifted up and down the street, noting that passersby were staring curiously at him. This was just another nameless town where folks speculated about his Indian heritage and reflexively labeled him as a no-account. Only when he pinned the badge on his chest did he draw a measure of wary respect.

Well, didn't matter, Jonah reminded himself as he strode off to make his purchases. He'd never spent time fretting about what white folks thought of him. He sure as hell wasn't about to start now.

Later he would have that much-needed drink—or three. First he was going to buy himself an expensive cigar and smoke it like the ritualistic pipes his forefathers had used while they sat around the campfire and contemplated the world. Then he'd find himself a willing female and relieve the days of frustration triggered by his tormenting association with Maddie.

That was his plan and he was sticking to it, he told himself as he veered into one of the stores on Main Street.

When Maddie had freshened up and buttoned herself into the one stylish dress she'd brought with her, she ambled off to enjoy a meal at the restaurant. She noticed that Jonah's coal-black gelding was nowhere to be seen. However, she had a pretty good idea where he'd gone. The same place most men frequented when they arrived in town to blow off steam.

The thought of Jonah in the arms of another woman stung like a wasp. Trying to outrun the painful vision, Maddie scurried across the street. To her surprise she saw Avery Hanson sitting alone at a table. The stout, bulky rancher, who was a good fifteen years her senior, smiled in greeting and motioned for her to join him.

"Ah, sweet Maddie, you are a sight for sore eyes," Avery gushed. "I've been worried about you."

She reluctantly took the seat he pulled out for her. Maddie wasn't in the mood for companionship, but Avery insisted on buying her supper. She inwardly flinched when he reached across the table to take her hand in his.

"With all the trouble you've been dealing with lately I had hoped you would turn to me for comfort and support. Have you raised the money for the ransom? If not, you know I will make you the loan, in exchange for your consent to marry."

Maddie withdrew her hand. All it took was that brief contact to remind her that she welcomed the touch of only one man. The one who was—at this very moment, no doubt—tumbling around on a bed with another woman. *Any* woman except her.

"I acquired the money I need," Maddie told the rancher, whose receding hairline made his forehead appear twice the normal size. It also emphasized his bushy brows, which reminded her of fuzzy brown caterpillars above his slate-gray eyes. "But I do thank you for your offer."

She noticed immediately the expression that crinkled his ruddy features. Avery was not pleased by the news, though he made a grand effort to assure her that he was.

"Good. Good, my dear." He levered his round body forward and leaned his elbows on the table. "I'm sure Christina will be home where she belongs very soon. Perhaps *then* you will be in a better frame of mind to accept my offer of marriage. You know how very fond I am of…"

His voice trailed off when the waitress appeared to take their order. Maddie was grateful for the momentary reprieve. She was not in the mood to hear Avery shower her with pretentious flattery or spout his supposed affection for her. She knew he was anxious to get his hands on the Bar G Ranch because of its abundant source of fresh spring water that nourished pastures, which in turn made Bar G cattle fat and marketable—until rustlers sneaked in to steal them during the night.

"There you are, sweetheart."

Maddie started at the rich baritone voice behind her. To her disbelief, she glanced over her shoulder to see Jonah towering behind her. She was also stunned when he leaned down to press a kiss to her forehead.

What the devil was he doing? she wondered bewilderedly.

Jonah thrust his hand toward Avery, who gaped at him in confusion. "Any friend of my wife's is a friend of mine. The name is Jonah Danhill."

He plunked down in the empty chair and motioned to the waitress. "I'll have what my wife is having."

"*Your wife?*" Avery wheezed, incredulous.

Jonah nodded his raven head as he reached into his shirt pocket to retrieve a shiny gold band. When he slipped it on her finger, Maddie stared at him, dumbfounded.

"I didn't want to waste any time replacing the ring you lost while swimming in the river," he said as he flashed her the most intimate smile she'd ever seen.

"Your wife?" Avery repeated. It seemed to be all he could think to say. Clearly he was shocked by the announcement that the ranch he coveted had been whisked from his reach. "When? Where?"

"In Coyote Springs," Jonah explained as nonchalantly as you please. "I actually met Maddie two years ago when I stopped at her ranch. I couldn't get her off my mind." He smiled adoringly as he reached over to trail his forefinger over her cheek, then tucked a recalcitrant corkscrew curl behind her ear. "I wrote to her monthly after that." He turned his attention back to the stricken rancher. "I considered it fate that we met in Coyote Springs."

Maddie had no clue why Jonah was carrying on this charade, but she heartily approved. He was providing her with a welcome buffer against Avery's repetitive proposals. She could have hugged the stuffing out of Jonah for this one last favor before he rode away. She would compensate him for the ring, of course. She didn't expect him to take the purchase from his pay.

"But I thought you and I—" Avery's accusing glare swung to Maddie and she winced at the menacing curl of his thin lips. Right there and then, she realized that when the rancher wasn't getting his way he could be a mite vicious, and that his charm—what little there was of it—was pretentious.

"I'm sorry, Avery," Maddie declared, her tone nowhere near as regretful as it might have been if he hadn't been glaring mutinously at her. "The fact is that I've harbored a secret affection for Jonah since we first met when he…" Maddie cursed herself soundly for rambling. She was too rattled by Jonah's unexpected arrival to embellish the tale, and had no idea where she was going with this.

"I herded horses to her ranch." Jonah took over from there. "Her father purchased several head from me."

Maddie tried not to slump in visible relief when he provided a plausible explanation. She turned her grateful gaze to Jonah, whose direct stare dared Avery to object to their supposed marriage.

When Jonah leaned close, as if to whisper sweet nothings in her ear—as if *that* would ever happen— Maddie shivered in helpless response. She noticed that Avery's eyes narrowed into thin slits when Jonah moved familiarly toward her.

"Your four friends have arrived in town," he murmured for her ears only. "Boone and I spotted them a half hour ago."

The news caused Maddie to tense apprehensively. She couldn't bear the thought of being this close to home with the ransom money and having it stolen from her. Damnation, didn't she have enough trouble coping with this unrequited affection for Jonah without going another round with those pesky thieves?

When their meal arrived, Maddie found that she'd lost her appetite, but she forced herself to eat. Jonah, she noticed, was the only one at the table who gobbled every bite of his food.

Avery Hanson shoved aside his half-eaten dinner and came to his feet. "If you will excuse me, I need to ensure that all my ranching supplies have been loaded in the wagon. My hired hands will be driving my cattle to Dodge City in two days and I want them to be prepared for the journey." Having said that, he lurched around and stalked from the café.

"One of your would-be fiancés, I presume," said Jonah.

Maddie nodded. "That's Avery Hanson. He has been itching to get his hands on my ranch."

Jonah smirked. "I doubt your ranch is the only thing he'd like to get his hands on, princess."

"Don't kid yourself. There is nothing endearing about me that entices a man into marriage except the prospect of controlling a prosperous ranch. Or at least it was prosperous until the rustling spree began. You are living testimony that my appeal is meager at best."

"What makes you think that?"

Maddie rolled her eyes in annoyance. "If memory serves, and it serves me very well, thank you, we have shared a pallet and bed and you felt no inclination to make advances."

He chuckled. "And you're basing your conclusion on that?"

Maddie bolted to her feet before she humiliated herself more than she already had. Jonah provoked too many emotions inside her. If she didn't leave right now there was no telling what idiotic comments she might blurt out.

Before she could exit the café Jonah was beside her, taking her arm to escort her onto the street. "Pay attention, hellcat," he growled in her ear. "You might be on familiar ground, but your friends still want your money."

Maddie pulled up short and gathered her composure. Jonah was right. She shouldn't barrel across the street after dark without paying strict attention to those around her. After the incidents in Coyote Springs and the Flat she knew trouble lurked in the shadows, waiting to pounce.

Her sharpened gaze darted down the street and she jerked upright when she saw Avery in conversation with one of the cowboys who had followed her back from Fort Worth.

"Son of a bitch," Jonah muttered beside her, then jerked her back inside the restaurant. He stared grimly down at her before he turned on his heel and shepherded her through the kitchen, as if he owned the place. Then he tugged her through the back door to the alley.

"This is beginning to make sense," Jonah murmured as he towed Maddie along. "I'm thinking your would-be fiancé might have sent a couple of his men to make sure you didn't return with the ransom money."

She stopped in her tracks, only to be uprooted and dragged along at his swift pace. "My God, do you think Avery would stoop that low, to get his hands on my ranch and force me to turn to him for help?"

"He's *your* acquaintance. You tell me. But I suspect he would be ready and willing to hand over the needed money if you agreed to marry him."

"Why, that devious, manipulative—"

Jonah clamped his hand over her mouth when her voice rose to a near shout. "Quiet down. The whole idea here is *not* to draw attention to ourselves. For sure, you aren't going through the front door to the hotel."

With a sense of urgency, Maddie hurried alongside Jonah.

Avery Hanson seethed as he watched Jesse Gibbs swagger toward him. "I hope you know that I'm not paying you until you handle this situation I entrusted to you."

Gibbs shrugged off Avery's fuming glare and propped himself negligently against the supporting post of the dry goods store. "And I hope *you* know this situation didn't turn out to be as simple as you said it would be," he countered insolently. "You are definitely going to pay me for my time and trouble. And by the way, Maddie has a husband. Why didn't you tell me that?"

"I didn't know it myself until a few minutes ago," Avery muttered sourly. "That ruins everything! I already have my hands full trying to keep my impatient creditors at bay. I had my plans for financial recovery laid out nice and neat, and everything falling into place. I was certain that Maddie would turn to me and her ranch would be under my control." Avery huffed out a frustrated breath. "And now this new development!"

"She still has the money she brought back from Fort Worth," Jesse reported as he tugged at the grimy bandanna that encircled his neck. "But the bad news is that she also has a husband and another bodyguard hovering around her. It won't be as easy to snatch that money with those two men around.''

Muttering, Avery paced back and forth on the boardwalk. "Easy or not, this is your only chance to steal that money before she returns to her ranch.'' He halted and swung his bulky body around to confront Jesse. ''And get rid of her husband while you're at it. It has to be tonight or I'm going to have to devise another plan, pronto. Damn it!'' he exclaimed irritably, then dragged in a deep breath and told himself to muffle his voice before someone overheard him. ''I'm sure Maddie is staying at the British-owned hotel. Saxon Hotel has the best accommodations and that's always where she stays when she comes to town.''

''I'll see what I can do,'' Jesse said as he pushed himself away from the post. ''But I want half my pay now.''

Scowling, Avery dug into his pocket and handed Jesse all the cash he had on him. ''This is all you're going to get until Maddie's husband is out of the way and I have that money.'' He glanced cautiously around, then stepped into the shadows near the door of the store. ''Make damn certain there are no witnesses. I don't want the blame to come boomeranging back to me. I've taken a chance just being seen on the street with you.''

When Jesse sauntered away, Avery swore foully. He hated having to alter his plans on short notice once he had them all laid out. It made him twitchy, wondering if he had remembered to cover all his tracks. But a sizable fortune hung in the balance and he

needed the money to keep afloat and to expand his
ranch operation. That new husband of Maddie's had
to go!

Avery double-checked the supplies in the wagon,
then paced nervously, still lost in thought. There was
something fishy about this sudden marriage, he
mused. It was too convenient. And why would Maddie up and marry a man who was obviously a half-
breed when she was a wealthy heiress?

Avery couldn't answer that puzzling question, but
he reminded himself that it wouldn't matter after tonight. Jesse Gibbs was handy with a pistol and, for a
price, he would eliminate any obstacle that stood in
Avery's way.

Comforted by the thought, Avery tossed his worries
aside and smiled in anticipation of returning home to
that certain someone who knew how to help him relax. And tomorrow, all his financial worries would be
over, he assured himself. Of course, he would be there
to console the young widow and convince her to
marry him. He would promise to protect her from
future harm—and put himself in position to expand
and take control of this entire area of Texas.

Once he had Maddie in hand he was going to focus
on ruining Ward Tipton's ranch the same way he had
undermined the Bar G Ranch. That uppity Brit needed
to go back to England where he belonged, Avery decided. The man's haughty airs annoyed him, and Avery was tired of the rival attention Ward bestowed on
Maddie. If Ward Tipton didn't back off and go away
he might find himself staring down the barrel of Jesse
Gibbs's pistol.

* * *

"How do you propose that I return to the hotel without being spotted?" Maddie asked as Jonah emerged from the alley to scan the street.

"The same way Gibbs and Newton sneaked into your room in the Flat." Jonah shielded Maddie from view as he bustled her across the street, then ducked into another alley.

"So you finally believe what I've been telling you?" she asked as she hiked up her skirts and sprinted down the alley.

"Yeah, I guess I do, princess," Jonah admitted. He grabbed her arm and directed her attention to the windows above them. "Which room is yours?"

Maddie gestured to the left. "There, but we don't have a convenient stack of crates at our disposal."

Jonah appraised the situation, then scooped Maddie into his arms. Before she realized what he was about to do he had lifted her over his head, planted his hand on her derriere and boosted her upward. Maddie balanced herself on the narrow ledge above the first-story window, grabbed hold of the edge of the building—and lost her footing.

Swearing, Jonah repositioned himself beneath her. She dropped into his arms, then he set her back to her feet. "Bad idea," he grumbled as he grabbed her hand and jogged down the alley. "Do you have the money with you?"

"Yes, it's tucked in the hem of my skirt.... Now where are we going?"

"To my room. We have a better chance of sneaking you in there, even if it isn't the fanciest place in town." He halted behind one of the saloons that rented rooms on the second floor. "It isn't much," Jonah warned her.

"At this point I don't care. As long as I don't have to wake up with a pistol in my throat again."

"Boone rented the room beside me, so if trouble arises, he'll be close at hand," he assured her.

Finding an abundance of whiskey crates behind the saloon, Jonah fashioned steps for Maddie to climb. Once she had thrust her leg through the window and disappeared inside, he disassembled the makeshift steps, then strode around the corner.

The four men that he and Boone had spotted earlier that evening were nowhere to be seen, but Hanson's loaded wagon still stood beneath the street lantern. The stocky rancher was pacing back and forth on the boardwalk, glancing expectantly around him.

Jonah had the unshakable feeling that Maddie's would-be fiancé had a hand in the trouble she'd encountered. Jonah felt like an overly suspicious fool for mistrusting Maddie. He suspected she had been set up to fail on her crusade. Unless Jonah missed his guess—and he doubted that he had—Avery Hanson had sent his henchman to steal the money so Maddie would have to turn to him in desperation.

"The sneaky bastard." Jonah scowled, clinging to the shadows as he slinked into the saloon. Tinkling piano music and rowdy laughter filled the room. A cloud of stale smoke hovered over the gaming tables, where calico queens cozied up to the men who had the largest stack of winnings sitting at their elbows.

Well, so much for trying his hand at the poker tables and inviting the nearest female upstairs to help him forget the woman who had tempted him to the very limits of his restraint. Jonah panned the saloon in search of familiar faces. Gibbs, Newton and Selmon were nowhere to be seen. Of course, Jonah hadn't met Rance Lewis, so he couldn't guarantee the man wasn't lurking about. Boone knew Lewis on sight, but Jonah had no idea where Boone had gotten off to.

Zigzagging among the tables, Jonah headed upstairs to his room—and to the woman who awaited him. Damn, he'd been so close to getting Maddie off his hands, but fate, that damnable devil, kept tossing her back in his lap.

And sure as hell, she was going to demand to know why he'd purchased that gold band that he'd placed on her finger while Hanson watched.

"What's this for?" Maddie asked the instant Jonah entered his compact room.

"Protection," he explained as she waved the ring under his nose. "I figured if you had a wedding band on your finger it would discourage the wanna-be fiancés who keep hounding you. All the better that I had the chance to meet one of your eager beaus in person. He can verify that I actually exist."

With a pensive nod she slipped the band back on her finger. It was a bit large, for Jonah had had to guess at the size. An odd feeling settled inside him when he glanced at her hand and that ring. Their pretend marriage didn't seem such a hoax since he'd made the purchase. It seemed as if she truly did belong with him.

Jonah gave himself a mental shake when the ridiculous thought jammed in his mind. He might not be the smartest hombre on the continent, but he had enough brains to know that he and Maddie were completely mismatched. He was a nomadic tumbleweed of a half-breed who only commanded respect and courtesy when folks noticed his badge. Maddie, however, was a land baroness who had men champing at the bit to claim her and take control of her property.

Not a bad bargain, Jonah mused. And despite what Maddie thought, she was more than enough incentive to entice a man into marriage—with or without her valuable property and trust fund.

Just not Jonah Danhill. He didn't deserve a woman of Maddie's wealth and obvious good breeding. Furthermore, he had not one damn thing to offer her. Except himself. And God knew that *he* was no prize.

Maddie smiled appreciatively as she twisted the ring on her finger. "That was very thoughtful of you, Jonah. I'm sure I can count on Avery to spread the word that he's met my husband." When she glanced up at Jonah another shaft of desire struck below his belt buckle.

"When the right man comes along, you can shed that band and announce that you're recently widowed or divorced," he suggested.

"The right man already came along." Her smile faltered as she stared at him. "He just doesn't want me."

"Maddie..." he said warningly. "If you're referring to me, I—"

Jonah's throat closed up when she walked purposely toward him and halted close enough for her unique scent to bombard his senses. Damn it, he'd made dozens of bargains with himself, trying to keep his distance from temptation. But he'd become a sentimental softy when he faced the realization that this was the last time he'd see this golden-eyed beauty who had an uncanny knack of getting under his skin—repeatedly.

"What is it about me that you find so lacking?" she asked somberly. "Not pretty enough? Too sassy and independent?"

Not pretty enough? Hell! She was the most bewitching, alluring female he'd ever encountered. Too sassy and independent? He liked that about her—even if she exasperated him occasionally with that willful mind of her own.

"Too unskilled in the art of pleasing a man?" she questioned when he didn't choose answer A or B. "If that's the case, perhaps I should *hire* you to teach me how to please you," she suggested impulsively.

Her comment sucked the breath clean out of his lungs and rendered him speechless. His heart slammed against his ribs and stuck there. He stared down at her luscious mouth and wanted it like nothing he'd ever known. He glanced up at the knot of curly hair that she'd coiled atop her head and he burned to get his fingers in the golden strands, knowing they would feel like silk sliding over his hands.

And that wasn't all he desired, he mused as his all-consuming gaze drifted over the swanlike column of her neck and dropped to the full swells of her breasts. He itched to touch her familiarly, to learn every shapely contour of her body by taste. And more than that, he wanted to mold her body against his, bury himself in her womanly softness and savor the tantalizing pleasure he had envisioned so often in his dreams.

He yearned for her to be his wife—pretend or otherwise—for just one night. He wanted the right and privilege to teach her what passion was all about. But she deserved better than that, deserved a man who didn't come with an unflattering stigma. A man who knew how to stay in one place and put down roots.

Jonah wouldn't know the first thing about that. He'd been raised with the Comanche, who followed the buffalo, then pulled up stakes to find winter campgrounds before moving on in the spring. He served with the Rangers, who rode from one trouble spot to the next. Jonah wouldn't know what to do with himself if he couldn't drift with the wind.

Maddie wanted to shake Jonah until his teeth rattled for simply standing there, staring down at her with those penetrating green eyes. She had brazenly asked him to make love to her one time before he went away. What did a woman have to do to tempt this invincible warrior?

Suddenly she recalled the teasing remark Jonah had made days ago. He'd said he would reverse direction and leave after he'd seen her naked. Determined of purpose, she veered around Jonah to lock the door. He arched a wary brow as he glanced over his shoulder. His gaze settled intently on her as she pivoted to snuff out the lantern.

"This is what you asked for," she reminded him as she unfastened the tiny buttons on the bodice of her gown.

"Damn it, Maddie, don't," he choked out.

The moonlight that filtered through the window provided more than enough light for Jonah to see her tapered fingers moving over the buttons. He swal-

lowed against the boulder that had somehow lodged
in his throat as the pale green fabric gaped to reveal
the thin chemise clinging to her breasts. He was hard
and aching in the time it took to swallow with a strangled gulp.

"Name your price, Danhill." She pushed the gown
to her hips, then stepped away from the pool of fabric
that encircled her feet.

She stood before him in the flimsy chemise and
pantaloons, and Jonah groaned at the enticing sight.
"Maybe it would be best for both of us if you took
this matter up with Boone," he chirped, his intense
gaze flooding helplessly over her.

"But Boone isn't who I want." She stepped toward
him. Her arms glided over his rigid shoulders as she
tilted her head back to stare directly at him. "It's *you*,
Jonah. I'm only asking for one night. Is that too much
to request of you?"

When she cupped her hand around the back of his
neck and brought his head steadily toward hers Jonah
knew he was going to buckle to the forbidden fantasy
that had been dancing in his mind since he'd first met
Maddie. His tormenting desire was going to lead him
straight to hell. He'd resisted maddening temptation
for as long as he could stand, and he was quickly
losing the ability to reason. For this one night he was
going to savor the passion and emotion she called
from him, and cast common sense to the wind.

"Damn, but you drive a hard bargain," he growled
as he nipped at her petal-soft lips and gathered her in
his arms.

"That's because I know exactly what I want," she
whispered between steamy kisses. "What I need right

now is *you* to help me forget the hellish day we've had.''

"All I want is to get you naked," he rasped as he tugged impatiently at the chemise. "And to keep you that way until dawn."

"I'm glad we finally agree wholeheartedly on something," she teased as she pushed the shirt from his shoulders.

The instant her hands and lips coasted over Jonah's laboring chest the frayed threads of his noble restraint snapped. He'd never felt so desperate and needy in his life, but he'd be damned if he'd rush through this night with Maddie. He vowed to savor her, to revel in every moment that she was in his bed. If he was going to make a colossal mistake, then it was going to be the best one he'd ever made.

He scooped her lush body into his arms, pulled back the quilts and bent his knee to lay her gently on his bed. In the dim light he could see the enchanting smile that played on her lips, and he grinned back at her.

"What?" he asked as he stepped back to unfasten his holster and drop it within easy reach of the bed. He pulled the dagger from his boot and unfastened the sheath on his arm. His gaze never left hers as he laid his weapons on the end table.

"It occurs to me that I should be thoroughly ashamed and demoralized that I have to *pay* a man to make love with me," she murmured as she reached out to draw him down beside her.

"You're right. And you *should* be," he agreed with a husky chuckle. "You're entirely too brazen to suit a proper gentleman. Lucky for you that I'm not one.

I also work cheap.'' His eyes twinkled with amusement. ''Being the businesswoman you are, you should appreciate the good deal you're getting.''

Maddie swore she'd fallen in love with Jonah all over again when he allowed her to see the playful side of his personality that he'd concealed from the world. The last of her awkwardness and apprehension fell away when he propped himself up on his forearms and made a thorough study of her.

''And, by the way,'' he said huskily, ''I don't want to hear any more of that nonsense about you not being appealing. You're beautiful, Maddie. Breathtaking is nearer the mark.'' His hand glided down her collarbone, then swirled over her breasts before circling her navel. ''Better decide right this minute if this truly is what you want, princess, because I've about used up the last of my restraint.''

''Right now, I can think of nothing I want more,'' she said with a satisfied sigh. ''All I want and need is you.''

Chapter Nine

Her body trembled in response to his featherlike touch and she swore she was about to melt bonelessly into the mattress. The emotional turmoil of the day drifted into oblivion as she focused absolute attention on the man who hovered over her, appraising her as if she were a priceless work of art. He made her feel incredibly desirable with just one heated glance, made her ache with each sweeping caress of his hand.

"Ah, Jonah..." Her breath hitched when he pulled the chemise over her head, then skimmed his warm lips over her beaded nipples.

When he took one sensitive bud into his mouth and suckled her, tingling sensations rippled through her. Maddie arched instinctively toward him as another fiery blast of pleasure sizzled through her body and burned into her very core. Impulsively she reached up to brush her fingertips over his muscled chest, but he grabbed her wandering hand.

"Not yet, princess," he whispered against her skin. "Don't distract me. I'm going to ensure you get everything you're paying for tonight."

"I asked you to teach *me* to please *you*," she reminded him with a shaky breath.

She felt him smile against the quivering flesh of her belly. "You are pleasing me. Touching *you* pleases me immensely. Now hush while I concentrate on making a thorough study of everything about you that bewitches me."

Maddie sucked in a ragged breath and dug her nails into the sheet as his hands and lips whispered over her flesh, igniting such white-hot pleasure that she moaned aloud. He divested her of her pantaloons, then flicked his tongue against her navel. The palm of his hand skimmed her nipples as his lips drifted over her abdomen.

"Jonah, please…" she murmured, unsure what she wanted from him. What could possibly appease this burning ache that pulsated in rhythm with her accelerated heartbeat?

"Not enough?" he taunted playfully as his questing hands brushed from her knees to her inner thighs. "Daredevil that you are, I'm not surprised. You want more?"

"Yes…" Her voice dried up on that shameless admission when his warm lips followed the titillating path of his hands. He sensitized every inch of her flesh and left her quivering in helpless response. The powerful undercurrent of desire he aroused dragged her into its hypnotic depths and left her shimmering with unrivaled pleasure. "Oh, my…"

Jonah brushed his free hand over the nest of curls between her thighs and felt hungry need clench inside him. When he glided his thumb over her softest, most sensitive flesh, he found her hot and wet, and he nearly lost it. She was like silky flames scorching his fingertips. Aching desire rocketed through him and exploded like fireworks.

He'd never devoted so much time and attention to a woman, but it seemed vital and necessary to discover how and where Maddie liked to be touched. He delighted in every muffled sound that he summoned from her, and he wanted to hear more, wanted to fill his senses with the taste and feel of this beguiling woman who had captivated him against his will.

When he dipped his finger inside her moist heat he felt her shudder in uncontrollable reaction. His own pleasure intensified tenfold as he stroked her intimately, and he heard her whisper his name with a ragged breath. She clutched at his arm, her nails unintentionally scoring the mending wound on his shoulder, but he didn't care. There wasn't enough pain in this world to override the masculine satisfaction he experienced when he made her luscious body burn with desperate need for him.

He shifted above her, nudging her thighs apart with his elbows, then glanced up her shapely body to see those amber eyes aflame with desire. He committed her expression to memory before he lowered his head to flick at her sultry flesh with the tip of his tongue. Her breath unraveled as he offered her the most intimate of kisses and caressed her gently with his thumb and fingertip.

Suddenly her body contracted around his gliding hands and lips, and he felt her wild release echoing through him. Urgent need—so intense that he shook with it—nearly overwhelmed him. But Jonah denied himself so he could bring her slowly to climax again.

His name was an incessant chant on her lips as he imitated his most fervent desire with the thrust of his tongue and fingertip.

And this time, when she came apart beneath his intimate caresses, he reached down to unfasten his breeches, then tossed them aside. He was more than ready and willing to be there for her at the moment she wanted him most.

Maddie was so desperate for him that she closed her fingers around his rigid length to guide him to that place deep inside her that burned with fiery need. He had teased and tormented her almost beyond bearing, and the empty ache he left burgeoning inside her demanded to be filled. She understood exactly what she had craved earlier—what she now needed madly, obsessively. He had aroused her to the point that she wanted him more than life itself, more than she wanted air to breathe. She *needed* to feel him inside her, needed to be flesh to flesh with him—right this very instant. In another moment the tormenting pleasure he aroused was going to be the death of her, she was sure of it.

His powerful body surged over hers and he settled exactly upon her. Nothing could have prepared her for the impact of delicious sensations that pummeled her as he braced himself on his muscled arms and moved gently, *tentatively* against her.

And *that* drove her crazy. He was trying to be too careful with her, and she was impatient to ease the wild ache that burned for him. He was intimately close, but he was still too unbearably far away to appease her.

"Not enough," she choked out as ardent need shook her.

His startled gaze dropped to her face and he stopped dead still, the muscles of his arms bulging as he hovered over her.

"Don't you dare hold out on me, Jonah," she demanded as she arched upward, urging him deeper. "I want all you have to give and I'll accept nothing less."

A scampish grin spread across his shadowed face, showing a flash of white teeth. "Insist on your money's worth, do you?" His playfulness faded and a tender expression softened his rugged features. "I was trying not to hurt you, princess. You should be thanking me."

"Well, I'm not grateful. I'm on fire and you're the one who started it. Now finish this before I die of unfulfilled torment."

Maddie grabbed a handful of his raven hair and dragged his head to hers. She kissed him demandingly, possessively, then gyrated her hips against his in a provocative plea for more.

Jonah decided he had unintentionally offended Maddie by treating her as if she were made of fragile crystal. Princess or not, the lady knew what she wanted and how she wanted it. He gladly accommodated her, because holding himself at bay was taking its toll.

He thrust deeply into her and felt the fragile barrier give way. But Maddie didn't cry out. Didn't so much as whimper or flinch. She held on to him as if she never meant to let go, wrapped those sleek, well-toned legs around his waist, clenched her thighs against his hips and moved with him in perfect rhythm.

That was so like his Maddie, he thought as raging pleasure streamed through him like a flash flood. Nothing timid or hesitant about her. She met him thrust for urgent thrust and nipped at his shoulder as he drove into her with no restraint whatsoever.

He was caught up in the tumultuous conflagration of passion that exploded around him. White-hot flames scorched him inside and out. Fiery need blazed hotter until it consumed him completely. His thoughts went up in smoke as immeasurable pleasure expanded, at such a phenomenal rate that he feared he would combust.

Windswept waves of heat crashed over him and he plummeted through time and space like a meteor blazing a path to its own flaming destruction. His body shuddered repeatedly in the aftermath of unbelievable passion.

It was like nothing he had ever experienced or could have possibly imagined.

Gasping for breath, Jonah wrapped Maddie possessively in his arms and held her against his thudding heart as the last of his strength and energy deserted him. Sweet mercy, he thought as he struggled to regather his scattered senses. No one had ever demanded so much from him, and he had never given of himself so freely before. This was something so far beyond sexual satisfaction that Jonah couldn't identify all the mind-boggling sensations and tangled emotions that rumbled inside him.

And that rattled him beyond measure.

When Maddie stirred beneath him, Jonah willed

himself to ease down beside her, but she grabbed hold
of his bare hips and held him in place. Another startling, indescribable sensation rippled through him
when she pressed a feathery kiss to his shoulder and
sighed in satisfaction.

Damn, sharing forbidden passion with Maddie
must have turned him into a sentimental sap. He felt
a goofy grin quirk the corners of his mouth as un-
paralleled contentment settled over him.

"Well worth the cost," she murmured, her raspy
voice whispering against his neck.

He lifted his disheveled head and found her smiling
impishly at him. Jonah committed that endearing expression to memory, too. In the years to come he
wanted to reflect on this remarkable night and remember everything she'd said and how she'd looked when
they surrendered to a wildfire of ineffable desire.

"Thanks, princess." He pressed his lips to her kiss-
swollen mouth, finding that he wasn't in his usual
rush to get up and dress before making a hasty departure.

"Jonah, I—" She clamped her mouth shut, then
smiled again.

"You what?" he prompted, but she shook her
head, sending a tangle of riotous curls over his fore-
arm.

"Nothing important."

He didn't press her for an answer, just dropped
another kiss to her dewy lips. When she moved sen-
suously against him and wrapped both arms around
his neck, he felt his male body stirring inside her. He
marveled at her amazing ability to arouse him so soon
after he swore she had worn him out completely.

"If I have only this one night with you, then I don't intend to waste time sleeping," she assured him as her hands glided down his back to caress his hips. "I want more...."

Jonah didn't deny her. Couldn't. Not when her lush body called to his and hungry need pelted him all over again. As they moved together as one, Jonah lost the ability to process thought and he soared off into a maelstrom of pleasure. He proved to himself once again that for all his tested strengths, he had one great weakness—his passion for Maddie.

And later, while they lay spent in each other arms, another corner of his hardened heart crumbled to pieces when she reached out to trace the curve of his mouth, his cheek and his chin, and then said, "You please me immensely."

Jonah trailed his forefinger over the gold band on her finger, then brushed one last kiss over her lips. She snuggled up against him as if that was where she belonged, and drifted off to sleep. Jonah draped a protective arm around her and tucked her head beneath his chin.

He could get used to this if he wasn't careful, he mused as he closed his eyes. But he wouldn't allow himself that luxury, because therein lay torment. This was the only night he'd ever spend with Maddie—and it was definitely one more than he should have spent with her. But at least he had treasured memories to cherish until the end of his days.

Maddie awoke the next morning to find Jonah gone. It was better this way, she assured herself. No tearful goodbyes to give her feelings away. She glanced sideways to see one of his pistols lying on the nightstand, although the rest of his gear was gone. Lost in erotic memories of the most incredible night imaginable, Maddie pushed herself upright. She plucked up the clothes that Jonah had thoughtfully draped over the edge of the bed....

Thoughtfully? She smiled in affectionate amusement. Hard-bitten though Jonah Danhill appeared on the outside, he had a tender streak. She'd seen plenty of evidence of his attentiveness and consideration the past few days—and last night.

Wincing at the unfamiliar tenderness between her thighs, Maddie walked over to pour water into the basin and wash her face. An impish smile pursed her lips when another round of erotic memories assailed her. She still couldn't believe she'd been so bold and demanding with Jonah. The man obviously brought out her most brazen characteristics. Heavens, the things she had said to him. The things they had done in the heat of mindless passion!

Maddie splashed more cold water on her pulsing face and forced herself to concentrate on the matter at hand. She needed to mount her horse and gallop home to receive updates on the activities that had transpired during her absence. She hoped she didn't have to contend with the loss of more livestock to rustlers. But no matter what the losses, she needed to concentrate on delivering the ransom to the specified location so she could get her sister back—and she damn well better get Chrissy back in the same condition she'd left in! Maddie vowed not to rest until those who were responsible for this hellish nightmare received their comeuppance.

With one last wistful glance toward the bed, she headed for the door. She had lived out her secret fantasy with Jonah, and she accepted the fact that he had walked out of her life. It wasn't what she wanted, but the past six months had taught her that Fate wasn't always fair.

She would do what needed to be done. Only in private moments would she look back and remember the night Jonah had introduced her to pleasure beyond description. Their splendorous tryst had launched into oblivion the maddening ordeals she'd encountered. She had needed that desperately. Now she had to focus on her responsibilities and concerns for her sister.

No regrets, Maddie told herself resolutely. She had turned to Jonah for strength, comfort and passion, and he had done likewise in a moment out of time. They had taken pleasure in each other after they had run the entire gamut of emotion the previous day.

Maddie was thankful she'd had the good sense to close her mouth before she had blurted out her affection for Jonah. He hadn't wanted personal involvement, after all. She had no intention of making him feel guilty because he couldn't return her love.

No, it was better that she'd kept her feelings to herself, she mused as she descended the steps to the empty saloon. Her affection, and the intimacy she'd shared with Jonah, was private and personal. She would keep it that way. As much as she might wish otherwise, what was between them was over. Done, Maddie told herself sensibly.

Starting now, her only purpose in life was to retrieve Chrissy and ensure nothing like this ever happened again.

* * *

Jonah watched Maddie's whiskey-colored eyes widen in surprise when she veered from the saloon and saw him leaning against the hitching post in front of the hotel. A wry smile twitched his lips as a becoming blush suffused her face. No doubt she was instantly reminded of the intimacy between them. That made two of them.

"You're still here?" Maddie said, astonished, as Jonah handed her the satchel she had left in her hotel room.

"Yup, so's Boone. He'll be along any moment. We've decided to come with you."

Her hands stalled in the task of tying the satchel behind her saddle. Her gaze riveted on him. "But you said—"

"I know what I said," he interrupted. "Changed my mind."

"You've been doing that a lot lately."

When an impish grin slid across her lush mouth, Jonah nearly groaned aloud. The expression was exactly like the one he'd seen last night when he'd glanced down at her—while they were as close as two people could get.

His body hardened instantly at the provocative memory.

"This new development with Avery and your two friends aroused my suspicions," Jonah informed her. "I've decided to check it out."

Maddie nodded as she pulled herself onto the mare and settled her skirts modestly around her legs. She glanced sideways to see Boone approaching, and she tossed him a smile.

"Morning, paleface. Sleep well?" Boone asked.

When Maddie blushed seven shades of red, Boone's perceptive gaze landed squarely on Jonah and locked there for a long moment. Feeling awkward and ill at ease, Jonah mounted up and headed west. He heard Boone's amused chuckle following him down the street.

Damn, sharing intimate glances with Maddie was awkward enough without Boone knowing what had happened between them. Soon as he got his ornery Kiowa cousin alone he was going to lay down the law before Boone embarrassed Maddie. These new-found feelings of possessiveness and protectiveness wouldn't permit him to let her suffer humiliation.

"See anything of Gibbs and Newton?" Jonah asked Boone a mile later.

"No, but then I was preoccupied for part of the evening," Boone said, casting Jonah a wry glance. "I did see Selmon and Lewis this morning. They'd passed out in the alley behind one of the saloons. The only thing I could get out of either of them was that they'd gotten paid in whiskey money for their efforts to overtake Maddie. From what I saw they drank all their profit last night."

"I will be tremendously relieved to deliver the ransom money," Maddie insisted as she trotted toward home. "No one will be able to take it away from me now and I'll have my sister home again."

If she was lucky, Jonah thought bleakly. He'd been involved in several hostage exchange situations. Some of them had turned out badly. He hoped Maddie didn't have to face another crushing blow. He could tell by the look that settled over her bewitching features that she had focused all her energy and thoughts on retrieving her sister. The closer they came to the ranch, the more determined her expression grew.

Two hours later, Jonah jerked his horse to a halt and let loose a string of oaths that startled Boone as much as Maddie. Jonah stared northwest to see a grand, two-story ranch house sitting near a spring-fed creek in a rugged canyon that formed a natural fortress. Holding pens for livestock lined the towering sandstone walls of the canyon.

It wasn't just *any* canyon, damn it to hell.

Harsh memories bombarded Jonah as he stared into the distance and remembered the past with painful clarity. This was the place his Comanche clan had named Forbidden Canyon after the army had descended from all directions at once to invade their winter encampment. This was where his father had died and his mother had been mortally wounded. This was where Jonah's life had changed forever.

Damn, didn't it just figure that Bar G Ranch would turn out to be his worst nightmare?

"Jonah? What's wrong?" Maddie asked when his expression turned to stone and he sat rigidly in the saddle, staring at her home as if it were the most distasteful, grotesque sight he'd ever clapped eyes on.

"Come on, Maddie," Boone murmured as he grabbed her reins and towed her forward. "I have a feeling that Danhill just came face-to-face with the worst of his past."

Maddie's gaze flew back to Jonah in alarm. Oh, God, no! Jonah had reluctantly told her about the massacre that had taken his family from him. This was the place where his bitterness originated? The place where he had been forced to bury his emotions to prevent them from overwhelming him? Sweet mercy! How many more times was she going to hurt him unintentionally?

When *she* looked at this valley she saw a green oasis filled with towering shade trees and an endless supply of clear spring water. But Jonah saw death, destruction and the brutal end of his childhood.

It had been the abrupt end to the only way of life he had known and understood.

Any whimsical hope that Jonah might come to care enough for her to stay died a quick death. If he refused to enter the valley, turned back and allowed Boone to take over she would understand completely.

Tears of guilt and regret blurred her vision as Boone led her across the lush valley, where cattle grazed on thick, verdant grasses, and eight-hundred-foot-high walls of stone formed a natural boundary behind the ranch house. The hired men waved their hats in welcome as Maddie rode past, but she could barely muster a smile of greeting. She felt compelled to reverse direction and wrap Jonah in her arms, offer sympathy and apology for bringing him to the place that must feel like the open jaws of hell to him.

No doubt, she had unintentionally associated herself with every tragedy and heartache he had suffered in the past.

Jonah stared into the distance, lost to painful memories, hearing the cries of his clan as the army thundered into camp, shooting at everything that moved— warriors, women, children, dogs and horses. In his mind's eye he could see pandemonium breaking loose, and watched as the glistening stream began to flow bloodred while his people crumbled beneath a ruthless barrage of gunfire.

To this day he still wondered why he had been spared, when so many of his clan had perished in this valley.

Jonah shifted uneasily in the saddle, closed his eyes and expelled a heavy sigh. Life, he decided, was one irony following closely on the heels of another. Forbidden Canyon was now the home of the forbidden woman he had come to know intimately the previous night. Her wealth and prosperity came at the sacrifice of Comanche blood. His family's blood and his clan's blood. This chasm was filled with unmarked graves of those who would forever be branded on his memory.

The impulse to reverse direction hounded Jonah as he stared at the looming canyon walls. But when his gaze instinctively shifted to Maddie's silhouette in the distance, he realized that his need to resolve her problems was stronger than his need to avoid his unpleasant past.

He had come this far, faced the worst of his living nightmares, and he would see this situation with Maddie through to the end, he told himself determinedly. After all, that was more or less the motto of Texas Rangers. You face hell and death and you just kept on coming, he reminded himself as he reined his black gelding toward the palatial ranch house.

Jonah also reminded himself that if not for this one unique woman and this fierce attraction he had developed for her—against his better judgment, he might add—he would not have set foot in Forbidden Canyon.

Maddie Garret was the reason—the *only* reason—he hadn't turned around and ridden the other way.

"Ah, ¡caramba! We were afraid you would never return!"

Maddie dragged her eyes from the brawny silhouette in the distance and glanced toward the house to see Rosita Perez, the housekeeper and cook, dashing toward her.

"What took you so long, *querida?*"

Maddie dismounted to find herself swallowed by Rosita's enthusiastic hug. She clung to the stout Mexican woman who had become her substitute mother for the past twelve years.

"Carlos!" Rosita called to her husband. "Come pronto. Our Maddie is home at last!"

Maddie pivoted to see the Bar G's foreman stride hurriedly from the barn. Although Carlos smiled in greeting as he approached, Maddie noticed the rigidity of his shoulders. His body language spelled more trouble. It was the same sense of foreboding she had experienced the day Carlos had found the ransom note and delivered it to her. Damnation, didn't she have enough trouble already? What now?

"Good to have you back, *querida,*" Carlos murmured as he hugged her close to his chest. "You are well, *sí?*"

"I'm fine." Maddie stepped away to make quick introductions to Kiowa Boone.

Boone nodded a greeting, then his gaze strayed to Jonah, who trotted toward them, wearing the bleakest expression Maddie had ever seen on his handsome face. She was surprised he'd come at all. But then, she reminded herself, Jonah lived on hell's fringe and faced constant danger. He was tough and enduring. Even facing the worst of all possible nightmares couldn't deter this remarkable man.

"And this is Maddie's husband," Boone announced abruptly.

Carlos's and Rosita's dark eyes popped in stunned amazement as they gaped at Jonah.

If there was one thing you could say about Boone, Maddie mused, he delighted in making shocking comments and watching everyone react.

"Your *husband?*" Rosita crowed as she made another thorough assessment of Jonah, then stared at the gold band on Maddie's finger. "When?"

Maddie's attention was so focused on Jonah that she didn't hear the housekeeper's question. She simply stood there staring up at him, totally amazed that he hadn't turned back.

"Come inside, *querida,*" Carlos insisted as he took her arm. "There is much we need to discuss."

Maddie's mind whirled with grim speculations as Rosita and Carlos bustled her into the house. Her emotions were already in a tailspin and her heart bled for Jonah. She wasn't sure she was ready to face another tormenting blow, but as usual, she was left with little choice.

Jonah stared up at the grand home and gigantic barn that were butted up against the towering sandstone walls of the chasm, and wondered what the hell he had done to deserve the emotional blow that had sent him reeling a few minutes earlier.

Fate, the cruel bastard, enjoyed kicking you while you were down—and never let you up.

Jonah tried to distance himself from the uneasy sensations and tormenting memories that hammered at him, and instead focus on Maddie's problems. But it was damn near impossible when the distinct image of that day fifteen years ago kept hounding his every step, causing his skin to crawl with bitter revulsion.

He could tell by the apologetic expression on Maddie's face that he had her pity and sympathy. That's the last thing he wanted from her. Hell, he didn't want anything from anyone at the moment. Didn't want to be *here*. The impulse to mount his horse and ride hell-for-leather back to the Rio Grande nearly overwhelmed him again.

There were dozens of legitimate reasons to leave, he reminded himself. And only one reason to stay.

"Sit, *querida*," the foreman requested, jostling Jonah from his troubled thoughts.

With dismal resignation, Jonah watched Maddie sink onto the elegant chair—one of many expensive furnishings in this opulent palace. There was no question now that her family was wealthy. The teasing nickname he'd given her truly did fit, he mused as he surveyed her majestic home.

Maddie quickly made introductions and then asked anxiously, "Has something else happened?"

"*Sí*, I'm afraid so," Carlos replied. "We received another message this morning that the ransom must be delivered tonight instead of tomorrow."

Jonah could tell by the Mexican's grim countenance that there was more. "And?" he prodded.

Carlos swallowed audibly. "The ransom has gone up to eight thousand dollars."

"Eight!" Maddie yelped in dismay. "I don't have that much left after making several purchases and paying expenses." Her wild gaze flew to Jonah.

"Boone and I will cover it," he promised. Anything to wipe that stricken look from her face. He'd worn that same expression himself today and he sure as hell didn't want to see it on Maddie.

"We will?" Boone choked out, incredulous.

"We can cover it," Jonah said confidently as he shot the Kiowa a silencing glance.

Jonah would bet his entire savings that the mastermind had received the message that Maddie had acquired the funds. To make things difficult for her, he had jacked up the price, anticipating that she would still have to turn to Hanson to meet the payment. Jonah suspected that bastard had another trick up his sleeve, too, and he had a pretty good idea what it was going to be.

His thoughts trailed off when he heard a muffled sound in the hall. He stepped around the corner to see that one of the hired hands had skulked in unannounced. Jonah's suspicious gaze homed in on the grimy, shaggy-haired cowboy who had taken it upon himself to carry their gear inside.

How convenient, Jonah mused cynically. He watched suspiciously as the cowboy flinched, realizing he had been spotted, and was forced to step into the room to explain himself. Jonah had the inescapable feeling that Maddie had an informant right under her nose, and that he reported back to the ringleader.

"Please put my husband's belongings in my room," Maddie said. "Boone will be using the spare room in the west wing."

Jonah's brows shot up as he dragged his wary gaze away from the bowlegged cowboy and stared curiously at Maddie. He hadn't expected her to carry this farce of a marriage right into her own home. But on second thought, if the lanky cowhand dropped Jonah's belongings in her room, it would pretty much guarantee that everyone *believed* the marriage was official and consummated.

A faint smile pursed his lips as he sent Maddie an approving glance. The little lady was as sharp as a cactus sticker. Apparently she was as mistrustful of the cowboy's convenient timing and possible eavesdropping as he was.

"One of these breeds is your husband?" the disrespectful cowhand snorted as his gaze bounced back and forth between Jonah and Boone.

Maddie surged to her feet, glaring at the hired hand. "Next time you decide to walk into this house uninvited, *don't,*" she scolded sharply, and then sent him a challenging stare. "I'm half Irish, Clem. Would you like to make something of *that,* too?"

"No, ma'am," the man mumbled, ducking his head and trying to look properly ashamed.

Jonah wasn't buying it. Apparently Maddie wasn't, either.

She snatched the gear from Clem's hands. "I'll take care of the luggage myself. *You* are dismissed— permanently."

Silence reigned as the hired hand turned and stalked off, but not before he cast Jonah and Boone a derisive glance.

Maddie wheeled back to her foreman. "Carlos, if anyone else is heard making disrespectful comments about my husband and my friend, I want them fired on the spot. Is that understood?"

"Sí, querida." Carlos fished the most recent ransom note from his pocket and handed it to her. "We lost another fifty head of cattle while you were gone," he reported. "Another Indian necklace and broken arrow was found in the area."

Maddie wilted into the nearest chair. "I'll deal with that tomorrow. Right now all I want is to get Chrissy home safely."

"Wise idea, princess," Jonah murmured as his gaze followed Clem out the door and down the steps. "First things first."

Chapter Ten

Avery Hanson glanced up from tallying expenses in his ledger when Jesse Gibbs walked into his office unannounced. "You damn well better have good news," he muttered as Jesse parked himself in the chair across from the desk.

"I didn't get the money or even get a shot at Maddie's husband," the man reported. "She never went to her hotel room last night. I don't know where the hell they got off to."

"Damn!" Avery's fist hit the desk with a hard thud. "Then please tell me that you had the chance to pick off her husband this morning."

Jesse shook his head. "Those two half-breeds watch their backs carefully. I couldn't get close enough to take a shot without being seen."

Avery slouched in his chair and drummed his fingers on the desk. Hell and damnation, he needed to get his hands on that ransom money before Maddie delivered it. He needed her to turn to him in desperation.

"If you want me to keep tracking Maddie's husband so I can get a shot at him, then it's going to cost you.'' Jesse extended his hand, palm up.

Avery gnashed his teeth, then reached into the bottom desk drawer to retrieve money. "I don't know why I'm paying you when you've botched up royally.''

"Because I can ruin you." Jesse grinned goadingly. "The sheriff would be interested in hearing what I have to say about your involvement with old man Garret's death and your other illegal activities. And I know plenty....'' he added, slowly and deliberately. "I'm sure Tipton would like to know about informants, rustling cattle and a few other matters that you have tried very hard to keep private.''

Scowling irritably, Avery handed over the money, then shooed Jesse out of the office. "Don't come back until you have something to show for the fee I've paid you. And make certain no one sees you sneak out the back door.''

When Jesse left, Avery treated himself to a few more succinct curses. Jesse Gibbs had to go. The man knew too much and he was causing more trouble than he was worth.

A wicked smile slid across the rancher's lips when an inspiration popped to mind. If all else failed he could send Clem Foster—his ace in the hole—to clean up this mess. Gibbs was getting too cocksure of himself. It might be time to shut him up—permanently.

"Mind telling me how we're going to come up with a thousand dollars we don't happen to have with us?'' Boone questioned as he and Jonah ambled through the upstairs hall to stow their gear.

"Old ranger trick," Jonah replied.

Boone snorted caustically. "I thought Indians were the only ones with old tricks." He halted and whistled softly when the plush furnishings in his room distracted him. "Would you look at this place? I've never stayed anywhere this fine."

Neither had Jonah. He hesitated to touch anything, for fear it would break and cost a fortune to replace. He couldn't imagine living in this house, either. Talk about feeling completely out of place!

Leaving Boone to stow his gear in the very lap of luxury, Jonah pivoted on his heel to stride down the hall. He stopped dead in his tracks when he reached the enormous suite that belonged to Maddie. Thick gold drapes hung from the vaulted ceiling to the polished wood floor. Bay windows provided a spectacular view of the towering canyon walls with their red, purple and white layers of stone. Jonah felt like the Great Spirit himself, gazing down on this panoramic valley dotted with grazing cattle, sheep and horses.

He turned to appraise the massive marbletop dresser and ornately carved wardrobes. The four-poster walnut bed was covered with a white lace spread and plump pillows fit to prop up a king.

Or a princess.

Jonah was still standing in the middle of the colorful Aubusson rug, his jaw scraping his chest, when Maddie swept into the room. She walked right up to him, flung her arms around his neck and kissed the breath out of him. He suspected she still saw him as her port in the storm, as she had last night. He'd become the place she came for solace when the world caved in on her. But right now, Jonah felt as if the world had caved in on him.

He responded ardently and immediately to the honeyed taste of her lips. As if they possessed a will of their own, his hands glided over the supple curves of her body, and he pulled her full length against him. He devoured her for one long, breathless moment before the voice of self-preservation reminded him that he couldn't let himself—or her—pretend this supposed marriage was more than it was. Which after last night was much *more* than it should have been.

It took all the willpower he could muster to break the kiss when his aroused body screamed for more. "Maddie, don't." He set her at arm's length. "Don't get caught up in this charade. Last night just happened. It shouldn't have, but it did. You were looking for consolation and I was willing and eager enough to help you forget the troubles you're facing and the bitter memories I had to deal with. We used each other, and that's all last night was about."

Maddie staggered as if he'd slapped her. Jonah despised himself for what he had to say and do, but if he was going to protect himself from these tender feelings that played hell with common sense, he had to make her understand that he was nothing more than the means to an end for her.

"Are you saying that last night meant nothing except—"

"We took pleasure and comfort in each other." He cut in bluntly. "You even offered to pay me, as I recall."

Damn, this was killing him by inches, but it had to

be done—for her own good and his. He couldn't allow her to confuse reckless passion with true affection. He was a realist, and realistically speaking, they had nothing in common but one incredible night in a space out of time. He would drive himself crazy if he let himself believe it could be more than that. He had to make her see what he'd known from the beginning.

He wasn't what she needed and he never would be.

When her chin snapped up he knew he'd hurt her feelings and her offended pride had rushed to her rescue. Good. If that sustained her until he retrieved her sister and made her world right again, then fine by him. Besides, he could deal better with this tempting female when they were at odds. He'd already proved beyond all doubt that the slightest invitation from her was his complete undoing.

"I'll have to write you an IOU for last night's lesson," she muttered, averting her gaze. "As you well know I don't have sufficient funds to cover the hike in the price of the ransom, much less pay you for what I owe you."

Maddie did an admirable job—if she did say so herself—of controlling the feelings of hurt and rejection that lambasted her. She knew Jonah didn't love her, even after she'd practically thrown herself at him last night....

Practically? Don't kid yourself, princess, jeered a taunting inner voice that sounded a lot like Jonah's. She *had* thrown herself at him. She had wanted one night of reckless pleasure in his arms. Like a fool, she'd hoped for more, and Jonah was making it crystal clear that he wasn't interested. Obviously he'd found her lacking, and preferred someone who was skilled at pleasuring an experienced man.

She had no right to be angry with him, she reminded herself. Jonah was only being his usual plain-spoken, straightforward self. Nonetheless, the rejection cut to the quick. He didn't want her. He'd had her once—well, twice, actually—and obviously that had been plenty for him. There was always another nameless female in another nameless town between here and the Rio Grande who could provide what he needed occasionally.

When humiliated tears threatened to cloud her eyes, she turned her back to him and squared her shoulders. "Where is this extra money you claim you can loan me to make an even eight grand?" she asked, her voice nowhere near as steady as she would have liked.

"You let me worry about that," he insisted. "Boone and I will take the money to the designated spot."

"No." She wheeled around, her spine stiff, her chin uplifted. "*My* sister, *my* problem. You have done more than enough. It's plain to see that you don't want to be here. Not with *me*. Especially not in this place."

He advanced on her, looking more ominous and formidable than she'd ever seen him. Maddie refused to cower. He could snarl and growl to his heart's content, but she knew he wouldn't physically hurt her. He'd had plenty of chances and he'd never been anything but tender when he touched her. Jonah Danhill might be hell on outlaws, but he wouldn't abuse her. She knew that as surely as she knew her own name.

But he could break her heart, without leaving a telling mark on her.

"You've got a problem, you send a Ranger. This is what I *do*, princess," he breathed. "You're going to stay right here in your palace and wait for Boone and me to deliver your sister to you."

"You made it perfectly clear that you didn't want to be involved in the first place." She hurled the retort back at him. "At every leg of this journey you have announced it was the end of the line for you, that it was as far as you intended to go. Frankly, I'm amazed you have come this far. And for the life of me I can't understand why you're still here."

He opened his mouth to interject a comment, but Maddie waved him off, determined to have her say. "It's obviously not because you have a strong and lasting attachment to me." When her lower lip quivered in response to the hurt and rejection twisting in her stomach, she bit down hard with her teeth, determined not to reduce herself to tears. "I don't want to be more beholden to you than I already am. You can stay here while I'm gone, if you please. Or you can leave for good. It doesn't matter one whit to me!"

"Damn it, Maddie." He grabbed her arm when she lurched toward the door. "I'm the expert here. Let me do my job."

Tears swam in her eyes again, but she held them at bay, held her ground. "Just leave this place. I know it haunts you, and with good reason. I will handle this matter myself!"

"Trouble in marital paradise?" Boone teased as he propped himself against the doorjamb. "I always enjoy a good fight, especially when I'm not involved. What's this one about?''

"About domineering, mule-headed, infuriating men!'' Maddie exclaimed as she jerked her arm from Jonah's grasp, then stormed from the room.

"She must be referring to you,'' Boone said, lips twitching. "I'm the most easygoing, good-natured man I know.''

Jonah raked his fingers through his hair and huffed out an agitated breath. "Miz I-Can-Do-It-Myself insists on delivering the ransom money,'' he told Boone.

Boone jerked upright. His playfulness vanished in one second flat. "Like hell!''

"That's what *I* said, more or less.''

"Leave that hellcat to me, Danhill. I'll talk sense into her while you're printing this money we supposedly have in generous supply.''

"Talk to her?'' Jonah snorted. "Waste of time. I want her tied up in knots so she can't follow us to the ransom site.'' He spun toward the door. "I have a few things to check on before dark, but I'll be back. Count on it.''

Boone blinked. "Are you kidding about the 'tied up in knots'?''

"No,'' Jonah called over his shoulder. "I've never been more serious in my life. I want her safe and sound until we deliver her sister to her. *If* we can do so....''

Maddie felt like a boiling caldron of nerves. She had no idea how she was going to pay the ranch expenses after the losses from rustling, but she'd have to worry about that another day. Rescuing Chrissy was top priority. Recovering from the sting of Jonah's rejection was a very close second.

She didn't know where Jonah had ridden off to, but he was gone and she was glad of it because it was difficult to maintain her composure around him. Boone she could tolerate. He didn't set off devastating explosions inside her when she glanced in his direction.

Boone had been following her around most of the afternoon, asking inane questions about the ranch and the hired help. The only time he'd left her alone for more than ten minutes was when he'd gone in search of the rude-mannered cowboy who had interrupted their conversation earlier. Maddie wasn't surprised to discover that Clem Foster had disappeared into thin air.

Maddie had wised up after all the misfortune she'd encountered these past months. In fact, she'd become as mistrusting and suspicious as Jonah. It hadn't taken her long to conclude that Clem might well be the informant who made it possible for rustlers to know where and when to strike without detection. Now that she thought about it, the rustling reeked of an inside job, and she should have suspected as much months ago. Unfortunately, she had been reeling from the endless search for her missing father and sidetracked by the mountain of responsibility heaped on her at short notice.

If Clem was in cahoots with the Comanche raiders—who might well be connected to Avery—Maddie would sic the sheriff on him. Her devious neighbor would find himself under arrest. Clem Foster, too. The nerve of that man making derisive comments about half-breeds, when *he* was probably a conniving outlaw who had betrayed her and robbed her blind!

Maddie released a frustrated breath as she tucked the money in the leather bag. When Boone ambled into the parlor she stared somberly at him. "I want your promise that you won't interfere with the captive exchange," she demanded. "I don't know where that mulish man went off to, but make sure he doesn't follow me, either."

"Whatever you say, Maddie," Boone replied as he plucked up the pouch. "But you can't leave until Jonah arrives with the extra money."

"Right." She'd have to see Jonah again before she rode off. That should put her in a fine temper.

The thought no sooner darted through her head than she felt a presence behind her. She pivoted to see Jonah standing in the parlor door, a saddlebag draped over his massive shoulder. "Do you have the money?" she asked stiffly.

He patted the pouch. "Got it." He stared her down. "But I repeat, you are *not* going, princess."

"I told you—" Maddie shrieked in furious outrage when Boone, the devious traitor, approached from her blind side to bind her hands behind her back. He crammed a gag in her mouth and tied her ankles with rope before she could escape him.

"Sorry, Maddie," Boone exclaimed. "This was Jonah's idea and it's for your own safety. You can thank us later."

To her further frustration Boone tossed her over his shoulder, stuffed her in the broom closet and tethered her to a hook on the wall so she couldn't hop away.

Neither could she pound her feet against the walls to summon help, because Rosita had already returned to her cottage for the evening.

Maddie slumped against the floor and called Jonah and Boone every name in the book. Those two men had better not get themselves killed on her behalf because she wanted them to come back alive—so she could shoot the both of them!

"There will be hell to pay when we get back," Boone prophesied. "If looks could kill we'd both be the deadest men who ever lived."

"At least she's out of harm's way," Jonah replied as he trotted toward the designated site. "I have a bad feeling about this rendezvous now that Maddie has acquired the money without relying on Avery."

Boone's thick brows furrowed. "What do you mean?"

"The ransom price went up immediately after Avery learned Maddie not only acquired the money but also a husband," Jonah explained. "I doubt this exchange would have been the end of Maddie's troubles."

Boone nodded pensively. "So you're thinking that if *Maddie* brought the money she might have been captured. That would put you next in line for extermination so this ranch would still be available to Avery Hanson."

"That's exactly what I predict," Jonah said grimly.

"Which means that now *we're* riding into a trap."

"*I* am," Jonah corrected as he urged his steed along the narrow old Indian trail that led up the canyon walls to the mesa above. "*You* will be guarding my back."

"So…you're laying your life on the line for Maddie."

"It's my job," Jonah reminded him as he followed the winding path.

"Maybe so." Boone chuckled wryly. "But I'm not so blind that I can't see this is personal. *She* is personal. Even if she is the kind of woman that men like us don't deserve."

Boone understood the ways of the world, Jonah mused. No matter how much Maddie meant to him, no matter what sacrifices Jonah was willing to make to keep her safe, she was still beyond him. That was the plain, irrefutable truth.

"What's really in the pouch?" Boone asked curiously. "I noticed you didn't bother to bring along Maddie's money."

Jonah smiled in the gathering darkness. "Shredded newspaper mostly. No way am I going to let these sneaky bastards get their hands on Maddie's inheritance."

"Figured it was something like that." Boone was quiet for a moment. "Do you think Maddie's sister is alive?"

Jonah winced. "I don't like the odds."

It would devastate Maddie if she lost her sister. He knew how it felt to be emotionally distraught and have the worst happen. Returning to Forbidden Canyon for the first time in fifteen years was a painful and vivid reminder that hope could be dashed so quickly it could rip the soul and spirit right out of you.

"It's going to be another blow if Maddie loses you, too," Boone predicted. "I think she's in love with you, Danhill."

Jonah snorted in contradiction. "If anything, she feels grateful for my assistance. As for the rest…" He shrugged evasively. "She only came to me for comfort and consolation." He glanced solemnly at Boone. "If things go sour, my last request is that you be there for Maddie until she has her life in order."

"I understand," Boone murmured. "Just make damn sure you come back so I don't have to keep that promise."

Jonah reached down to retrieve the bow and arrows he'd brought with him. "Remember how to use these, my Kiowa cousin?"

Boone snickered. "It's always been my weapon of choice. Yours, too, I suspect. Where'd you find them on short notice?"

"There's an obscure cave behind the waterfall that feeds the creek in Forbidden Canyon. My clan always left supplies and weapons there in case of emergency. The damp cavern preserved the bowstring." He handed the weapon to Boone. "Bullets will draw too much attention."

The Kiowa nodded in understanding. "Silent but deadly, so the kidnappers aren't aware that their numbers are dwindling."

"Precisely," Jonah confirmed.

Jonah reined to a halt on the moonlit ridge that led into another rugged canyon. This was familiar territory and he'd trekked through the area earlier this afternoon to determine the most likely places for his enemies to take cover. Unfortunately, the narrow chasm provided excellent hiding places behind cedars and inside the fingerlike crevices of eroded rock that fanned from the canyon floor. But if a man listened carefully he could hear the crunch of pebbles beneath booted feet. Which was why *he'd* worn moccasins.

Jonah suspected these rustlers were charading as Comanche to throw the authorities off track. He had searched the area and seen no evidence of Indians or the small campfires and obscure campsites that were the trademark of his people.

It wasn't the first time Indians had been blamed for criminal activities machinated by devious whites. It probably wouldn't be the last, either.

"Here," Boone said as he untied the sheathed Bowie knife that was strapped to his thigh. "A man can never carry enough hardware." He pulled another knife from his shirtsleeve.

Jonah accepted the daggers. Thanks to Boone, he would have one tucked in each moccasin, one in each sleeve and one on his thigh. His six-shooters would be his last resort, because spitting fire and rolling smoke made a man an easy target in the darkness.

"I'll be at the base of the canyon," Jonah murmured. Then he added, "Make every arrow count."

"I'll be your second set of eyes and ears," Boone promised.

"I'm counting on it," Jonah said before he began his winding descent into the labyrinth of ravines.

Maddie decided there were times when being a woman had its advantages while dealing with men. Boone had bound her up securely, but he'd also ensured that the ropes around her ankles and wrists didn't bite into her skin. That provided her with space to worm and squirm. She couldn't accurately measure the time it took to wiggle her feet free, but she accomplished the deed with determined effort. Freeing her hands, however, took considerable energy. She had to pause occasionally to give her aching arms a rest.

Finally Maddie worked free of the rope and came to her feet. When she pushed on the door, she met with restraint. No doubt Boone had blocked the exit with a chair braced beneath the outer knob. Backing up a step, Maddie kicked at the door. After four frustrating attempts the door wobbled on its hinges, causing the chair to topple sideways.

Free at last, she bounded upstairs to change into her riding breeches and grab her pistol. If her assumptions were correct, Avery Hanson would be waiting at his ranch while his henchmen were making the exchange. Although she couldn't overtake Jonah and Boone, she did have the perfect opportunity to ride to Avery's ranch and eavesdrop on damning conversation between him and his henchmen.

She silently fumed when she recalled the gentlemanly flattery and pretended concern Avery had bestowed on her after both her father's and Christina's disappearances. And all the while Avery had been treacherously plotting to gain her trust. Not to mention his offer of marriage, she fumed. He had purposely placed himself in position so he would be there, hoping she would turn to him to help her resolve the crises facing Chrissy and the ranch.

Oh yes, Avery Hanson was going to get what he

deserved for his duplicity and double-dealing. He was going to find himself under arrest.

The thought prompted Maddie to race downstairs. She skidded to a halt and growled furiously when she noticed the saddlebag filled with money was still sitting on the sofa.

Damn it! She didn't know what Jonah had stuffed in his bulging pouch, but she'd bet the ranch it wasn't money. If he got Chrissy injured or recaptured because of his daredevil tactics she was going to strangle him.

Maybe even twice for good measure.

Still fuming, Maddie tucked the saddlebag out of sight then dashed from the house to request Carlos's assistance.

"What is going on, *querida?*" Carlos asked as he stepped onto the cottage porch. "I thought you rode off to retrieve Christina, as the ransom note ordered."

"Change of plans," Maddie muttered. Damn if she didn't sound as short and to the point as Jonah. She was going to have to break that habit if she planned to get over loving him sometime in the next century. "I think Avery Hanson is behind this kidnapping. Maybe even the rustling. I need you to ride into town and bring Sheriff Kilgore out here."

"And what will you be doing while I'm gone?" Carlos asked, flashing her a wary glance.

"Watching and waiting," she replied evasively.

Carlos fastened his holster in place, then shook a stubby finger in her face. "You be careful, do you hear me? We don't have the little bambino home safe yet. I don't want something to happen to you in the meantime.... Rosita!"

His wife appeared at the door and wrapped her robe around her. "*Sí*, Carlos. I heard. I won't let Maddie out of my sight."

When Carlos dashed off to fetch a horse, Maddie turned to Rosita. "I'll be at the house." She didn't bother to mention that her favorite gelding stood at the hitching post, where it had been tied in preparation for her riding to retrieve Christina. "Come up there when you're dressed."

When Rosita pivoted to fetch her clothes, Maddie sprinted outside and jogged uphill. She was on the strawberry roan gelding in a single bound and raced off into the darkness.

Jonah halted and pricked up his ears when he heard scrabbling noises to the right and left of him. Pebbles cascaded down the rugged hillside, assuring him that the outlaws were closing ranks. He also heard the sound of bullets being shoved into the chambers of rifles.

He smiled in wry amusement when he saw what he was undoubtedly supposed to assume was an Indian warrior—in full war-party regalia—rise from behind a boulder. Colorful war paint was slashed across the man's face and his bare chest was covered with a bead-and-bone breastplate. Jonah's gaze swung to the pinto behind the supposed chief. A motionless bundle covered with a buffalo hide quilt was draped on the horse.

Jonah's gaze swung back to study the man, who wore a feathered headdress, doehide breeches and leggings. The chief didn't walk or move like an Indian.

Being one himself, Jonah could recognize an imposter at a glance.

"Where is the girl's sister?" the would-be Indian demanded in stilted English.

"She's having a nervous breakdown," Jonah supplied smoothly. "I came in her stead because I'm her husband."

The news didn't appear to faze the charlatan chief. No doubt he'd been informed that Maddie had acquired a husband.

"You brought money?" the imposter questioned.

Jonah hitched his thumb toward his horse. "In the saddlebag. I want to see the girl first. If she isn't in good condition I will only pay for what I get."

The comment caught the chief off guard. He glanced sideways, alerting Jonah that one of his cohorts was hiding behind a nearby boulder. That accounted for two outlaws. He suspected there were more perched above him, waiting to ambush him the instant the chief had the money in hand. Jonah sure as hell hoped Boone had located the bushwhackers by now. Otherwise, Jonah might be nursing more than an injured shoulder.

"Show me the girl," he demanded in Comanche dialect. The supposed chief blinked. Well, that verified Jonah's assumption. Not only was the man an imposter, but he didn't have the slightest command of the language. "Show me the girl now," he repeated in English.

The man glowered at him. Jonah ignored the intimidating stare and focused on the unmoving bundle on the horse. Christina was either dead or drugged. Jonah hoped it was the latter.

Without turning his back, the chief stepped toward the pinto to jerk the sack off the girl's head. Pale golden hair tumbled over the horse's flank. Jonah felt a jolt spear through him and he wondered if he was encountering a younger version of Maddie. Christina's face was peaked but flawless in the moonlight. According to Maddie, the girl was uncommonly attractive. He prayed that she hadn't been used to appease the lusts of these outlaws.

Rage boiled inside him at the thought. He was going to resort to old ways of retaliation and take a few scalps if this girl had been abused and left to deal with emotional wounds that could take years to heal. Jonah knew firsthand what that long, tormenting process was like, and he wouldn't wish that kind of long-term misery on anyone. Least of all this lovely young girl.

"In one piece," the chief declared. "Now, the money for the girl."

As calmly as you please, Jonah replied in Comanche, "You're loco if you think you're going to walk out of this canyon alive."

The chief stared at him in confusion, so Jonah repeated the comment in plain English. When the chief made a grab for the pistol he had tucked under the breastplate, Jonah snatched the knife strapped to his thigh and hurled it. The chief went down soundlessly. In one fluid motion Jonah pivoted and grabbed the knife in his sleeve. The instant the hombre who was hiding behind the boulder raised his head and prepared to fire, Jonah hurled the dagger, then dived to the ground to dodge the bullet aimed at his chest. The pinto tried to bolt and run when the gun discharged so close to its rump, but Jonah leaped to his feet to grab the reins.

To his relief, gunfire didn't break out from the outcropping of rock above him. He smiled in approval. Boone had done his job well.

"You okay, Boone?" Jonah's voice echoed along the craggy precipice into the silence.

"I'm fine. Just wrapping up a few loose ends. How about you, Danhill?"

"Not a scratch on me." Jonah turned his attention to the lifeless bundle wrapped in the blanket. Untying the ropes, he pulled Christina into his arms. The waterfall of shiny blond hair tumbled over his elbow as he placed her gently on the ground. A sigh of relief gushed from his lips when he surveyed the sleeping beauty. She didn't appear to have been beaten, but he couldn't swear that she hadn't been misused.

Although she was filthy and a musty smell clung to her hair and clothing, she seemed to be safe and sound. Her shallow breathing disturbed him, however. He had the uneasy feeling she had been given an overdose of a sedative. Jonah removed the dingy blindfold and untied her hands and feet. He gave her a gentle shake, but she didn't respond.

"Is she alive?" Boone asked as he approached.

"More or less." He scooped Christina into his arms and nodded toward the pinto. "Climb aboard the horse, Boone. You can carry this sleeping beauty home."

Boone mounted up, then leaned down to take the unconscious female from Jonah. A smile played on his lips as he studied the angelic young face. "Reminds me of her sister."

"Yeah," Jonah murmured. "Hope this one survives to grow up to be as feisty and independent as Maddie."

"Her color worries me," Boone murmured. "Too pale." He plucked gently at the skin above her wrist. "Dehydrated is my guess."

Jonah swung into his saddle and reined toward the house. "What condition did you leave the other bushwhackers in?"

"*Dead* condition," Boone replied. "Thought I might be rusty with a bow but I found my mark easily enough. You?"

"I left the masquerading Indians in the same condition. Unfortunately. I was hoping for a survivor to interrogate. Did you recognize Gibbs or Newton?" Jonah asked.

"No," Boone said as he followed behind Jonah. "But at least we accomplished our mission. Maybe Maddie will be so relieved to have her sister back that she won't skin us alive."

Jonah smiled wryly. "Yeah, I'm counting on that myself, though it's probably too much to ask for. I figure she's going to let me have it with both barrels."

"I figure she is, too." Boone grinned wryly. "Sure glad I'm not you, Danhill."

Chapter Eleven

Maddie tethered her winded steed to a scraggly cedar in an obscure ravine, then hiked toward Hanson's ranch house. A log bunkhouse stood off to the west, protected by the overhanging canyon wall. An oversize corral filled with bawling cattle sat near the gigantic barn that dwarfed the house.

Veering west, Maddie checked the brands on the penned cattle. She swore softly when she noticed the Bar G brand on the rumps of several steers and heifers. Damn that Avery. He'd told her that he was herding cattle to the railhead in Dodge City in the morning. He hadn't mentioned that he was taking *her* stolen cattle with him.

Confound the man! He'd made her life hell. He'd been preying on her emotions and spouting pretend sympathy, while he kidnapped her sister and stole her livestock—and most likely disposed of her father.

Her furious gaze swung to the modest stone-and-timber house, where a single light speared the darkness. No doubt Avery was waiting for his henchman to return with the money and report on the rendezvous with Jonah and Boone.

And Jonah and Boone better not have gotten shot, and Christina better be in good condition, or Avery wouldn't live long enough to stand trial for kidnapping, extortion and quite possibly murder, Maddie thought vengefully.

Scolding herself for wasting time with vindictive thoughts, she crept toward the house. She was not going in half-cocked and risk having that sneaky bastard get the drop on her. She might find herself abducted and held for ransom, too, if she didn't watch her step.

Since she'd been in Avery's home on several occasions, she knew the blazing light at the front of the house came from his office. That was where he'd made his first proposal two years earlier, catching her completely off guard. It had come the day after Ward Tipton had proposed to her. Upon reflection, she wondered if Avery also had an informant planted on Ward's ranch to keep him updated on his neighbor's business. She wouldn't put it past that cagey rancher.

Maddie shook off her wandering thoughts and scurried toward the back door, which led to the kitchen. The hinges whined when she opened it and Maddie clutched her pistol in her hand before tiptoeing across the room. The house held an eerie silence and an odd, unfamiliar scent, she noticed, as she inched along the wall toward the spacious dining room. The cook and housekeeper—a small, wiry Chinese man who had been in Avery's employ since their arrival from Arizona Territory four years earlier—was nowhere to be seen. Maddie had no idea where the employee was quartered, but she presumed it was somewhere in the house.

Halting by the door, she glanced across the foyer to determine if Avery was lounging in the dark parlor. She could see no one in the shadows. Inching down the hall, she found the office door partially open, so she cautiously craned her neck to look into the room. Maddie nearly choked when she spotted Avery Hanson—and his informant, Clem Foster.

'Hardly daring to breathe, she recoiled and plastered herself against the foyer wall. Maddie was suddenly struck with the feeling that coming here wasn't one of her brighter ideas.

This situation had disaster written all over it.

Uneasy sensations slithered down Jonah's spine as he and Boone approached the grand home. He frowned warily when he saw Rosita Perez pacing across the covered veranda.

"Dios!" Rosita cried when she spotted the two riders. She clutched at her skirts and hurried down the steps. "Is my *bambino* all right?"

Jonah couldn't answer that question satisfactorily until he and Boone had time to thoroughly examine the girl.

"What's happened to her?" Rosita gasped when she noticed Christina's motionless body draped over Boone's lap.

"Heavily sedated," Jonah replied as he took Christina in his arms and turned toward the house.

A raft of Spanish curses flooded from Rosita's lips as she bustled up the steps and led the way to Christina's room.

"Do you have smelling salts on hand? Coffee?" Jonah asked as he headed up the staircase.

"*Sí, señor.*"

Jonah halted when Rosita wheeled abruptly on the step above him to make her hasty descent. He stared down into the girl's face, noting the dark circles under her eyes and her bloodless lips. Despite her weakened condition Maddie's sister was indeed strikingly attractive. Her features were so dainty and delicate that Jonah predicted she would one day become a heartbreaker, the likes few men could resist.

Just like her sister.

Something that must have been akin to brotherly concern washed over him as he carried Christina into her room. Suddenly he understood Maddie's devotion and protectiveness. This was all that was left of her family and she guarded her sister closely.

Jonah started when Boone's hand shot out to turn down the quilts. Jonah had been so preoccupied that he hadn't heard his friend's approach. But then, Boone was half Kiowa, Jonah reminded himself. Moving as silently as a shadow was second nature to him, too.

"I'll tend the angel while you let the wildcat out of the closet," Boone insisted. "I'll wait my turn to get my eyes clawed out and my head bit off. You go first."

"Thanks for leaving me with the tough assignments," Jonah grumbled.

He stepped into the hall and passed Rosita—who'd returned with medical supplies—on his way down the stairs. Jonah heaved a resigned sigh as he veered down the dark hallway. He was not looking forward to facing Maddie's wrath. His only hope was that she would be so relieved Christina was upstairs that she wouldn't jump down his throat for leaving her tied up.

Jonah's thoughts trailed off when he noticed the overturned chair in the hallway. Scowling, he whipped open the door to the broom closet—and found nothing but mops and brooms. Damn it, he had given Boone specific instructions to tie Maddie up securely, and he'd botched it!

Lurching around, Jonah pelted down the hall and took the steps two at a time to the bedroom. Rosita and Boone were hovering over the bed, attempting to rouse their patient.

"She's not where we left her," Jonah snapped accusingly.

Boone jerked upright and stared at him incredulously.

"Ah, *¡caramba.*" Rosita wailed. "How could I have forgotten?" She rattled in Spanish about madness and forgetfulness, but even though Jonah spoke the language fluently he had no clue what the woman was yammering about.

"Do you know where Maddie is?" he demanded urgently.

Rosita's shoulders lifted in a helpless shrug. "No, I don't know, but she said she suspected Avery Hanson was involved. She sent Carlos to fetch Sheriff Kilgore, then she thundered off before I reached the house."

Jonah swore under his breath. He had the unmistakable feeling that Maddie had raced off to confront Hanson with her suspicions. Damn it, she couldn't read Avery every sentence and paragraph of the riot act without the risk of getting *herself* abducted and granting Avery the opportunity to cover his tracks.

The wobbly groan that sounded from Christina's ashen lips drew Jonah's attention. He glanced back to watch Boone wave smelling salts under her nose. Eyes as blue as a mountain stream fluttered open.

"Hey, angel, can you hear me?" Boone questioned when Christina's eyes swept shut again.

Those incredible eyes opened for a few more seconds before drifting closed. "Maddie..." she whispered hoarsely.

Rosita burst into tears, but Boone ignored her in his haste to grab the smelling salts again. Christina jerked reflexively, then inhaled a shuddering breath, but dozed off again immediately.

"I think she'll be okay," Boone predicted as he ran his hand over her concave belly. "My guess is that she's about half-starved. If we can get her to wake up long enough to get food and water down her she should come around quickly."

Rosita snapped up her head, wiped her eyes and scurried off to fetch food and drink.

Jonah watched in wry amusement as Boone grabbed a wet cloth to cleanse the girl's face and neck. Hell, the Kiowa was a regular handmaiden when he needed to be. At the moment he didn't appear to be a tough, hard-bitten half-breed. If this was any indication of what a female could do to a man, Jonah didn't know what was.

"Since you have things under control I'm going to track Maddie before she gets herself in trouble," he said.

"If you were going to prevent her from doing that you probably should've left two hours ago," Boone said, never taking his eyes off Christina. "You think she went after Avery?"

"Don't doubt it for a minute," Jonah muttered as he turned on his heels. He hoped Maddie hadn't fouled up this investigation by striking off to portray the avenging angel of justice. If she had, he was going to rake her over live coals—provided she hadn't gotten herself killed already.

The unnerving thought caused Jonah to grimace as he mounted up and nudged his steed to a gallop. If Avery Hanson harmed one hair on Maddie's golden head he wouldn't survive the night. That was one promise Jonah vowed to keep.

Maddie braced herself against the foyer wall and sucked in a steadying breath. When a movement in the shadows caught her attention she swung her pistol into shooting position. The Chinese housekeeper squawked in surprise, spun around, then dashed back in the direction he'd come.

This was not good, Maddie thought as she scurried toward the dining room. Chiang Ti could attest to the fact that she was in the house, and she didn't want to have to explain what she was doing here—especially not now!

Frantic, Maddie burst through the back door with more speed than caution and ran smack-dab into an unyielding obstacle. When the man—she assumed it was Chiang Ti—grabbed hold of her she swung her pistol wildly, hoping to stun her captor so she could escape.

"Ouch, damn it! Gimme that thing before you crack my skull open with it!"

Maddie half collapsed in relief when she recognized Jonah's scolding voice and felt him jerk the pistol from her fingertips. She peered over her shoulder to note the annoyed frown that puckered his brow. Well, too bad. She wasn't all that happy with him right now, either.

"Is Christina okay?" Her voice evaporated when Jonah suddenly shoved her back against the side of the house and covered her body protectively with his. Only then did Maddie hear the scrabbling noise and look west to see someone clawing his way up the side of the craggy cliff.

"Is that Avery?" Jonah growled against her ear.

"No, I suspect it's Chiang Ti, the cook and housekeeper," Maddie wheezed. "I must have scared him half to death when I pointed my pistol at him. Is Christina all right?" she asked in the same breath.

"She'll be fine. Sedated heavily and undernourished but alive," Jonah reported. "Boone and Rosita are tending her. Now tell me why you scared the cook."

"Because I was standing outside Avery's office when I saw a moving shadow. He was it. He turned and ran." Maddie glared at Jonah. "And thank you so much for leaving me bound up in the closet!"

He ignored her sarcasm. Had to. He was too distracted by the tantalizing feel of her breasts pressed into his chest and her hips meshed suggestively against his. He cursed his unruly body and stepped back from her.

"Did you overhear Avery making damning comments about the abduction or find incriminating evidence of extortion?'' he asked in a raspy voice—the side effect of standing entirely too close to Maddie.

She avoided his direct stare. "Not exactly."

He frowned when she shifted uneasily from one foot to the other. "Exactly what does 'not exactly' mean?"

"It means that Avery and my disloyal cowhand, Clem Foster, weren't talking."

When Maddie pivoted and reentered the house, Jonah was hot on her heels. He followed her into the office, then screeched to a halt.

"Well, damn." He scowled as he surveyed Avery, who was dressed in a red silk robe. His upper body was draped over his desk and he stared sightlessly at Jonah. Clem was sprawled faceup on the floor. His vacant stare told the gruesome tale. Both men were dead, but they hadn't been that way very long. When Jonah noticed there was no indication that a fight had taken place, his accusing gaze landed squarely on Maddie.

"Don't look at *me,*" she snapped indignantly. "They were dead when I got here. I didn't fire a single shot, either, and I'm not carrying a knife." She waved a trembling hand toward Avery. "Stabbed in the back. I didn't touch Clem, but I suspect he has an identical wound. Neither of them must have realized what was coming until it was too late."

Jonah squatted down to roll the bowlegged cowhand onto his belly. Sure enough, there was a telling stain between his shoulder blades. Muttering, he resituated Clem as he'd found him. "Do you think Chiang Ti might have done this?"

Maddie shuddered repulsively. "I have no idea."

The gory scene was getting to her, Jonah noted. He surged to his feet to shepherd her out the back door. Here was yet another glaring reminder that the world he lived in was rife with violence and death, while Maddie was unaccustomed to dealing with such unsettling encounters.

"If anyone shows up, head for the hills," he instructed as he positioned her outside the back door and handed her the pistol. "I want to have a quick look around the house before we leave."

She nodded jerkily, but didn't object. Impulsively, Jonah angled his head to kiss her quickly and soundly. He'd developed a bad habit of doing that during the past week. But damn it, she looked so rattled that he thought she needed a good kissing to bring her back to her senses.

Jonah strode off to check the house. The front door showed no signs of forced entry. Neither did the office window. Jonah noticed that the bottom drawer of the desk was standing open. An empty leather pouch suggested Avery kept a stash of money there, and it had been stolen.

Grabbing the lantern, Jonah ambled down the hall to survey the bedrooms. The first one was unoccupied, but a quick look in the second bedroom caused a muddled frown to gather on his brow. He stared at the unmade bed in what he presumed was Avery's room. An incense burner on the nightstand gave off an exotic scent, as did the elaborately carved pipe that sat beside it. The likeness of a Chinese dragon carved from stone was perched on the commode. Jonah walked over to the wardrobe closet to confirm his worst suspicions. Scowling in disgust, he reversed direction to rejoin Maddie.

"Did you find anything?" she asked expectantly.

"Yup." He propelled her toward their horses.

"Well?"

"Has Avery ever been married?"

She gave him a strange look to match his strange question. "Not to my knowledge."

"Didn't think so. If you had consented to marry Avery you wouldn't have had to share his bed," Jonah said in a hushed tone as he veered around the bunkhouse.

"What does that have to do with this situation?" she asked, bewildered.

"Avery already has a bed partner. Chiang Ti. And from all indication they are both opium addicts."

"What! You must be—" Her voice evaporated when Jonah clamped his hand over her mouth to prevent her from drawing unwanted attention from the bunkhouse.

"I doubt Chiang Ti will want to hang around these parts after the truth comes out," Jonah whispered.

"Which only confirms what I've said all along." Maddie stuffed her booted foot in the stirrup and swung onto her strawberry-roan gelding. "Avery wanted to marry me to acquire control of the ranch. He didn't give a fig about me personally. But then, what man ever did, besides my father?"

Jonah rolled his eyes, wondering if Maddie would ever realize how attractive and fascinating she truly was. He was certainly aware of it and he imagined he could speak for the rest of the male population. Maddie seemed to be the only one who was oblivious to her incredible allure.

He shook off his wandering thoughts and said, "The question still remains, who killed Avery and his informant? My money is on your two friends, Gibbs and Newton. They must have been keeping watch when the hostage exchange went sour tonight. Gibbs and Newton might have returned with the bad news, then decided to rob Avery to ensure they made some profit on the scheme."

His gaze landed squarely on Maddie as they trotted southwest. "But thanks to your arrival at the house you will be a prime suspect because it was *your* sister who was kidnapped and *your* cattle penned up with Avery's. You have motive galore. I wish the hell you'd stayed home."

Maddie's shoulders slumped defeatedly. She had made a critical error in judgment tonight. But surely her friends and neighbors wouldn't believe she was capable of this crime...would they?

"I didn't do it, Jonah. I swear!" she exclaimed. He hadn't trusted her in the beginning and she doubted that he trusted her now. Not really.

"I believe you, princess," he murmured.

"You do?" Maddie was so relieved that she leaned out to hook her arm around his neck, then gave him an off-balance hug.

She found herself lifted from her horse and deposited on Jonah's lap, facing him. Her legs were draped over his muscular thighs and her hips rocked rhythmically toward his as the horse moved beneath them. Heat suffused her body when he stared at her for a long moment. Maddie nearly melted on the spot, vividly reminded of how intimate they had been the previous night.

Although she knew Jonah had no deep feelings for her, she was still helplessly attracted to him. Impulsively, she looped her arms around his shoulders and leaned forward to kiss him—and forgot for a few timeless moments that her life was in turmoil. All she needed to revive her flagging spirits was the taste and feel of him.

Maddie gave herself up to the longing Jonah constantly inspired in her. She reveled in the fact that his lips devoured hers as thoroughly as she devoured his. She could feel the hard length of his arousal pressing against her thigh, and hungry need burned through her like a blazing torch, making her ache for the intimacy they had shared last night.

Her mind reeling, her breath coming in ragged spurts, she leaned back in his encircling arms to peer up at him. He had a strange, indecipherable look on his shadowed face, quickly replaced by a disapproving frown.

"Well," she said challengingly, "*you're* the one who dragged me over here. Even as dense as you can be sometimes, surely you know that I've developed a fond attachment for you, despite what you think of me."

The comment seemed to irritate him. Muttering, he promptly deposited her back on her own horse.

"You and Boone can leave now," she said, bombarded by rejection—again. "I can handle this situation."

Jonah looked at her as if she were insane. "You struck out on your own tonight and became a prime

murder suspect. If I leave you to take care of yourself
now, you might wind up arrested. I sure as hell can't
verify that you didn't grab a knife and stab both men,
then drop the weapon down the privy. And if Chiang
Ti does decide to point an accusing finger at you, and
claims he managed to escape before you killed him,
too, your goose will be cooked. So don't ask me to
leave until you have your life in order!'' he all but
yelled at her. ''Now, are we clear on that, princess?''

Maddie winced at his razor-sharp tone. The man
could go from wildly passionate to royally annoyed
in the time it took to hiccup. She was never going to
figure him out, she decided. Not that she would have
the time. As he pointed out, she would be lucky to
keep herself out of jail after she had been spotted at
the scene of the crime.

Maddie inwardly groaned when she recalled that
she had sent Carlos to summon the sheriff. She could
be under arrest by morning. Once again she'd proved
that she'd made one bad choice after another the past
few months. Tonight especially. She had no one to
blame but herself for the mess her life had become.

Jonah stood aside to watch the emotional reunion
between the Garret sisters. The affection between
Maddie and Christina was unmistakable. It had been
half a lifetime since Jonah had felt that sort of close
connection to anyone.

Even Boone had propped himself against the wall
to observe the interaction between the two women
who had a life and a past in common. Jonah had also
noticed that Boone had been oddly attentive to their
recovering patient since the moment Christina had

opened her baby-blue eyes and stared up at him. Boone had hand-fed Christina, poured water, then more broth down her parched throat. He'd murmured constantly to keep her awake. In fact, when Jonah and Maddie arrived, Boone had Christina up on her feet, walking off the effects of the sedative.

Jonah's thoughts trailed off when Christina laughed at something Maddie whispered to her. Then the girl's gaze landed on Maddie's left hand. Uh-oh, thought Jonah. He could see the curious question forming in Christina's eyes.

"You're married?" Christina croaked in astonishment. "How long have I been gone? When did this happen?"

Maddie half turned from her position on the edge of the bed. Jonah came to attention when her gaze landed directly on him. It seemed as if Maddie was debating whether to continue the hoax or tell her sister the truth. The light in those mesmerizing amber eyes dimmed and her smile wobbled around the edges, but she held out a hand to Jonah, as if requesting his presence beside her.

Fool that he was, he came to heel like a devoted pup.

"Jonah and I were married this week," Maddie reported.

He didn't know why she thought it necessary to continue the lie until she added, "And you need to know that if something should happen to me, you can depend on Jonah to be the big brother you never had. Boone, too. They rescued you tonight, not without great risk to their own lives."

Jonah shot Boone a stony glance. Obviously Boone

had offered the details of the ambush to Maddie while Jonah had been tending the horses.

"I'm eternally indebted to you both," Christina rasped.

When her gaze drifted from Jonah and landed on Boone, he could see the open adoration in her eyes. Oh hell, Jonah muttered under his breath. Boone seemed as bewitched as Christina looked bedeviled. This infatuation was as ill-fated as his attraction to Maddie. Doomed from the onset.

Was Jonah the only one here who had at least one foot planted in reality? And what the devil was the matter with Boone? The girl was too young for him and decades too inexperienced. Just a few hours ago Boone had commented that men like them didn't deserve women like Maddie. The same held true of young Christina. Apparently Boone had stared into Christina's luminous blue eyes and lost the common sense he'd spent twenty-six years cultivating. And hell, Boone was half Kiowa. That should have given him the edge.

Once again, Jonah was reminded how quickly a man could lose his perspective when a beautiful woman crossed his line of vision.

"I think we should let Christina rest and recuperate," Jonah said sensibly. "We also have a few matters to work out." He stared pointedly at Maddie.

She gulped uneasily, then forced a smile for her sister's benefit. "You're home safe and sound, Chrissy. Nothing is going to happen to you now or ever again."

Christina nodded tiredly, then her lashes fluttered

against her pale cheeks. Jonah grabbed Boone's arm and half dragged the besotted man from the room.

"You're drooling," he chided sternly.

Affronted, Boone jerked upright. "I am not."

"Yes, you are," Jonah countered. "Now pay attention here. We have a major problem." He gave Boone the condensed version of the situation at Avery's ranch. Boone swore at the unexpected turn of events, but Jonah kept talking. "I need you to ride out to intercept Sheriff Kilgore and Carlos. Divert them to Hanson's ranch so we can recover the stolen cattle and investigate the scene of the murder thoroughly. I'll join you as soon as I stash Maddie away for safekeeping."

Boone nodded grimly. "Where are you going to hide her until we get this sorted out?"

"I'll find a suitable place," Jonah assured him. "My instincts tell me that Gibbs and Newton are responsible for the murders, but they might be long gone by now."

Boone's expression hardened. "If they had a hand in keeping that poor kid locked up, sedated and starved, then I'm going to make it my mission to track them down."

"Poor kid?" Jonah smirked. "You weren't hovering over Christina as if she were a helpless *child.* It looked pretty damn personal to me. Better watch your step, Boone."

Boone opened his mouth—to protest, no doubt—then shut his trap. He glared pitchforks at Jonah before he wheeled around and stalked off. Jonah sincerely hoped his Kiowa cousin got over being angry and offended, and took what Jonah had said to heart.

Christina was a fifteen-year-old woman-child who was clearly suffering hero worship because Boone had come to her rescue like a white knight. He had been hovering around like a guardian angel since the moment she'd regained consciousness.

If Boone didn't get his head on straight he would be stumbling over the same impossible pitfalls that had tripped up Jonah. If Boone and Jonah didn't remember their places in regard to the princesses of the Bar G Ranch, the rest of the world would be sure to remind them—repeatedly and emphatically.

Jonah turned his full attention on Maddie when she exited her sister's bedroom. He clutched her hand and led her down the hall. "Grab a few things," he ordered. "You're going into hiding for at least a day while I investigate those murders."

"But my sister—"

"—will understand and be properly cared for," Jonah interrupted as he snatched up the discarded satchel. "I want you and your money safely tucked away, and I want to be sure Newton and Gibbs have left the area. I'll have the sheriff put out a warrant for their arrest."

Maddie grabbed a fresh set of clothes and stuffed them in her bag. "You promise that Chrissy will have constant care and attention?"

"Yes," Jonah said without hesitation. "Rosita will keep constant vigil."

Jonah shuffled Maddie out the front door and headed for the barn to retrieve the horses.

"Where are we going?" she asked as he led the saddled mounts from the barn.

"To the safest place I know," he assured her as he trotted toward the towering walls of the canyon to the north.

Jonah led Maddie deeper into the twisting ravines of Forbidden Canyon. Moonlight glinted off the stream that meandered through the valley as Jonah followed the spring to its source—a waterfall that tumbled from one overhanging ledge to a lower out-cropping of rock, where a thin veil of water tumbled gently into the pool below.

Maddie stared bemusedly at Jonah when he dismounted beside the gleaming pool. "This is one of my favorite places on the ranch," she said, "but I don't think..."

Her voice trailed off as she watched Jonah scale the jagged rocks, then disappear behind the falls on the cliff. He expected her to spend the day with her back plastered against the stone wall, while cascades of water shielded her from view?

Maddie huffed out an exasperated breath, then grabbed her satchel. She followed Jonah's zigzagging path to the elevated falls, then sidestepped along the ledge—and blinked in astonishment. She hadn't realized a spacious cavern was hidden behind the upper falls. Ordinarily she experienced uneasy sensations when she was enclosed in tight spaces, but this cave was larger than her own bedroom and provided indirect light from the trickling falls. Here she could breathe without feeling as if the walls were shrinking in on her.

"I've lived here for years and never knew this

place existed,'' she marveled as Jonah lit the torch that he'd retrieved from the corner.

As golden light blazed around her, Maddie's jaw sagged on its hinges. There was no question that this had once been an Indian haunt. Beaded necklaces, leather leggings, buffalo hide quilts and outdated weapons were stacked against one wall.

Eerie sensations trailed down her spine—and not because she was experiencing the usual fear of being buried alive in a narrow space. Instead, she felt as if she'd been transported back in time—and into an alien culture. Sketches of tipis, Indians, horses and buffalo had been carved in the stone, creating a historical account of those who once had the freedom to roam this area of Texas.

Maddie suddenly remembered the Comanche and Kiowa vision quests that Jonah had mentioned. She had the unmistakable feeling that this private sanctuary behind the upper falls was a special site for meditation and reflection.

Jonah made a pallet on the floor and motioned for her to sit down. Then he squatted on his haunches to confront her. ''You've missed out on a night's sleep, so take advantage of this refuge.'' He trailed his forefinger over the dark circles she was certain ringed her eyes. ''Promise me that you'll stay put this time until I come back for you.''

''You're taking my horse with you, I presume, so I won't be able to get very far very fast.''

He nodded his raven head and smiled faintly. ''I prefer that no one knows where you are until I've convinced the sheriff that you weren't involved in the double murder,'' he explained reasonably. ''Extinguish the torch when I leave. There's enough light spearing through that thin curtain of water so you won't feel the darkness crowding in on you.''

He leaned forward to press a soft, lingering kiss to her lips. ''I'll be back as soon as I can. I stuffed some trail rations in your satchel, in case you get hungry. You'll have all the fresh water you need right here.''

Jonah retrieved his badge from his pocket and pinned it on his black shirt. ''This is for you, princess. I'm going to use my rank with the Rangers to clear you of wrongdoing. I'm going to get your world back in order before I do us both a favor and get out of your life for good.''

He kissed her tenderly one last time before he rose to his feet, then stared at her for a long moment before he turned and walked away.

When he disappeared into the tumbling falls like a wraith evaporating at dawn, Maddie brushed her fingers over her lips, savoring the incredibly tender kiss. The man's constant change of demeanor and conflicting words had her thoroughly confused. One moment he was pulling away from her, as if he resented physical contact. The next he was initiating kisses, as if she meant something special to him.

Perhaps he *did* care, but resented the attraction, she mused pensively. Just because Jonah didn't *love* her as much as she wanted him to did not necessarily mean that he didn't *like* her with all that he was capable of giving to a woman.

Well, whatever motivated Jonah's actions was too complex for Maddie to sort out tonight. Sighing tiredly, she stretched out on the padded quilts to rest.

She'd been riding an adrenaline high for days on end and fatigue had definitely caught up with her.

Odd sensations spilled over her as she closed her eyes and nestled in the warm cocoon of Indian blankets. This was the second time in the past few days that she'd felt as if she partially understood what it was like to be inside Jonah's skin—and in his head. She was practically entombed in his past, ensconced in a sacred haunt greatly revered by his people. Knowing Jonah had come here often as a child was comforting to her.

Maddie smiled drowsily. When Jonah walked out of her life for good she could come here and absorb this deeply ingrained part of him that she felt reverberating within these stone walls. Indeed, she could almost feel a spiritual presence now, the same presence that his people must have instinctively gravitated toward in this place in days gone by.

Relaxed and content for the first time in hours, Maddie fell asleep.

Chapter Twelve

Jonah arrived at the Hanson ranch to find Sheriff Kilgore and Boone inspecting the corral. According to Boone, the sheriff had already questioned several hired hands, who claimed to know nothing about the stolen cattle. Jonah wasn't surprised. He'd spent half his life taking statements of proclaimed innocence from criminals who were as guilty as sin.

While the cowhands prepared for the trail drive to the railhead at Dodge City, Jonah ambled over to formally introduce himself to the sheriff.

"I recommend that you wire the sheriff in Dodge and have him oversee the accounting for the sale of Hanson cattle," Jonah suggested. "It's fairly obvious that Hanson has been stealing from the Bar G Ranch, and the Garrets should be compensated for their loss by paying them with the profits from the trail drive."

Sheriff Kilgore, a crusty law officer with a handlebar mustache, weathered face and a permanent squint in his brown eyes, nodded agreeably. "I'll do just that, Danhill." He sent Jonah a solemn frown.

"Boone tells me that you had a *situation* in one of these canyons last night."

"An extremely deadly encounter," Jonah clarified. "And before wild rumors run rampant, you need to know that the bushwhacking brigade consisted of white outlaws masquerading as Indians. I asked Boone to guard my back with bows and arrows because we had to rely on silence and stealth. The odds were stacked heavily against us."

"Were you able to identify the outlaws?" Kilgore asked.

Jonah shook his head as he glanced at the cowboys who were stowing their gear in the two wagons. "Some of these hired hands might recognize them, but obviously they're pleading ignorance to avoid involvement."

Kilgore hitched his thumb toward the milling cowhands. "You need to know that some of these men are quick to presume that you and Boone are involved with the Indian raids and that you're using your badge as protection. One of the men referred to you as the rogue Ranger."

Jonah wasn't surprised. Because of his heritage he'd been blamed and accused of all sorts of things. He'd conditioned himself not to be concerned with white folks' low opinion of him.

He gestured toward the ranch house. "Let's check the office. I'm sure Boone told you what I found last night."

"Yeah, hell of a mess that poor Maddie has found herself in," Kilgore remarked as he hurried to keep up with Jonah's long, swift strides. "First her father's disappearance and our ongoing search for him. Then rustling and kidnapping, and now her neighbor ends up dead, along with one of her cowhands.''

Jonah stopped short and stared down the older man. ''Just so you know, Maddie found the bodies when she came here last night to confront Avery with her suspicions. It rattled her badly. I can attest to that. It's my opinion that she wasn't involved in the killings. I'll stake my reputation on that.''

Kilgore stared at the tin star pinned on Jonah's shirt, then nodded. ''Your word is good enough for me, son.''

Jonah breathed an inward sigh of relief when the sheriff took him at his word, half-breed or not. It was the first time since he could remember that he'd cared what someone else thought of him. But it was for *Maddie's* sake, not his, that it mattered. His top priority was to clear her name. He'd made a promise to set her world to rights, and Jonah wasn't leaving West Texas until he'd tied up all the loose ends in this case.

Maddie stirred sluggishly when she felt the whisper of warm lips against her cheek. She opened heavy-lidded eyes to see Jonah crouched beside her, and she smiled drowsily.

''You can go home now, princess,'' he murmured as he combed his fingers through the curlicue strands that tumbled over the side of her face.

''I'm no longer a potential murder suspect?'' She sighed in relief when he nodded.

And then it hit her like an unseen blow to the solar plexus that Jonah was going to leave for good. Everything inside Maddie rebelled against the thought.

This would be the last time she would be alone with him, the last time she ever saw him.

Forbidden Canyon was the last place on earth he wanted to revisit.

The need to share the incredible intimacy she had known with him overwhelmed her. She wanted to brand herself on his mind and heart for all eternity, because she would never love anyone as deeply and devotedly as she had come to love Jonah.

Maddie reached up to trace the rugged features of his face, then cupped her hand around his neck to bring his head to hers. "Maybe you don't want to hear the words whispering in my heart, but I need to say them," she murmured against his sensuous lips. "I love you, Jonah Danhill. I will always love you, even if it has to be from afar."

"Maddie, it's just gratitude—"

She kissed him to shush him, and held on tightly when he tried to retreat. She stared him squarely in the eye and said, "In case you haven't figured it out yet, I'm a woman who knows her own mind."

Jonah chuckled softly. "I might not be the brightest star in the heavens, but, yeah, I've figured that out." Then his expression sobered as he stared down at her. "I'm not what you need, princess. I have nothing to give that you don't have already."

"You have *you*," she insisted as she clutched her fist in the front of his shirt and pulled him down on top of her. "That's all I want, and you're kidding yourself, Mr. Ranger, if you think you're leaving this cave until I've had my way with you one last time."

She flashed him what she hoped was a provocatively playful smile, even if she was crying on the inside, knowing she couldn't keep him forever. She was going to touch him as intimately as he'd touched her, arouse him to the limits of his sanity. He would remember her, she vowed determinedly. She might be left behind, but she couldn't bear to be forgotten by the man who held her heart and soul.

Her free hand drifted down his chest to unfasten his holster, then his breeches. Jonah's hand folded over hers to forestall her. "Stop that before I lose the ability to think straight," he said hoarsely.

"I don't want you *thinking*," she said as her hand drifted lower to trace the hard bulge in his breeches. "I want you *naked*." She grinned saucily and added, "You assured Major Thorton at Fort Griffin that your life is easier when you just give me what I want."

Jonah sucked in a breath when her nimble fingers escaped his grasp to loosen the placket of his breeches. He hissed in tormented pleasure when her hand folded around his aching flesh, then stroked him from base to tip. He'd never allowed a woman such liberties, but he was helpless to stop Maddie because he welcomed only her touch. She explored the textures of his body and purred in feminine satisfaction when he groaned in pleasure.

"You need to lose that badge and those clothes, Mr. Ranger," she insisted playfully. *"Now."*

He should pull away. He should surge to his feet and run for his life. Should, but couldn't. Maddie held the kind of power over him that defied physical strength and iron-willed resolve. She could make him a slave to passion with one intimate touch, one mind-boggling kiss.

A trembling sigh tumbled from his lips as he allowed her to divest him of his shirt, then peel his breeches down to his knees. Jonah wasn't sure how he'd landed on his back with Maddie hovering over him. She was like a mystical siren who'd captured him in her potent spell, and he melted into the pallet. Her adventurous hands mapped the expanse of his chest, swirled over his belly, then stroked his throbbing erection again—and again.

Jonah could barely remember the feeling of surrender or defeat. He'd been trained to refuse to accept either one in his years with the Rangers. But he was definitely becoming reacquainted with those vulnerable feelings and he was at Maddie's mercy. Her gentle hands were driving him out of his mind—and making him savor every moment of it.

Desire slammed into him with the force of a cannonball when her silky hair grazed his chest and her moist tongue flicked out to tease the tip of his arousal. Jonah forgot to breathe—and couldn't recall why doing so was necessary—when she took him into her mouth and suckled him. Fire raged through his blood, and the fierce impact of her intimate caresses and kisses left him burning alive. Before he passed out from the intense pleasure, he reached frantically for her, but she pressed him to his back again and held him captive with that hypnotic smile that had been his downfall since the day he'd met her.

''I want it understood that when you leave me for good and say 'I'm pleased to have made your acquaintance,' that you mean it in every sense of the word.''

Her tongue glided over his pulsing length, and Jonah swallowed a howl of maddening pleasure.

"I am *pleasing* you, aren't I?" she asked.

Jonah was beyond speech, beyond thought. He could barely nod his head as dizzying pleasure kept tossing him off balance.

"And does this please you, too?" she whispered before she took him into her mouth and nipped lightly with her teeth.

"Mmm…" It was all he could get out while she introduced him to her exquisite brand of seductive torture.

The world went out of focus and Jonah clawed at the pallet, trying to anchor himself in reality, but it was damn near impossible when Maddie kept launching him from one disorienting plateau to another. Bulletlike sensations pelted him as she stroked him repeatedly. Heat coursed heavily through him when she flicked him with that teasing tongue and caressed him gently, over and over again. He shuddered in wild desperation when she levered over him to kiss him hungrily, and he tasted his own passion on her lips.

"Come here," he rasped, frantic for her.

"Do you want me?" she asked as she stroked him, then enfolded him in her hand. "I need to hear that you want me."

"I don't remember when I didn't want you," he admitted as another rolling wave of pleasure cascaded over him.

He reached for her again, but she rocked back on her knees and knelt between his legs to remove her blouse. He drank in the alluring sight of her, marveling at her feminine perfection. All the while her eyes remained locked on his, watching him stare at her in masculine appreciation. She seemed unashamed of baring herself to his hungry gaze and unafraid of confiding her feelings for him—misinterpreted though he knew those feelings were.

When she had shed all her garments and hovered above him, guiding his hard arousal to her, Jonah nearly passed out again. His ragged breath wobbled in his chest when she sank onto him and he felt her softest flesh burning around him like a living flame.

For sure and certain Jonah knew this spell-casting siren had bewitched him for all eternity. He was hopelessly entranced as she moved above him. He arched up to meet her and her golden gaze never left his as they rocked together, then apart, setting a frantic cadence of passion. Jonah watched desire overtake her, heard her gasp in pleasure as he buried himself to the hilt, then retreated. She took all he had to offer and gave herself generously, wholeheartedly to him.

Pleasure mushroomed inside him, converging then scattering like debris in a cyclone. Jonah struggled to draw breath and swore he was about to fly off in every direction at once. Complete and total surrender had never been so welcomed, so inevitable. When unleashed passion exploded inside him, he curled upward to topple Maddie against his chest. Shudder after helpless shudder riveted him as he clutched her shapely body in his arms and held her close to his heart. His mind reeling, he inhaled the scent of her hair, savored the unique scent of *her* and felt the last remnants of pleasure burn a fiery path to the depths of his soul.

The most remarkable sense of contentment flooded over him as his spent body sagged on the pallet. Jonah had gone so many hours without sleep that exhaustion overtook him immediately. His eyes fluttered shut and he drifted into oblivion, letting his erotic dreams take up where reality left off.

Maddie smiled in feminine satisfaction when she felt Jonah slump beneath her and heard him breathing deeply. She'd had her way with him. It was an empowering feeling that she wouldn't soon forget. Her only regret was that both times they'd made love she had initiated the trysts. She would have given almost anything if just once *he* had come to *her*.

Perhaps then she would have known that what he felt for her had transformed from physical desire to love—or at least something very much like love. She suspected that Jonah had so little association with love and affection in his life that it was foreign and unfamiliar to him.

Easing away, Maddie gathered her clothes and dressed quietly. All the while she made a dedicated study of this man who had become her guide, her guardian spirit and her one true love. "As a child I dreamed of a dark, daring knight, my own unique prince," she murmured to him, though he heard not one word. "Regardless of what you believe, my Comanche knight, I will always love you. And if we have created a child together he will know that his father is the most remarkable man I've ever known and that I chose you without hesitation or regret."

Maddie twisted the gold band on her finger, knowing she should return it to Jonah, but she was reluctant to give it up. "We are married in all the ways that truly matter," she whispered. "You make me feel whole and alive and incredibly happy. I draw from your strength, your invincible capabilities and your determination, Jonah. I will always admire and respect you.''

Impulsively, Maddie knelt beside him to press one final kiss to his unresponsive lips. Her warrior had worn himself out in setting her world to rights again. ''I'm grateful for all you've done,'' she murmured as she withdrew. ''But gratitude is only part of what I feel for you, even if you won't believe it. Wherever you are will always be the place I long to be.''

Turning away, Maddie exited the cavern. She mounted the spare horse that Jonah had provided for her, and left his black gelding grazing near the pool. When Jonah awoke and returned to the house to gather his gear and say farewell, Maddie vowed she wouldn't throw herself at his feet and beg him to stay.

He knew how she felt about him. She had made it abundantly clear that he had her heart. If Jonah felt anything strong and lasting for her, if he wanted to return one day, then *he* would have to make that decision.

Maddie rode home, knowing she was leaving the best part of herself behind with the man who had been born under a wandering star and who would never be content to live in the valley where painful memories tormented him. When she considered what she would be doing, asking for him to put down roots in this place, she knew she wanted the impossible—even of a man who dared to face impossible odds in the name of duty.

But not in the name of love for her.

Destined to live with this empty ache in her soul, Maddie returned to her life, vowing to ensure her younger sister was well on her way to recovery and to turn this ranch into the prosperous property it had been—before Avery Hanson undermined it with his treacherous schemes.

Smiling ruefully, knowing her sister was destined for disappointment, Maddie stood outside the bedroom and watched her sister practically drool over Boone. It didn't take a genius to realize that Chrissy was completely infatuated. The girl was all smiles and laughter when Boone teased her playfully.

Unless Maddie missed her guess, Boone was smitten, too. He was hand-feeding Chrissy bites of beef, bread and cheese, although Chrissy appeared to have recovered the strength to feed herself. But given the hellish week Chrissy endured, she was entitled to all the pampering and pleasure she could get. She was, however, setting herself up for the kind of heartache Maddie experienced. But when a woman met her prince—no matter how poor the timing or ill-fated the situation—she listened to her heart, not her head.

"Maddie, you're finally back!"

Maddie shook herself from her wandering thoughts and returned Chrissy's smile. She ambled into the room, aware that Boone had eased back into his own space, in case Maddie disapproved of the familiarity between them.

"Thanks to Jonah and Boone, I'm back for good," Maddie said as she eased down on the edge of the bed. "You look much better today, Chrissy."

"I'm feeling much better," she confirmed as her gaze darted helplessly to her companion. "If not for Boone, I might never have returned home."

"Jonah had a definite hand in your release," Boone

insisted, then lost himself in Chrissy's luminous blue eyes. "Well, I better go. I'm sure you ladies would like to visit privately."

When he stood to leave, Chrissy clutched his hand. "I can never repay you, Boone," she murmured, her heart in her eyes. "I'm forever indebted."

"Take care of yourself, angel," he said as he patted her hand.

Maddie bit back a grin when Boone took his leave and her sister's longing gaze followed him until he disappeared from sight.

"Isn't he the most incredibly handsome and charming man you ever laid eyes on?" Chrissy said with an adoring sigh.

"Oh, definitely," Maddie agreed, eyes twinkling with amusement.

"Well, except for your husband, Jonah," she quickly amended.

"Yes…and about that." Maddie gathered her thoughts and said, "Jonah and I are not actually married. It was just a charade to protect me from trouble and to force Avery's hand."

"But you love him, I know you do," Christina insisted. "I've never seen you look at a man the way you look at Jonah."

"It's not that simple," Maddie said quietly. "Just because you have special feelings for a man doesn't mean that he *can* or *wants to* make a place for you in his life."

"Well, it should be that simple," Christina said idealistically.

Maddie chortled. "I wish it were, but you're going to discover in the years to come that life doesn't fall into place just because you wish it so. Papa amassed a great deal of wealth, but you will find that it can be as much a curse as it is a blessing. Some men will show interest in you because they see you as a meal ticket, the means to elevate their social status. Others will perceive you as unattainable because they have nothing to give that you don't already have.''

Men like Jonah and Boone, Maddie mused, and wondered if her sister would make the connection.

Maddie reached out to take Christina's hand and gave it a fond and supportive squeeze. ''The most important lesson you have to learn is to become strong and independent and not allow yourself to put blind faith in any man who catches your eye. You have to learn to look for hidden motives. Some men you can trust explicitly and others only want to use you.''

''Well, Boone isn't the kind of man who would use a woman to get ahead in life.''

''No, he isn't. But Boone is very much like Jonah in that he perceives himself far too different to fit into your world, or for you to fit into his. And you need to prepare yourself for the inevitability that Boone will be leaving with Jonah and we might never see them again.''

''Leaving?'' Chrissy's face fell like a rock slide. ''How soon?''

''Today, I expect.'' Maddie tried hard not to let her voice betray her. She smiled a little too brightly to counter the gnawing ache in the pit of her stomach. ''The most important thing is that you're home and safe at last.''

Her attention drifted to the pile of discarded clothes

in the corner of the room. She walked over to pick them up and took a whiff of the musty scent. She remembered the smell that had clung to Chrissy after she returned home. The scent seemed strangely familiar, but Maddie couldn't place it.

"Do you have any idea where you were held captive?" Maddie asked curiously.

Chrissy, who'd been lost in thought—and Maddie had no doubt that Boone weighed heavily on her mind—jerked to attention. "No, I was set upon by five men I'd never seen before. They blindfolded and sedated me. I awoke occasionally and I remember the scent of cool, stale air, but that's all I recall."

Maddie frowned ponderously as she made note of the scent of the clothes and the reddish-brown stain on the sleeve of the blouse. The smell was not the same as in the cavern where Jonah had stashed her for safekeeping. True, the rugged ravines and canyons in the area abounded with small niches and caves, but this scent was different and Maddie couldn't recall why it seemed familiar to her.

A light rap on the open door drew Maddie's attention to Rosita poised in the hall. "Amos Mosely and his son, Terrance, are here to pay their respects and check on the bambino," she announced. "Shall I send them up?"

Maddie nodded, distracted, then set aside the garments.

When the Moselys arrived, Maddie smiled in wry amusement while Terrance, the eldest son of a struggling neighbor rancher, poured on his limited charm and yammered about his concern for Christina's ordeal, and how delighted he was that she had returned home safely. The long-winded spiel definitely sounded rehearsed—at Amos's insistence, no doubt.

Maddie stood aside to see how Christina dealt with her would-be beau after their heart-to-heart talk. It seemed her sister was trying to decide if Terrance's concern was sincere or if he was simply buttering her up for a future courtship.

A moment later Terrance stuck his foot in his mouth by saying, "I would like to call upon you again tomorrow. Perhaps you will feel up to strolling around the spacious grounds of your grand home."

Christina's delicate brow arched as she shot Maddie a discreet glance. "Spacious grounds? Grand home? Why, Terrance, if I didn't know better I might think that you are more interested in the place I live than you are about my recuperation. I seriously doubt that I will be ready for a vigorous hike around our ranch tomorrow."

Maddie muffled a snicker when Amos gouged his son in the ribs with an elbow. Here was yet another example of men who viewed the Garret women as an opportunity for wealth and elevated social stature.

When Christina sighed heavily and scrunched down in bed Maddie took her cue and said, "As you can see, my sister's energy is failing her and she needs to rest." She took Amos's arm and steered him toward the door. "Thank you for stopping in to check on Christina."

Rosita returned a few minutes later to announce that William Gilmore, another young, potential suitor, had arrived to see Christina.

"I think you're right," Christina muttered while she waited for William's arrival. "Wealth does indeed bring suitors out of the woodwork. All they need is an excuse to show up.''

Maddie was impressed with how speedily and skillfully Christina dealt with the fawning admirer and his gallant offer to visit her daily while she recuperated.

William worked as an assistant at the nearby trading post and had about as much ambition as a slug. It seemed that what he lacked in ambition he made up for in gumption. He appeared more than eager to attach himself to a young heiress who could keep him in the manner to which he aspired.

William Gilmore had been gone only a few minutes when Rosita—who looked exhausted from so many trips up and down the stairs—poked her head around the corner again.

''Senor Tipton is here,'' she said, huffing and puffing for breath. ''And if you don't mind, I'll just send up any other visitors who arrive. These steps are wearing me out.''

When Rosita trounced off, Christina fluffed her pillow and propped herself up. ''At least this suitor is only using me as an excuse to see you,'' she said. ''You can deal with him.''

Maddie was not particularly in the mood to visit with one of her would-be fiancés, but she vowed to play the gracious hostess before sending Ward on his way. Besides, she needed to inform him about her supposed marriage to Jonah. Then she would have limited association with her British-born-and-bred neighbor, who oversaw the ranch owned by several English investors.

Maddie didn't understand the British fascination with Texas, but there were several foreign-owned ranches in this area, plus the elegant Saxon Hotel and two upscale restaurants in Mobeetie.

She mustered a smile when Ward entered the bedroom. She appraised him, noting that he looked his usual stylish, well-heeled self. Ward was classically handsome, with refined features and blond hair. Though not as tall as Jonah or Boone, he was a distinguished figure and had been nothing but polite to Maddie. She marveled at the fact that, despite his good looks and blue-blooded breeding, she had never felt the fierce attraction and rapt fascination that Jonah held for her.

Obviously Maddie had a weakness for rugged, swarthy warriors, not dignified gentlemen. So did Christina.

"Good afternoon, ladies," Ward said with a customary bow. "I was at Palo Cinto Trading Post this morning and heard the news that Chrissy had been returned safely. I wanted to see for myself that she was unharmed."

Maddie nodded graciously. "It was kind of you to drop by, Ward. As you can see, Chrissy is well on her way to recovering from her ordeal."

"That is grand news." Ward strode over to press a kiss to Chrissy's wrist. "I do hope you're up and about soon...." His voice trailed off and he frowned when his gaze glided to Maddie's left hand. "You're married?" he questioned, stunned.

Although there was no need to continue the charade, Maddie nodded. She was not taking off this gold band—ever—because she had decided never to settle for a substitute for the man she loved. Becoming a spinster was her only option.

"Yes, I am," she replied. "To make a long story short, I was reunited with Jonah recently. Although his profession demands constant traveling, we were wed this week."

"You must know I'm disappointed."

Maddie offered an apologetic smile. "I'm sorry, but I followed my heart. I hope you can understand."

When he nodded in reluctant acceptance, Maddie breathed a sigh of relief. That had gone better than anticipated. But then, she reminded herself, neither Ward nor Avery held any true affection for her. It was this ranch they coveted.

"Since Hanson Ranch will be up for sale, I suppose you'll be interested in the property," she said conversationally.

Ward smiled. "I'm sure my investors will want to expand. I wondered if you might be competing with me for the land."

"I have all I can manage. No need to worry about me driving up the price."

"Glad to hear that…"

His voice trailed off as he glanced over Maddie's head. Maddie turned to verify who had nabbed Ward's attention, but she already knew. She could feel Jonah's presence because she'd developed such an acute awareness of him.

Although her heart was breaking, she walked over to take Jonah's hand. She noticed the star had been unpinned from his shirt, and his fresh, clean scent indicated he'd made use of the spring pool to bathe before riding back to the house. "Ward Tipton, this is my husband, Jonah Danhill."

The two men nodded shortly, then sized each other

up. Ward tipped his hat politely and said, "I should be going. It's a pleasure to make your acquaintance."

Maddie bit back a grin when Ward's remark reminded her of the playful comment she'd made to Jonah. Clearly, he remembered, because he flicked her a quick glance and his eyes glinted with suppressed humor.

When Ward exited, Jonah turned his attention to Chrissy. "You look much better this afternoon. Thank goodness."

"I feel better." Chrissy's gaze drifted past Jonah to see Boone hovering in the hallway, staring solemnly at her. "You're leaving," she said in a deflated tone.

"Yes, we came to fetch our gear," Jonah affirmed.

Maddie wondered if anyone else in the room could hear her heart breaking and clattering to the floor. Even knowing this moment would come hadn't prepared her for the hollow ache that swallowed her alive. Maddie drew a restorative breath, squared her shoulders and vowed to remain dry-eyed—until Jonah rode away. His last memory of her was not going to be of a weepy female.

Jonah pivoted on his heels and said, "By the way, I don't like Ward Tipton."

Maddie smiled, amused, as she followed him down the hall. "As I recall, you said you didn't like anyone very much."

Yes, he had, but knowing that dignified dandy of a rancher had set his sights on Maddie made Jonah like him even less. But that's what ill-founded possessiveness did for you, he decided. He couldn't allow himself to think of Maddie as *his*. They were worlds apart and he couldn't let himself forget that.

This love she claimed to feel for him would fade soon enough. Then she would realize that she had been caught in an emotional whirlwind and had simply turned to him for comfort and support. In time she would probably thank him for not taking advantage of her vulnerability more than he had already.

When Jonah lurched around to say his final farewell, he gazed into Maddie's luminous amber eyes and felt as if he'd been gut-punched. Damn, he'd grown accustomed to having her underfoot and dealing with her stubborn defiance. It would take time to adjust to not having her around. Even longer to forget the way she made him feel, deep down in those secret places he shielded from the rest of the world.

His thoughts disintegrated when she impulsively flung her arms around his neck and kissed him senseless. He was still standing there, his senses overloaded with the taste, feel and scent of her, when she abruptly released him and fled from the room.

Jonah swore inventively as he scooped up his gear. He had to get out of here before he started questioning why he should leave and not look back.

He cast one last glance around the spacious room and his gaze landed on the plush four-poster that he would never share with Maddie. Resolutely, he turned and walked away from the place he didn't belong, away from the woman who deserved far more than he had to offer.

Chapter Thirteen

"Christina kissed me, right on the mouth," Boone confided as he and Jonah headed east thirty minutes later.

"Must be a Garret family trait," Jonah murmured absently. "Kiss and run."

"She also told me that I was always welcome at the ranch and she would be there waiting for me." He shook his head in amazement. "Is that girl blind? Can't she see me for what I am?"

"She's blind," Jonah muttered. "So is her sister."

Boone was silent for two miles, then he said, "It's hell doing the right thing, isn't it, Danhill?"

"Pure hell," Jonah agreed.

Since he'd left Maddie behind, the hole in his chest kept expanding until it felt as if it would rip him in two. He'd been alone countless times, but he'd never felt as lost and lonely as he did right now—even when Boone commenced jabbering on about Christina.

Jonah was so tangled up in his emotions that he wasn't paying the slightest attention to his surroundings. But the crack of rifles splitting the air just at sunset nabbed his attention and jerked him back to the present. Jonah instinctively ducked. Boone did likewise. Two bullets whizzed between them and plugged into the wall of the rocky ravine.

Jonah dropped to the side of his horse so he wouldn't be a sitting duck. Boone did the same. They barely dodged two more flying bullets, which zinged off the rocks and caused the horses to sidestep skittishly.

Jonah panned the cliffs, which provided excellent cover for the bushwhackers. "Newton and Gibbs," he speculated.

"That'd be my guess," Boone said. "Why the hell are they shooting at us? They should know we don't have the money. Maddie does."

The comment caused an uneasy feeling to slither down Jonah's spine. He dropped to the ground behind a fortress of stone to return fire at the bushwhackers. "If those two hombres are still after the money, why wouldn't they go after Maddie now that we're out of the picture?" Jonah mused aloud as he scanned the rugged ledges, looking for signs of the bushwhacking duo. "And damn it, what is there about me that inspires folks to try to blow off my head?"

"Must be your dazzling personality…whoa!" Boone ducked when an oncoming bullet tried to put a new part in his hair.

"Something doesn't add up here—" Jonah hit the ground when another bullet whined past him and scattered dirt beside his boot.

He recoiled to get off a shot when he saw a rifle barrel glinting in the evening sunlight. His aim was on the mark. He heard a surprised squawk above him and saw the rifle cartwheel over the ledge.

"Nice shot," Boone exclaimed. "Too bad you hit that bastard's rifle instead of his head."

Jonah half turned when he caught movement out of the corner of his eye. "There." He and Boone took aim. Their rifles barked in unison and one of the ambushers crumbled on the cliff to their left.

Jonah was on his feet in a single bound, darting in and out of the scrub cedars and mesquite as he clambered up the hillside to reach the downed outlaw. Without being told, Boone provided cover by firing several rounds at the other outlaw, who had grabbed his six-shooter and was blasting away, even though he was too far out of range to do any serious damage.

Jonah crouched beside the injured man, whom he recognized as one of the cowboys who had followed Maddie from Fort Worth. It was Newton or Gibbs, but he wasn't sure which.

"Boone!" he yelled in between volleys of bullets. "Get up here. I'll cover you." Jonah fired off several shots while Boone scrabbled up the steep incline. "Which one is this?"

Huffing and puffing, Boone squatted beside the injured man. "Beau Newton." He smiled nastily at the grimacing outlaw, then glanced at Jonah. "You wanna torture him for information Comanche style or shall I do it Kiowa style?"

Jonah smiled maliciously. "Let *him* choose. It's his hide."

"I don't know nothin'!" Beau wheezed as he watched blood soak both sleeves of his shirt.

Jonah drew his dagger from his boot and tested the

sharpness of the blade. "That's the beauty of torture, Newton," he said conversationally. "The more intense the pain, the clearer your recollection becomes."

"Let me do it." Boone spoke up, waving his knife in front of Newton's face. "I haven't carved on any palefaces lately."

"Me, either. I almost forgot how much I enjoyed slicing up spineless white men."

"Jesse!" Beau railed at the top of his lungs. "Help me!"

Jonah glanced over at the spot where Jesse Gibbs had last been seen. "Looks like your sidekick bailed out on you. Guess it's just us against you now." His intimidating gaze settled directly on Beau. "Pick your method of torture or we'll start carving from both sides at once and meet in the middle."

Beau's frantic scream echoed across the ravine as darkness settled around them.

"You big sissy," Boone mocked. "We haven't even laid a hand on you—yet."

Jonah doubted the gutless man would hold out too long before he sang like a canary. Any man who got his greatest thrills in life by terrorizing women would crack easily under pressure. Jonah vowed to have his revenge on this cowardly son of a bitch for falsely accusing Maddie of theft and trying to blow her to kingdom come on two occasions.

Maddie stood at the parlor window long after Jonah and Boone disappeared from sight, watching the sun make its leisurely descent in the cloudless sky. He was well and truly gone, and she would never see him again. A tear dribbled down her cheek and she wiped it away. Maddie drew in a cathartic breath, squared her shoulders and told herself not to spend the rest of her days staring into the distance, wishing Jonah would have a change of heart and return.

He's gone. Get that through your thick skull, princess.

Maddie smiled ruefully, recalling that she never had broken Jonah of the habit of calling her princess. He was the only man alive she had allowed to get away with it.

"Maddie?"

She glanced sideways to see her sister, garbed in a pink satin robe, clinging to the stair railing for support. Her face was still pale, but she'd mustered the strength to venture from her bedroom. That was a good sign.

"You should be resting." Maddie strode into the foyer to frown disapprovingly at her sister. "Go back to bed."

"I just remembered something about my captivity. I took off the ring Papa gave me for my thirteen birthday and dropped it on the floor between the cot and the wall that first night, before someone poured drug-laced wine down my throat." Her curious gaze settled on Maddie, who stood at the bottom of the staircase. "Do you suppose Avery had a musty-smelling wine cellar of some sort? It's the taste of wine that I recall. Never water. Just wine."

When Christina swayed slightly, Maddie dashed toward her. She lifted the hem of her skirt to keep from tripping, then glanced down at the step. An uneasy feeling settled in the pit of her stomach when she noticed the clump of red mudstone on the stair. She hurriedly scooped it up on her way to assist Christina back to bed.

A niggling feeling hounded her as she escorted Chrissy to her room. With sickening dread, Maddie plucked up her sister's soiled blouse and held the mudstone near the fabric to compare the stains.

"Maddie? What's wrong?" Christina said worriedly. "You look as if you've seen a ghost."

Maddie drew herself up and manufactured a smile for Chrissy's benefit. "I'm fine. Just tired is all. I think I'll lie down while you're resting."

When she stepped into the hall she uncurled her hand and stared at the telltale clump of reddish-brown mudstone. A vivid image formed in her mind, causing her to mutter an unlady-like curse. She had the unmistakable feeling that she knew where to find Christina's ring. But now that Jonah and Boone were gone and the sheriff was a three-hour ride away, Maddie was left to tend to the matter herself.

She scurried down the hall to change into her riding breeches and grab her pistol. Then, gritting her teeth with determination, she walked outside to fetch her horse. As the sun sank on Forbidden Canyon, leaving the world in darkness, Maddie rode off to investigate.

"I'll tell you what you want to know!" Beau yelped when Jonah drew a bead of blood on his index finger.

Jonah was amazed at Beau's odd tolerance for pain. He'd been winged by a bullet in both shoulders, but the equivalent of a paper cut on his finger sent him over the edge. "You'd never qualify for warrior status with the Kiowa or Comanche," Jonah said as he sank back on his haunches. "Now, who sent you after Maddie Garret and then after us?"

"He'll kill me," Beau muttered apprehensively. "You have to promise you won't tell him that I told you."

Jonah and Boone exchanged glances. Obviously, Beau wasn't acting under Avery Hanson's orders, because Avery was dead. When Boone got that impatient look on his face and grabbed Beau's right hand, the man commenced squealing like a stuck pig before the dagger even touched his flesh.

"It was Ward Tipton!" Beau wailed. "Two years ago he discovered that Avery had an informant relaying information about his ranch operation. Ward decided to get even by paying the spy more money to work for *him*."

"Clem Foster?" Jonah asked.

Beau shook his head. "Jesse Gibbs."

Jonah and Boone stared curiously at him.

"Then how did Clem fit into this scheme?" Jonah asked.

"He spied at the Garret ranch for Avery," Beau wheezed. "Ward and Avery were both after the Bar G Ranch. When Ward found out that Avery sent Clem to kill Maddie's father, he knew Avery was making a play for Maddie."

"So Ward Tipton had Christina Garret kidnapped and held for ransom?" Boone growled.

Beau swallowed apprehensively, then glanced this way and that, as if he expected someone to leap up from nowhere and shut him up with a well-aimed bullet. "No, that was Avery's doing."

Jonah was thoroughly befuddled. Apparently Boone was, too. He wore the same muddled expression.

"Then how does Tipton fit into this tangled mess?" Jonah demanded impatiently.

"Jesse informed Ward that Avery was sending him after Maddie to make sure she didn't acquire the ransom money on her own. Then Ward sent me along with Jesse to steal the money so Avery couldn't get hold of it."

"So Ward took Avery's scheme and played it to his advantage," Jonah surmised.

Beau swallowed hard and bobbed his head. "Yeah. He intended to expose Avery's involvement, then convince Maddie to turn to him for help. He was angling to negotiate a wedding between them so he could take over her ranch."

Jonah swore under his breath. Ward Tipton was one manipulative son of a bitch.

"When we told Ward that you'd married Maddie, he ordered us to dispose of Avery and Clem and make it look as if *Maddie* had struck out in revenge for her sister," he said with a ragged breath.

"That might have worked if Jonah hadn't used the power of his position and insisted Maddie wasn't responsible," Boone mused aloud.

"Why take potshots at Boone and me?" Jonah questioned.

He scowled in irritation when Beau's eyes rolled back in his head and he passed out before answering the question. Jonah hurriedly bandaged Beau's gunshot wounds while Boone tied him up to ensure he'd still be there when they got back.

"I still don't get it," Boone said as he strode toward his horse. "Why would Ward dispose of us if he already got rid of his rival and now has the chance to buy Avery's ranch?"

"There's only one way to find out," Jonah said as he swung into the saddle.

"Right. Ask Ward Tipton in person. Damn that English dandy and all his polished manners. He almost got away with murder."

Jonah jabbed his heels into his mount's flanks and took off at a gallop. He wasn't leaving this part of Texas until he knew exactly how Ward Tipton fit into this convoluted scheme, and was positively certain that Maddie wasn't on a collision course with more trouble.

Maddie trotted her strawberry-roan gelding along the moonlit path. She knew of only one place in the area that fit the description of the dank niche where Christina had been held captive. If Maddie found the ring in that makeshift wine cellar, she anticipated that it would raise more questions than provide answers. She had been in that musty wine cellar with Ward Tipton only once—which was one time too many, because it had made her break out in a cold sweat. That was when she'd first realized she had an unnatural dread of being confined in tight spaces. She had experienced those sensations momentarily when Jonah led her into the cavern behind the falls, but the apprehensive feelings were nothing compared to the ones that tormented her that day almost a year earlier.

Despite the thought of closeting herself in narrow

spaces again, she intended to retrieve Christina's ring and solve this perplexing riddle once and for all.

Dismounting, Maddie tethered her horse, then hiked up the rugged slope to locate the door that opened into a hand-dug hole in the canyon mudstone. Leaving the door ajar, she made use of the ladder, then inched along the rough wall until she located the lantern. Even when light blazed forth Maddie didn't breathe easy. The narrow cubicle reminded her of a tomb, where not one ounce of air stirred to indicate the slightest sign of life. She felt clammy and short of breath, and unreasonable panic tried to sink its claws into her hard-won composure. When she tried to inhale, the air was so heavy with moisture that it seemed to be sucking the oxygen from her lungs. The stench was as cloying as she remembered from her one and only visit here, and she recalled that she hadn't been able to escape this place fast enough.

Hounded by a fierce urgency, she hurried to the narrow cot butted up against a damp mudstone wall, where water droplets had condensed. Maddie eased down and shoved her arm between the wall and cot, groping about for the missing ring. Sure enough, her hand closed around it almost instantly. She held it up to the flickering light, noting the red mud that clung to the jeweled stones.

"You devious sidewinder," she muttered aloud.

"Are you referring to me, my dear?"

Maddie started when the taunting voice wafted toward her. Her left hand inched toward the pistol she had tucked in her waistband.

"I wouldn't do that if I were you," Ward Tipton warned.

The click of a trigger broke the vaporous silence, indicating that Ward had a pistol trained on her back. Maddie thought quickly and decided she *did* dare because her fear of being closeted in this dingy hellhole was greater than her fear of being shot at.

Employing Jonah's technique of dropping and rolling, she dived from the cot and reached simultaneously for her pistol. Ward's bullet whizzed over her head and struck a glass bottle. Wine dribbled onto the rock floor. Maddie aimed at the weasely scoundrel who had sneaked up on her through the narrow tunnel that connected the wine cellar to his ranch house. Unfortunately, Ward ducked around the corner into the tunnel and her shot ricocheted off the stone wall.

Ward's next shot shattered the lantern, plunging the small cavern into darkness. Before Maddie could control her apprehension he was upon her like a pouncing panther. He wrested her pistol from her hand, grabbed her by the hair and jerked her roughly to her feet. His chokehold on her neck only intensified the panicky sensation of being enclosed in these dark, narrow confines that reminded her more of a sepulcher than a cellar.

"Nervous, Maddie?" Ward jeered. "I noticed you were uneasy that time I brought you with me to fetch a wine bottle during one of my dinner parties. I'm surprised you found the gumption to come back here."

"I've developed considerable gumption during the past six months. And I will never forgive you for stashing my sister in this wretched place," she muttered. Then she winced when he crammed the pistol against her jugular vein, making it even more difficult to breathe in this vacuum of darkness.

"You'll forgive me, all right," Ward said confidently as he frog-marched her into the tunnel that led to his house. "If you care about your sister you will cooperate completely."

Maddie tensed as Ward forced her through the dank passageway, which was barely five feet high and two feet wide. Her nerves screamed and her severe case of the jitters had her gasping for breath.

Ward smiled devilishly as he hunched over and propelled her along in front of him. "When we're married you can expect to be punished for your insolence by spending time in the cellar. That should serve to make you a cooperative wife."

"I'm already married."

"Widowed by now," Ward predicted as he hurried her along toward the ladder that led to the trap door in the floor of the pantry. "Your husband and his friend have met with a stroke of bad luck—not uncommon in this wild part of the country, what with all the Indian renegades, outlaws and rustlers running loose around here. In fact, rumor has it that those two half-breeds were connected with the rustling."

Maddie was having trouble maintaining her composure, but Ward's comments practically knocked her to her knees. The thought of Jonah and Boone having their reputations ruined and then perishing because of their association with *her* deflated her spirits in one second flat.

She moved numbly up the ladder as Ward shoved her forward. But defiance and fury returned in full force when she reached solid footing in the pantry and dragged in a fortifying breath of air. Maddie plunged forward in an attempt to escape.

"Bloody hell!" Ward snarled as he snaked out his hand, grabbed her ankle and jerked her off balance.

She landed hard on the planked floor, scraping her chin and snapping her teeth together so quickly that she bit her tongue and tasted blood.

"Behave yourself, you little twit," he snapped as he hoisted her to her feet. The spitting end of his pistol jabbed her between the shoulder blades. "You are trying my patience, woman. It's bad enough that I have to saddle myself with an untitled nobody of an American wife in order to expand my holdings. But you can bet your life that I will do what I must to return to the earl's good graces and collect my rightful inheritance. When that controlling bastard finally keels over, I will claim my title and no longer have any need of you."

Maddie found herself shoved into Ward's elaborately decorated office and pushed into a chair.

"Now then," he said briskly. "Here are the terms of our agreement." He smiled tauntingly as he held her at gunpoint. "I will allow your sister to live, provided you agree to marry me and turn control of your ranch over to me."

"You sniveling bastard. You are not going to hold my sister's safety over my head and I will not be intimidated into marrying you!"

Ward clucked his tongue and shook his blond head in disapproval. "You were much easier to deal with before you allowed your feisty temperament to rule you." One refined brow lifted in aloof challenge.

"Just as Avery made your father disappear, so I can arrange for your sister to conveniently vanish."

"You won't be able to blame Avery for her disappearance this time. Obviously you disposed of Avery when you no longer needed him as your scapegoat."

"That queer bastard tried to outmaneuver me," Wade said, and scowled. "I simply turned his own underhanded tactics on him, and he got what he deserved. I should think you would be grateful that I had him killed for disposing of your father, in his treacherous crusade to marry you so *he* could take control of your valuable property."

Maddie sneered at the arrogant dandy. Having her worst fears about her father confirmed caused angry resentment to coil in her belly. Her anguish and grief over her father's death—and quite possibly Jonah's and Boone's—made her daring and reckless, and she vented her frustration on Ward. "I am *not* appreciative. You are no better than Avery was and I won't marry you under any circumstances. I can't believe innocent people have died just to ensure you are re-elevated to some ridiculous stature in British society." She flashed him a scathing glare. "You are unworthy of any title other than *bastard,* and you are beneath contempt!"

Ward took offense at her disrespectful slur and glowered disdainfully. "If you refuse to cooperate then I will marry a child bride after *you* suffer an untimely accident. It hardly makes any difference to me. Christina will serve my purpose just as well."

He contemplated that prospect for a moment, while

Maddie battled the insane urge to go for his throat, despite the loaded pistol aimed at her chest.

A sinister smile stretched across his lips, making them all but disappear from his face. He didn't look as handsome when the dark side of his personality came pouring out, Maddie noticed.

"As it turns out, I really don't need you, after all," Ward declared. "Christina will welcome my consolation and support after your mangled body is found at the bottom of a canyon. No one will question the fact that your horse lost its footing on the crumbling edge and sent you plunging to your death."

Maddie swallowed the lump of fear that jammed in her throat. For all Ward Tipton's proper British manners and blue-blooded breeding, he definitely had an evil mind and a black soul.

"I doubt Chrissy will be as easily manipulated or eager to accept your pretentious compassion as you seem to think," Maddie snapped. "Turns out that she's fallen in love with someone else and I doubt she'll settle for less, even after she learns of my demise."

A muffled noise in the foyer caught Ward's notice. The instant Maddie realized she wasn't the absolute focus of his attention she launched herself off the chair, lowered her head and plowed into his midsection. Howling in outrage, Ward stumbled over his feet and fell to the floor in an unceremonious heap. While they wrestled for control of the pistol that was clenched in Ward's fist, the roar of a familiar voice distracted Maddie. She made the crucial mistake of glancing toward the doorway.

And found herself clamped in Ward's arms, used

as a shield to protect him from the men who burst into the room.

Maddie was so relieved to know Jonah and Boone were alive that she didn't react immediately when Ward shoved the pistol into her neck again. Her wild-eyed gaze flew to Jonah in silent apology as Ward climbed awkwardly to his feet without releasing his stranglehold on her.

The deadly expression on Jonah's chiseled features indicated that he was mad as hell at her for getting herself into another scrape, and furious with Ward for using her as his defense.

"Drop your guns," Ward demanded as he poked his pistol a little deeper into the underside of Maddie's chin.

"I don't think so," Jonah snarled, his murderous green eyes boring holes into the rancher.

The comment flustered Ward momentarily and he pulled Maddie so tightly against him she found it difficult to breathe. Stalemate, she mused.

"She's your wife, Danhill," Ward mocked in that uppity British accent that was beginning to grate on Maddie's frazzled nerves. "Drop your weapons or she loses her head because of you. Not that I give a bloody damn if her death is on your conscience. If, in fact, mongrel half-breeds like you even *have* a conscience."

"Just shoot him," Maddie demanded of Jonah and Boone. "He's the one who had Avery and Clem murdered. He kidnapped Chrissy and held her captive in that tomb of a wine cellar!"

Jonah frowned, bemused. "I thought Avery kidnapped your sister."

"You've been misinformed. I want this selfish bastard punished for the hell he put Chrissy through. He even tried to intimidate me into marrying him after he'd marked you and Boone for death. He intended to blackmail me into cooperating to spare Chrissy's life!" Maddie stared Jonah squarely in the eye and said, "Just *shoot* him, even if you have to go through me to get to him. He deserves to die!"

"You're insane," Ward snorted, incredulous. His gaze bounced from Jonah to Boone, both of whom kept their six-shooters trained on him and Maddie.

Jonah decided Ward Tipton was right; Maddie had gone a little crazy. There was a wild, reckless gleam in her eyes that scared the bejeezus out of him. He sensed that she was about to do something rash—and he had no idea what in hell it was. His only clear shot was at the arm Ward had wrapped diagonally across Maddie's chest. If Jonah missed his mark by mere inches he could hit Maddie. He stepped sideways, hoping to draw Ward's attention and get a better angle for a shot that would spare her from injury.

Damn it, he'd been in some tough scrapes before, but he'd only had to worry about spilling his own blood. The thought of Maddie injured at his hand was enough to give him the shakes—which was the very last thing he needed right now.

"Just shoot him!" Maddie choked out impatiently.

Jonah nearly suffered heart seizure when she abruptly raised her knee and kicked backward like a mule, catching Ward in the shin. And suddenly all hell broke loose and years of experience and instinct took over. Although Maddie dived sideways to avoid the line of fire, the English dandy was so outraged by her maneuver that he took his fury out on her.

Jonah and Boone fired simultaneously, but Ward managed to get off a shot before he crumpled in a lifeless heap atop Maddie. Jonah thought he screamed her name as he rushed forward to shove Ward aside, but he couldn't swear to it because his pulse was pounding so loudly in his ears that he wondered if he'd been struck deaf.

He sank to his knees, so shaken by the sight of the bloody wound on Maddie's shoulder that he couldn't think straight. He'd forgotten what disabling panic felt like. But he was sure this was it—this helpless sensation that swirled through him, paralyzing his reflexes and robbing him of strength. Feeling as if he was moving in slow motion, he tugged her body into his arms and tilted her ashen face to his with a trembling hand.

"Damn it, woman, are you out of your mind?" he yelled, his fear for her making him lose his tentative grasp on his temper.

A faint smile wobbled on her lips as she stared at him with unfocused amber eyes. "Did you get him?" she croaked.

"Got the son of a bitch," Jonah confirmed, his voice quaking as badly as his body.

"Good." She swallowed with noticeable effort, then said, "I love you...."

When her thick lashes drifted against her pallid cheeks and she slumped heavily against him Jonah hit another level of frenzied panic. He knew how to stem the flow of blood from a wound—or at least he *used* to know. But that was before Maddie intentionally got herself shot. Suddenly his mind went blank and, like a witless imbecile, he just stared at the spreading bloodstains.

After what seemed like minutes of indecisiveness Jonah's survival skills finally kicked in and he tore off his shirt to use as a makeshift tourniquet for her arm. "Find some whiskey to cleanse the wound," he barked at Boone, who was hovering over him. "There has to be some around here somewhere."

Boone darted to the massive oak desk and rummaged through the drawers until he located an unopened bottle of wine that would serve as antiseptic. To Jonah's dismay, Maddie didn't rouse when he dribbled liquor over her shoulder. That was not a good sign.

"Let's see how bad it is," Boone insisted as he hunkered down beside Jonah.

"If she survives I'm gonna kill her for that daring stunt," Jonah growled in frustration.

Boone peeled away the tattered sleeve to inspect the wound. "You're in luck. She'll live. Doesn't look as if the bullet shattered the bone." He glanced at Jonah. "You wanna go ahead and kill her now or shall we patch her up first?"

Jonah scowled darkly. "You are *not* amusing."

"Maybe not, but *you* are." Boone's mouth quirked as he cleansed the wound. "Never saw you fall apart before. Now *that's* amusing."

"I am *not* falling apart!" Jonah bellowed.

"Right. My mistake. What was I thinking?" Boone shoved the wine bottle into Jonah's free hand. "Here. You need a drink. Or three."

Jonah chugged three swallows, but it didn't take

the edge off his shattered nerves. He was rattled, when he never got rattled. He was always cool under fire. Well, usually, he amended. Watching Maddie purposely draw gunfire was not a good example of how well he reacted in lethal situations.

"You need to calm down," Boone advised as he wrapped a strip of Jonah's shirt over her wound. "You're starting to make *me* nervous."

Jonah closed his eyes, inhaled a steadying breath and told himself that Mad Maddie Garret was going to live to see another day. They were going to have matching scars on their upper left arms, but that was better than the alternative.

The thought of a single scar marring her silken flesh tempted Jonah to grab his pistol and shoot Ward Tipton a few more times for good measure. That cocky bastard couldn't end up fried to a crisp in hell fast enough to pacify Jonah.

"Want me to carry her outside while you pull yourself together?" Boone questioned.

"I've got it together."

Boone frowned doubtfully. "If you say so."

Jonah struggled to his feet and resituated Maddie's motionless body in his arms. He couldn't make himself release his possessive hold on her for even a second. Furthermore, he predicted the sight of her ashen face was going to haunt his nightmares for the next several weeks. He never again wanted to live through anything as terrifying as this showdown with Ward Tipton.

The incident had shot his nerves of steel to pieces. It would probably take him longer to recover from this harrowing encounter than it would for Maddie to recuperate from her injury.

"What in tarnation was she thinking?" Jonah muttered as he rode toward Bar G Ranch with Maddie cuddled protectively against him.

"She was thinking of *you*," Boone murmured in the darkness. "My guess is she invited the shot to ensure Tipton didn't turn his weapon on you first." He glanced sideways at Jonah and stared at him for a long moment. "What does it feel like to have a woman love you so much that she would take a bullet for you?"

Jonah didn't have an answer. He couldn't speak. Hell, he could barely even breathe!

Chapter Fourteen

By the time Jonah reached the ranch house he had composed himself—somewhat. He carried Maddie upstairs to her room, then sent Boone to deliver the news to Christina that Maddie had been injured. Although the girl was still unsteady on her feet, she insisted on seeing for herself that her sister was alive and would recover from her wound.

"Do you have laudanum in the house?" Jonah questioned Christina, who was clutching Boone's arm to hold herself upright.

She nodded jerkily without taking her worried gaze off her sister.

"Good. Do you feel up to fetching it for me?"

When Christina reversed direction, still clinging to Boone for support, and exited the room, Jonah gently peeled off Maddie's boots, breeches and shirt and tucked her in bed. He was so aggravated at Maddie for confronting Ward alone and then drawing his gunfire that he wanted to shake the stuffing out of her. Yet, simultaneously, he wanted to clutch her possessively to him and hold on to her until all these wild emotions that were whirling through him finally settled back in place.

Jonah half collapsed on the edge of the bed and heaved a frustrated sigh. No one had ever gone to such dangerous extremes to protect him from harm and he didn't know how to deal with it. But then, he didn't know how to deal with half the emotions Maddie triggered inside him.

This daring female always kept him off balance and distracted. He never really found solid footing when she was around. Forbidden desire and sensible logic constantly warred inside him, and Jonah had bedded down, battle-weary, every night since Maddie had barged into his life and turned it upside down.

He glanced up when Boone and Christina arrived with the sedative and a pitcher of water. "I'll sit up with her tonight," he volunteered as he gave her a double dose of laudanum to ensure she slept through the worst of the pain. "Go back to bed, Christina. You need to rest, and I will make certain your sister gets any medical attention she might need."

When Christina simply stood there, staring down into Maddie's peaked face, Jonah glanced at Boone, silently requesting that he attend to her.

"Maddie is in capable hands," Boone soothed as he gently turned Christina around and shepherded her toward the door. "You can check on her first thing in the morning."

Christina glanced up at Boone with such trust and affection that Jonah rolled his eyes in exasperation. The girl was growing entirely too dependent on his friend.

In addition, Maddie had convinced herself that she was in love with him, Jonah mused as he cupped his hand behind her neck to force her to take a drink of water. What was the matter with the Garret sisters? Couldn't they understand that he and Boone were only temporary intrusions in their lives? Jonah and Boone had been trained as warriors—guns for hire, more or less. They never stayed in the same place for very long and they weren't supposed to become emotionally attached before they moved on.

Jonah pulled up a chair and plunked down in it. He expelled a loud sigh, then scrubbed his hands over his face. He had to focus on wrapping up this case, then get out of Maddie's life before he lost the will to leave at all. Despite what she thought, he was the last thing she needed, and Forbidden Canyon was still the last place he wanted to be.

When Maddie grimaced, then moaned groggily, Jonah's thoughts scattered like buckshot. Watching her suffer was killing him, bit by excruciating bit. He kept reliving that unnerving shoot-out in Ward's office and it kept giving him cold chills.

"Damn it, princess," he muttered at her. "*I* should be the one lying there, not *you.*"

What does it feel like to have a woman love you so much that she would take a bullet for you? Boone's words came back to him in a frustrated rush.

It felt like hellish torture, pure and simple, Jonah mused. Maddie had been willing to make the supreme sacrifice for a man who was unworthy and didn't deserve her. *He* could see that as clear as day. Why couldn't *she?*

* * *

Maddie awoke to find that she and her sister had reversed roles. Christina looked the picture of health while she perched on the edge of Maddie's bed. Maddie felt as if she had been trampled in a stampede. Her body was stiff and achy, and her left arm refused to move without every muscle pitching a fit.

"Thank goodness you're finally awake," Christina said in relief. "I've been worried about you, and Rosita has been beside herself for days on end."

"Rosita always overreacts," Maddie said in a voice that she barely recognized as her own. It sounded as if her vocal cords had rusted from lack of use.

Christina dimpled and grinned. "Yes, she does. And she still refers to me as the bambino, even though I'm rapidly approaching my sixteenth birthday."

Maddie wondered why Christina thought it was imperative to mention her age, and decided it probably had something to do with her obvious infatuation for an older man.

"Things are pretty much back to normal around here. I only wish Papa..."

When Chrissy's voice trailed off, Maddie reached out to grab her hand. "I know," she murmured softly. "But I think Papa would be proud of us for standing up to adversity the way he always did."

"Yes, he would." Chrissy muffled a sniff and tilted her chin to a determined angle.

Maddie smiled, realizing that mannerism was definitely a Garret family trait.

After a moment Maddie glanced sideways to note

that morning sunlight was pouring through the windows. "How long have I been stuck in bed?"

"Four days," Chrissy reported.

"Four?" Maddie gasped, astonished.

Chrissy nodded her silver-blond head. "You have Jonah to thank for that. He wanted to ensure that you slept through the worst of the fever and pain. I tried to convince him, having been overdosed with laudanum myself recently, that you wouldn't want to be drowsy constantly. But Jonah insisted that was the only way to keep you in one place long enough to recuperate. And if you vaguely remember being roused hourly during the night to sip water and take nourishment, that was his doing. He's been fussing over you as much as Rosita has."

Maddie vaguely recalled Jonah's voice in the darkness, but she presumed she had been plagued with whimsical dreams of his gentle touch and the light whisper of kisses against her cheek.

Christina smiled impishly. "Your pretend husband has taken over around here. I've been calling him General Danhill. He's been spouting orders left and right to ensure you are well cared for, and he and Boone have been cleaning up this area of Texas in typical Ranger fashion."

Maddie frowned, bemused. "Cleaning up?"

"They have been sorting the good guys from the bad guys, and Jonah has interrogated every hired hand at both the Hanson and Tipton ranch," she explained. "He and Boone were confused about exactly who had ordered my abduction, and they were determined to sort it all out and get the story straight."

"I told them it was Ward," Maddie insisted.

"Apparently they had been given conflicting information by one of the men who followed you back from Fort Worth. It seems Ward was very careful not to let the right hand know what the left hand was doing. Or in this case, his right-hand men and the left ones. One band of henchmen kidnapped me and two of his hired guns followed you to and from Fort Worth. Ward planted informants here and at Avery's Ranch, and he received constant updates about the goings-on."

Maddie sighed heavily. "All because Ward refused to let Avery get the better of him and because he was obsessed with impressing his father so he could become the next earl of Longwood."

"*Lang*wood," Chrissy corrected. "Boone and I rummaged through Ward's desk, and we found several letters from his uppity father. Ward was exiled to Texas and his father insisted Ward had to redeem himself by becoming an honorable gentleman and a capable financial manager, if he hoped to save face after some sort of scandal that involved his best friend's wife."

"That two-faced, back-stabbing scoundrel," Maddie muttered.

"You can say that again. Boone and I also found two bottles of laudanum in Ward's desk, along with the tin cup I remember having shoved against my lips when I was constantly sedated."

"I'm almost sorry that man is dead because I don't think I'll feel vindicated unless I can shoot him myself!" Maddie grumbled as she tried to lever herself up in bed.

Chrissy's hand shot out to hold her in place. "You

are not getting up. I have been given specific orders to ensure that you stay put. For some reason your pretend husband is very touchy and adamant about you staying exactly where he left you.''

Maddie shifted uncomfortably. ''Perhaps I was better off being sedated. That way Jonah couldn't jump down my throat for daring to break the stalemate that night in Ward's office.'' She stared somberly at her sister, trying to make Chrissy understand why she'd done what she had. ''I refused to see Jonah or Boone hurt on my behalf. They have suffered more than you know because of me. Better a wound in my shoulder than a hole through Jonah's heart. And I will argue that point with him to my dying day.''

''And what point would that be, princess?''

Maddie glanced over Chrissy's shiny blond head to see Jonah looming in the doorway, looking grim-faced, tough and so ruggedly handsome that her pounding heart did a back somersault in her chest and slammed into her ribs.

Chrissy popped up like a jack-in-the-box. ''I think I'll see if Boone would like a refreshing drink.'' She grinned playfully at Jonah on her way out the door. ''Don't yell at my sister, *General*. She hasn't fully recovered yet.''

Jonah ignored the teasing request and never took his eyes off Maddie as Chrissy brushed past him. He had spent the last four days racing from one place to the next, ensuring that all those who were responsible for causing an upheaval in Maddie and Chrissy's lives were behind bars.

All except for that elusive Jesse Gibbs, who must have lit out for parts unknown. But Jonah was making it his personal crusade to hunt the man down and see him punished for the torment he had inflicted on Maddie.

Jonah had encountered some wily mastermind criminals in his time, but Ward Tipton headed up the list. The man had been exceptionally shrewd, intelligent, manipulative and conniving. He never told his henchmen the same story—hence Beau Newton's misinformation.

To this day Beau maintained that Ward had sworn to him Avery was responsible for the kidnapping. According to Beau, neither he nor Jesse Gibbs had been allowed any association with the men who had perished the night of the hostage exchange. Ward always rendezvoused with Jesse and Beau in a remote canyon, out of sight from the ranch house.

Ward Tipton had taken his cues from Avery Hanson, in attempting to gain control of Maddie's ranch. But Ward had made Avery look like a second-rate crook in comparison.

Tossing aside his wandering thoughts, Jonah approached the bed. "Are you feeling better?"

Maddie eyed him warily as he towered over her. "That depends."

He frowned at her. "That depends on what?"

"On whether you're going to flay a few strips off my hide with your tongue if I feel up to it."

She tilted her chin in typical Maddie fashion that was both adorable and exasperating. Jonah said, "You look well enough to hear the scathing lecture you deserve after that death-defying stunt." He leaned down, bracing his hands on the edge of the bed, got right in her face and shouted, "Do. Not. Ever. Do. That. Again! Damn it!"

"Then do not ever try to draw gunfire to spare me," she yelled back, then winced when she unintentionally jarred her left arm. "I saw you move sideways while Ward was holding me hostage. You practically dared him to turn his pistol on you, and I refused to stand for it!"

"Look, princess, I—"

She cut him off at the pass. "No, *you* look, Jonah Danhill. *I love you.* Can't you get that through your thick head?"

"It isn't love," he insisted. "It's gratitude."

Maddie glowered at him. "You might tell me what to do occasionally and I might *allow* you to get away with it, but do *not* presume to tell me how I feel. I know what is in my heart. And it doesn't matter how you feel about me because what is most important to me is that you are safe and in one piece."

"Maddie—"

She hurried on before he could interrupt again. "I have decided to deed the land at the north end of this canyon to you because your family and clan bought and paid for it with their lives. It is your heritage and I'm giving you the responsibility of ensuring that the valuable water source that nourishes this valley is protected. It will be a place you can always call your own."

"You don't have to—" he tried to protest, for all the good it did him.

"I *do* have to," she insisted loudly. "And besides, I owe you my life several times over!" Maddie decided that being shot had made her short-tempered and cranky, because her tone of voice was getting sharper by the second. But she didn't care. She was going to speak her piece and that was that.

"I can endure almost anything if I know you're out there somewhere in the world," she told him honestly. "But I *couldn't* bear the thought of standing there in Ward's office, watching you take a bullet for *me*."

"And how do you think *I* felt?" Jonah demanded harshly. "You drove me half-crazy when you lurched away from Ward and he turned that pistol on you! I've spent every damn night sleeping in that chair beside your bed, changing the bandages on your wound and wishing it had been *me* who'd been shot, not *you!*"

"You already took a shot in the left arm," she retorted. "I didn't think you needed another one!"

"Children, children." Boone heaved a theatrical sigh as he invited himself into the room. "We can hear you yelling at each other from downstairs. Christina asked me to come up here and tell you to pipe down and be nice to each other."

Jonah pushed himself upright and smirked at Boone. "And of course you rushed off to do Princess Christina's bidding."

Maddie bit back a grin when Boone blushed. The poor man had it as bad as Christina. At least the feelings were mutual, unlike her own one-sided affection for Jonah.

"I came up here to tell Maddie that the criminal elements have been weeded from Avery and Ward's ranches." He shot Jonah a sardonic glance. "I wasn't sure you would get around to it," he said, then turned his attention back to Maddie. "The sheriff appointed a replacement at Ward's ranch, until the British investors decide who will take over the operation. Avery's ranch will be put up for sale, and your stolen livestock has been returned. You will be fully compensated for the cattle Avery sold as profit. In short, this ranch operation is back on track.''

Maddie sighed in relief. ''That eases my mind considerably. Thank you, Boone. I intend to pay you and Jonah for your assistance. I can't begin to express how much I appreciate what you've done for Chrissy and me.''

''No pay necessary,'' Boone insisted.

''Do not argue with me,'' Maddie said tersely. ''I'm cranky.''

''I'll say she is,'' Jonah muttered, eyeing her accusingly.

Maddie leveled him a silencing glare.

''Angel asked me to escort her into Mobeetie to gather supplies—''

''*Angel?*'' Jonah stared at Boone in blatant disapproval. ''You've given Christina a pet name? You've been here four days too long and you are *not* taking her to Mobeetie without a chaperon.''

Boone jerked up his head, squared his broad shoulders and tapped himself on the chest. ''*I'm* the bodyguard and chaperon.''

''Like hell you are.'' Jonah scowled.

''Leave him alone, Jonah. My sister likes him.''

''That's what worries me,'' Jonah grumbled as he shot Boone another meaningful glance.

''I'm certain I can count on Boone to ensure my sister's welfare and safety.''

''No, you can't,'' Jonah contradicted.

Exasperated, Maddie glanced at Jonah. "Oh, for heaven's sake, Boone is hardly what I call lecherous and unscrupulous."

The Kiowa beamed. "Thank you for your vote of confidence."

"Maddie is still delirious from fever and pain and doesn't know what she's saying." Jonah wagged his forefinger at Boone. "As for Christina, she's been through enough lately. Don't make matters worse...and you *know* what I mean."

Maddie wasn't certain what Jonah implied, but apparently Boone was, because both men exchanged significant glares for a long, tense moment. Finally Boone spun on his boot heels, and stalked out.

"He's too old for her," Jonah muttered.

"Perhaps," Maddie agreed. "But Chrissy is infatuated for the first time in her life."

"And nothing good can come of it."

Maddie glanced up to see his penetrating green eyes boring into her. She had the feeling he was no longer discussing Boone and Christina, but rather her affection for him.

"It's not as if I have made demands on you after what happened between us," she said quietly as she shifted her left arm to a more comfortable position on the pillow. "As soon as I pay you for your time and trouble you are free to leave. You can accompany Boone and Chrissy into town if you wish, especially since you insist they need a chaperon."

"Maybe I *will* go with them. If your sister is as forward as you are, I don't want to lay odds that Boone can resist her. Then where will they be?"

Maddie glowered at him, affronted. "If I had the

strength to climb from this bed, I'd slap you silly for that insulting remark.''

Jonah glared back at her, hoping to further incite her anger, making it easier for them to part company once and for all. Jonah felt the need to burn his bridges behind him so Maddie would realize they could have no future contact. It was easier this way, he told himself. Parting on a sour note would sever these ill-fated ties between them.

''Did you or did you not seduce me twice?'' he demanded.

Maddie averted her gaze. ''Yes. You are completely irresistible and I'm shameless. Is that what you want to hear? Well fine, I've said it and you have made it abundantly clear on several occasions that I'm not what you want or need.''

''I did not say that you aren't what I want,'' he replied, frustrated torment making his voice harsh. ''This is for your own good, damn it!''

Maddie flashed him a withering glance. ''God save me from men dedicated to protecting me from myself!''

Jonah raked his hands through his thick hair and expelled a breath. ''Look, princess—''

''I have one last request before you leave,'' she interrupted. ''Do *not* call me princess ever again.'' She flicked her wrist, dismissing him. ''Go away, Jonah. You are giving me a raging headache and my arm is killing me.''

''Fine. This is my last goodbye,'' he told her stiffly, refusing to buckle to the emotion that was eating him alive. ''I promised to get out of your life and I'm going. Now. This is the end of the line.''

"That's what you said when we reached Fort Griffin," she didn't fail to remind him. "You said the same thing in Mobeetie. You said it again—twice—at this ranch." She stared him down. "So why are you still here?"

He opened his mouth to tell her that he was still here because he was having one hell of a time letting her go. Fortunately, he caught himself in the nick of time and shut his yap—fast.

Jonah spun on his heel and strode toward the door without looking back. He didn't have to glance back at Maddie because her image had been emblazoned on his mind and he suspected it would stay there until the end of eternity. He would keep his promise to get out of her life, but, sure as shootin', he was never going to be able to *forget* her.

He suspected it would take dying to get that done.

Later that afternoon, while Christina was in the boutique at Mobeetie, making her purchases, Boone and Jonah treated themselves to a whiskey at the saloon.

"I was wrong, you know," Boone said out of the blue.

Jonah glanced at him over the rim of his glass. "You're wrong a lot. You'll have to be more specific."

Boone ignored the taunt. "I was wrong about you and Maddie."

Jonah set down his glass very deliberately and said, "Don't start. I don't want to have this conversation."

Boone ignored that, too. "That's too bad, because we're having this conversation anyway." He leaned back in his chair and stared pensively at him. "Think about it, Danhill. Although you balked at getting involved with Maddie's problems from the onset, something made you serve as her guide and protector so she could reach Fort Griffin."

"That something was two men with loaded guns," Jonah rapped out. "Can we talk about something else?"

"No." Boone smiled wryly. "Was that the *reason* or the *excuse?*"

Jonah shifted awkwardly in his chair. "Doesn't matter. The outcome was the same. I took Maddie where she needed to go and I protected her from getting shot and robbed."

"Even when you swore never to set foot in the Comanchería again?" Boone waved his arms expansively. "But here you are, as deep in the heart of Comanche country as you can get." He stared pointedly at Jonah. "As deep in the *heart* as you can get. You tried not to get involved, but you couldn't help it. Not with *her.* You were involved and you kept getting in deeper and deeper with every mile you rode west." He smiled wryly. "Rather symbolic, don't you think, Danhill?"

"Is there a point to this philosophical prattle?" Jonah asked irritably. "If there is, then get to the point. I'm not growing any younger."

"You're not getting any wiser, either. Obviously." Boone leaned his forearms on the table and stared Jonah squarely in the eye. "You're in love with her and you know it. A man doesn't keep contradicting himself, drawing lines and then crossing over them if he isn't in so deep that he can't find his way out. And

Maddie loves you like crazy. She proved it that night in Ward's office. Declarations of love don't get any louder or clearer than that, Danhill.''

Jonah took another drink, then stared into the amber contents of his glass, wincing when the color of the whiskey reminded him of Maddie's eyes. Reminded him that the whiskey was nearly as intoxicating and addictive as her kisses.

This was not a good time to be remembering that. He had resolved to be sensible and do the right thing by letting go.

''Well, at least admit it to me, even if you won't admit it to her,'' Boone prodded. ''You might as well admit it to yourself while you're at it, because denial sure as hell isn't working for you.''

Jonah clamped his jaw shut and glared at his pesky Kiowa cousin, Chief Know-It-All.

''Damn, Danhill, you're a stubborn cuss. And you call Maddie stubborn and defiant?'' Boone scoffed. ''I'm losing all respect for you. This just proves that Kiowas are smarter than Comanches.''

''All I want to do is enjoy my drink. Go harass someone else.''

''You need to hear this. No one understands you better than I do and no one understands me better than you do. I know that blue-eyed angel is too young for me and that she's suffering her first bout of puppy love. I also know she can do better than me and I have to back off and give her a chance. The timing is wrong for me, but it's different with *you*.''

Jonah shook his head obstinately. ''Nothing's changed. I'm still who I am and she's practically royalty in this part of Texas. Hell, she practically *owns* this part of Texas.''

"So did our people, before the white invasion. We've faced our loss and our bittersweet memories. I like to think I'm a better man for confronting those painful memories and getting past them, once and for all. Maddie made that happen and I'll always be grateful to her for that.'' He was silent for a moment, then said, "Princess or not, Maddie loves you, Danhill. That changes all the rules. She sees our kind as equals and even became our champion when prejudiced men insulted us in her presence. As for me, I've discovered there are only a select few whose opinions matter a whit to me, and her opinion matters.''

"Fine, her opinion matters to me, too.''

"So what this all boils down to is that you make her happy. And she makes you happy, even when the two of you are in the middle of one of your heated debates or power struggles. You like the fact that she has spunk and stands up to you and meets you on her own terms.''

Yeah, he did. He'd never felt more alive and exhilarated than when he was matching wits with Maddie—or making love with her. She triggered all of his emotions.

Boone glanced at the clock over the bar, then came to his feet. "Well, I guess I'll meet you in Coyote Springs after I ensure Tina returns home safely.''

"Now it's *Tina?* You have definitely been here too long, Boone.''

A rueful smile pursed Boone's lips. "Coming here is the best thing that's ever happened to me, though. I found myself while I was here.''

"Interesting. I didn't even know you were lost."

Boone chuckled and shook his head. "Maddie's smart mouth definitely rubbed off on you. Now I'd say you are her equal, her match. And vice versa."

Her equal, her match. The words rang in Jonah's ears long after Boone exited the saloon.

If only that were true.

When a red-haired calico queen parked herself in Boone's vacated chair and suggested Jonah buy her a drink, he handed over the bottle of whiskey. He ignored the come-hither glance she directed at him, then surged to his feet. The very thought of touching another woman when he had Maddie on his mind felt like betrayal.

Jonah ambled onto the street to watch Boone and Christina climb into the wagon, which was heaped with supplies, and head west. They were all smiles and quiet laughter as they rode out of sight.

Lost in conflicting emotions that pulled him in two directions at once, Jonah strode off to fetch his horse, and headed east before he could change his mind.

Chapter Fifteen

Maddie felt well enough to make several trips up and down the hall the following day. The day after that, she tackled the staircase to build up her stamina. Although Rosita fussed over her unnecessarily, Maddie was determined to regain her strength. Lying abed, wallowing in misery and self-pity, was not aiding in her recovery.

Activity and distraction was what she needed to revive her spirits. She felt the impulsive urge to revisit the cavern behind the falls. It was there that she had discovered a sense of connection to Jonah and his past. And right now she needed to feel his comforting presence, because watching Chrissy practically float on air while Boone was underfoot was depressing. The twosome had become inseparable, making the most of every moment before Boone's impending departure.

How the blazes was Maddie going to keep Chrissy's spirits up after Boone left when *her* spirits were scraping rock bottom?

Wobbling slightly, she braced her hand against the

marble-top dresser while she pulled on her riding breeches.

"What do you think you're doing?"

Maddie glanced sideways to see her sister standing in the doorway, hands on her hips. "Getting dressed, as you can plainly see."

"For what purpose?" Chrissy demanded. "You are not leaving this house."

"I'm your older sister," Maddie reminded her as she shoved one foot, then the other, into her boots. "Don't boss me around. I plan to go riding because these walls are closing in on me." When Chrissy opened her mouth to protest, Maddie flung up her hand. "If Jonah could ride cross-country, outrunning outlaws with an injured arm, I can certainly ride around the pasture. I need fresh air."

"Then open the blasted window," she suggested flippantly.

"Maddie, listen to your sister," Boone chimed in as he appeared in the doorway. "She's right. Besides, it's almost dark. At least postpone your ride until morning."

Just what she needed. Two mother hens. Three, if you counted Rosita, who brought food and drink every hour on the hour to ensure Maddie had plenty of nourishment and attention.

"The two of you are in charge," Maddie announced, then walked over to the safe to count out financial compensation for Boone's extended stay and invaluable assistance. "Here," she said, thrusting the roll of money at him. "Take this. And I want you to remember that no matter where you go, no matter how long you're gone or what you do, you will always be welcomed and wanted here. *Uncondition-ally.*'' She stared meaningfully at him. ''This land was once your home, Boone. It will always be your home. I want you to feel that this ranch is the one place you can always come back to.''

Boone smiled as he tucked the money in his shirt pocket. ''You are one hell of a woman, even if you are a paleface, Maddie Garret.''

''Thank you, it's nice to be appreciated.'' She walked gingerly toward the door. ''I will inform Carlos that anything you need for your journey tomorrow will be provided.''

Maddie eased down the steps, then halted on the front porch to inhale a long-awaited breath of fresh air and admire the panoramic sunset. This had always been her favorite time of the day, when the restless wind usually died down and the world seemed to be at peace with itself.

Shortly afterward she was riding north into the canyon. Magnetically drawn toward the cave hidden behind the falls, Maddie nudged her mount forward, then dismounted by the sparkling pool. Livestock that had come to drink shied away as she approached, then wandered off to graze on the plush grass that filled the scenic valley.

The sound of pebbles trickling from the rocky cliffs overhead drew her attention, and she pivoted toward the sound, her foolish heart filling with the hope that Jonah had changed his mind and returned. The blinding sunlight made it impossible to identify the dark silhouette—until the man bounded from the ledge and crouched in the shadows.

Her enthusiastic smile transformed into a gasp of

alarm when she recognized Jesse Gibbs as the man
who was sidestepping down the steep slope. Maddie
cursed herself soundly for neglecting to arm herself
before she rode away from the house. With Jesse hot
on her heels, she made a mad dash for her horse.

She shrieked in pain when he slammed into her,
sending her stumbling off balance. She proved to be
no match for his strength as he hauled her up against
him. Every attempt to squirm free sent agony shooting down her mending arm, but that didn't stop her
from trying to escape him.

"Hold still," Jesse snarled against her neck.
"You're going to help me get out of here before that
Texas devil you married catches up with me."

Damnation, not again! Maddie mused, exasperated.
Just when she thought her troubles were over, here
they came, sneaking up on her. Wasn't it enough that
the past few months had been one tormenting stumbling block after another? No wonder Jonah had become so cynical and mistrusting. Every time you
turned around some worthless bastard was making
your life miserable. And hadn't Jonah told her to always pay attention to her surroundings for fear of
encountering an unpleasant surprise? She should have
listened to him.

To Maddie's dismay, Jesse bound her arms behind
her back, causing excessive strain on her left shoulder. Only now did she fully appreciate the discomfort
Jonah had endured while he recovered from his own
injury. Physical exertion played havoc with her temperament. Jonah's, too, she realized in retrospect.

Maddie wasn't sure what this scraggly ruffian intended until he pulled a folded paper from his pocket

and half dragged her toward her horse. She watched Jesse tuck the note between the saddle and the blanket, then slap her horse on the rump. The strawberry roan thundered toward home, scattering the grazing cattle as it went.

"If you're lucky, your sister will follow my instructions and exchange money for your life," Jesse said as he watched the horse gallop toward the distant barn. He glanced down at Maddie. "If that husband of yours shows up here then all bets are off."

"Jonah left for Coyote Springs two days ago," Maddie informed him.

"Good. Suits me just fine if I've seen the last of him." He propelled her up the steep incline, then down into the narrow ravine where he had tethered his horse.

Confound it all, Maddie muttered to herself as Jesse tied her feet with a rope, then anchored her to a scraggly juniper. She'd thought the only hurdle she had left to encounter was teaching herself to live without Jonah. Apparently not.

A sudden passing shadow prompted Maddie to look skyward. Wouldn't you know that if birds were circling above her they were bound to be buzzards? She sighed in frustration and shifted uncomfortably while Jesse paced.

"Someone's coming," Jesse announced as he watched the two riders approach. He glanced suspiciously at Maddie. "I thought you said your husband left."

"He did," she confirmed. "But Boone is still here.

Did you really expect him to allow my sister to ride out here alone?''

Jesse scowled sourly at the news. "Damn breeds. Can't trust any of 'em to react like a white man. If he tries something sneaky you are sure as hell gonna suffer for it."

Maddie grimaced when Jesse jerked her roughly to her feet and propelled her along the spine of rock to watch Boone and Christina approach the spring.

"Leave the money," Jesse called down to them as he held Maddie on the crumbling edge of the cliff. "Don't try to play the hero, Boone, or the little lady is going to take a nasty fall."

Maddie watched as Boone made a spectacular display of holding up the saddlebag and waving the money above his head. Then he crammed the cash back in the pouch. "I'm not leaving without Maddie," he said in no uncertain terms.

Maddie listened to Jesse snarl and growl in irritation. She had the feeling that, despite what Jesse had said, he'd planned to drag her along with him for insurance until he was well out of Texas—and far from the long arm of justice.

"No Maddie, no money," Boone called out. "That's the deal. Take it or leave it."

Maddie smiled ruefully. Boone reminded her of Jonah. Tough, fearless, uncompromising.

Her thoughts scattered when her captor grabbed her arm and shoved her forward. "You listen to me, breed," Jesse jeered. "I'm in charge of making this deal! Leave the money and go!"

When Jesse jerked her sideways, her left foot dropped off the ledge. Her stomach pitched forward and plunged fifty feet—straight to the bottom of the canyon. It was all Maddie could do to bite back the scream of terror that rushed to her lips. But she refused to give Jesse the satisfaction of intimidating her and twisting her perilous situation to an advantage against Boone. If things ended badly, Maddie vowed to be an example of courage for her sister, who would have to carry on alone.

"Don't hurt her!" Christina shrieked frantically.

"If you knock her off that ledge you sure as hell won't get the money!" Boone bellowed at Jesse.

Maddie reared back and braced both feet on the ledge. She was not going to be used as a pawn again. Ward Tipton had tried this tactic and it wasn't going to work any better for Jesse than it had for him.

She stared down at Boone. "Does this look like another stalemate to you?"

"Oh, hell!" Boone scowled when he realized Maddie was giving subtle notice that she was about to act. "Just wait!"

"Jesse, you son of a bitch, I told you to keep your hands off my wife! You don't listen worth a damn."

Maddie started at the booming voice that exploded from above her like rumbling thunder. The last time Jonah had showed up unexpectedly she had suffered a moment of paralyzed surprise. This time she reacted immediately. She dropped to her knees, pulling Jesse partially off balance.

Swearing, Jesse let go of Maddie and wheeled toward Jonah. "You can go straight to hell and take that other half-breed with you!"

Maddie flattened herself on the ledge and looked up to see Jonah looming on the bluff like the dark angel of vengeance. She wanted to strangle him for drawing Jesse's attention and standing there like an unmoving target, daring the outlaw to take his best shot.

Jesse raised his pistol to take deadly aim, but Maddie swung her legs upward, catching Jesse in the back of the knees. His legs buckled, causing his shot to go astray.

When Jessie tried to get off another shot, Maddie watched in awed amazement as Jonah's pistol cleared leather in a blur of speed. Jonah's well-aimed bullet plugged Jesse's gun hand. He yelped in pain and clutched his injured wrist against his ribs.

Like a pouncing cougar, Jonah bounded from boulder to boulder, then hopped onto the ledge. Holding Jesse at gunpoint, he squatted down to retrieve the fallen pistol, then untied Maddie's hands.

"Let this be a lesson for you, princess. The loose end you don't tie up always comes back to haunt you," Jonah said as he glanced pointedly at her. "And I'm not just talking about Jesse Gibbs."

Although she was pleased to know she had been on his mind, she still flashed him a reproachful glance. "You could have gotten yourself shot."

He smiled dryly as he bound Jesse's hands behind his back. "Not much fun watching someone put his life on the line for you, is it?"

"No, it isn't. And don't you ever do it again," she muttered darkly.

"Now you know how I felt that night in Ward's office. And you nearly gave me a heart attack a few minutes ago when you tried to break the stalemate while I was trying to move into position to take out Jesse.''

"You said you were leaving for good. So why did you come back?'' she asked as Jonah hoisted her to her feet.

"Is everything okay up there?'' Boone called out. "Damn, that was close. I was afraid Maddie was going to do something drastic before you could get in position.''

Jonah eased closer to the edge of the bluff to see Boone and Christina staring up at him. "We're fine. We're bringing Jesse down.''

"You didn't answer my question,'' Maddie prompted, as Jonah grabbed the outlaw by the collar of his shirt, then marched him down the winding path. She thought she knew, but she desperately wanted to hear him say it. "Why *did* you come back?''

"Because I knew you couldn't stay out of trouble for more than two days.'' Jonah tossed the words over his shoulder.

She wrinkled her nose at him. "You are such a charmer, Danhill. Makes me wonder why I love you so much.''

Jonah chuckled. "Makes me wonder, too, princess. I still haven't figured it out.''

Well, at least he had stopped trying to deny *her* feelings for *him,* she mused. That was progress.

When they reached the canyon floor, Christina dashed forward to hug Maddie. "Thank God you're all right!''

"I'll take Jesse to Mobeetie,'' Boone volunteered. "There's a jail cell there with his name on it.''

Maddie glanced up in time to see the look that

passed between Boone and Jonah. Her niggling suspicion was confirmed when Boone turned his attention to Christina. "Take care of yourself, angel. Do me a favor and don't follow in your sister's footsteps. She's too much of a daredevil. Just steer clear of trouble. *Please.*"

"Boone?" The question in Christina's eyes was so poignant that Maddie felt a sentimental lump clog her throat. "You *are* coming back, aren't you?"

Maddie's eyes clouded over when Boone leaned down to press a chaste kiss to Christina's forehead. He was telling her goodbye without voicing the words.

When Boone strode off to put Jesse on a horse, Christina tried to go after him, but Jonah grabbed her arm and held her in place. "You have to let him go," he murmured.

Her eyes flooded with tears. An anguished expression settled on her young face as she stared up at Jonah. "I can't let him go. I *love* him."

A tender smile pursed Jonah's lips as he brushed his thumb over her cheek to wipe away her tears. "I know you do, kid. And that's why you have to let him go."

"I'm not a kid!" Christina railed in frustration as she watched Boone ride off into the night. "Do not treat me like a child!"

"Then don't act like one," Jonah said sharply.

Maddie smiled in amusement when Jonah's comment snapped Christina out of the beginning of a childish tantrum. "Jonah, would you mind fetching the spare horse that Jesse left in the ravine to the east? Christina and I need a moment alone."

When Jonah strode off, Christina rounded on Maddie. "If you are going to tell me that I made a fool of myself because I fell in love with Boone, save your breath. You feel the same way about Jonah, so you have no room to talk."

Maddie didn't deny it. Instead she said, "The difference is that I'm nearly twenty-one and you aren't quite sixteen."

"We know several girls my age who are married," Christina reminded her.

"Yes, we do, but you aren't going to be one of them and Boone didn't ask you to be." Maddie stared directly at her sister. "Why do *you* think Boone feels that he needs to leave here?"

Christina's shoulders slumped dejectedly. "Because he thinks I'm too young for him."

"No, he *knows* you're too young for him," Maddie corrected as she curled a comforting arm around her sister's waist, then ambled toward the lone horse that stood beside the spring. "Boone is a good and honorable man. Is it so hard to understand that he might just be waiting for you to grow up?"

When Christina glanced up hopefully, Maddie smiled. "I know it's hard to be patient, Chrissy. But there truly is a time and a season for things to come."

Christina nodded reluctantly. "So you really think Boone will come back someday?"

"He'll be back," Jonah confirmed as he led the spare mount down the path. "I know for a fact that Garret women are impossible to forget. Believe me, I tried." He smiled wryly at Maddie as he approached. "Used to think I was a man of my *word,* until someone around here had me contradicting myself left and right. I was five miles east of town when I realized I couldn't leave you behind because I've become a man of my *heart*."

Maddie beamed at him. He hadn't said the exact words she wanted to hear, but it gave her hope.

"I had some arrangements to make before I came back to the ranch to see you." He stared disapprovingly at Maddie. "Should have known you wouldn't have the good sense to stay in bed instead of riding off, daring trouble to catch up with you."

Christina managed a faint smile. "He chewed Boone and me up one side and down the other when he discovered that we'd let you go riding alone." She stared accusingly at Maddie. "As if we had any choice. Then Jonah burned my ears off with curses, the likes I've never heard before, when that ransom note arrived."

Maddie tossed Jonah a frown of feigned annoyance. "If you can't be a positive influence on my sister then I will have to ask you to leave."

"You can ask," Jonah said as he scooped Maddie up and gently set her atop her horse, "but I'm not going away again. In fact, Boone and I formed a partnership to purchase the Hanson Ranch so we can raise and train horses. Boone will be a silent partner for a time, but all the same, half the ranch is his."

Maddie sat there in stunned amazement as Jonah swung up behind her in the saddle. She nearly melted into a puddle of hungry need when he slid his arm around her waist to pull her back against him, and pressed his sensuous lips against the side of her neck.

"In case you haven't figured it out yet, princess, I'm here to stay this time. *This* is the end of the line for me."

Maddie's heart swelled with so much pleasure that she swore it was about to burst. "You aren't just saying that to make me feel better because I almost got myself killed again, are you?"

"No," he murmured. "You know me better than that. I don't say anything just to be nice or accommodating."

"You broke my heart when you rode away. I'm not sure how long it will take me to forgive you for that," Maddie said as Jonah walked the horse toward the house.

"I'll always be right here when you need me," Jonah promised as he cuddled her possessively against him. "I intend to prove exactly how much you mean to me when we get home."

Home. The word hadn't held any meaning for Jonah in years. But now, wherever Maddie was felt like home to him, even this canyon that had once held bitter memories. It was his past, yet it was his future—filled with hope and a promise of better days to come. He thought perhaps his Comanche clan might approve of the fact that he had returned to claim this land that had been his by right of birth.

And the woman who held his heart.

Jonah's pensive thoughts trailed off as he dismounted, then eased Maddie from the horse. He glanced sideways at Christina, who had a lost look on her face. Jonah had worn that same expression the past two days. He knew it was going to take a while before Christina accepted the inevitability of the time and distance Boone felt compelled to put between them.

Jonah felt a fond smile curve his lips when Christina slipped her hand in his, then pushed up on tiptoe to press a sisterly kiss to his cheek.

"I'm glad you're here to stay," she whispered. "I've always wanted a big brother." She smiled a little too knowingly as she glanced back and forth between him and Maddie. "I'll see you both in the morning."

Jonah frowned as he watched Christina climb the steps and disappear into the dark foyer. "Are you sure that kid is only fifteen?"

"Fifteen wishing she were twenty." Maddie stepped onto the porch, then pivoted to smile invitingly at him. "Come to bed, Jonah. It's been a long, tiring day."

Jonah grinned as he followed her up the steps. He was going to enjoy hearing Maddie tell him to come to bed—every night for the rest of his life.

When Maddie closed the bedroom door she glanced back to see Jonah doffing his shirt and his holsters. He had said he was here to stay and she believed him. But this time she needed to hear the words that bound him to her forever, and he was going to have to come to *her*. She was not going to throw herself at him the way she usually did. Not this time, at least.

When Jonah ambled toward her to wrap her in his sinewy arms, she smiled in pleasure. Finally! This was the first step in the right direction.

"I hope you know that you scared ten more years off my life out there tonight. For a moment I wasn't sure you were going to live long enough for me to tell you how I felt about you." He inhaled a deep breath, stared her straight in the eye and said, "I love you, princess. It has taken me two days to work up the nerve to say the words because I've never said them to anyone before."

When Maddie didn't fling her arms around his neck and kiss him breathless, Jonah angled his head to the side and said, "Something wrong, princess?"

"Yes, I'm waiting."

He frowned, confused. "Waiting for what?"

"You said you were going to prove that you'll never leave me again." She tilted her chin challengingly. "So prove it, Mr. Ranger."

"I'm not a Ranger anymore. I resigned. Boone is my replacement.... Will you marry me?"

"Yes," she said without hesitation.

Still she made no move toward him. Jonah blew out an exasperated breath. "Now what?"

Maddie sent him a withering glance. "When you left here two days ago you accused me of seducing you twice, and insulted me by saying that I was too forward."

Jonah grinned. "Now I get it."

"Not from me, you won't," she sassed him. "Am I going to have to hit you over the head before it finally soaks in that I'm not going to throw myself shamelessly at you ever again?"

"Never?"

"Absolutely not," she confirmed.

Chuckling, Jonah scooped her up in his arms and

carried her to the four-poster bed. "You want me to seduce you, I take it."

"That's exactly what I want."

Jonah grinned rakishly as he tugged off her boots, then removed her shirt—carefully, so as not to aggravate her mending shoulder. When he had her out of her riding breeches, lying naked on that fancy bed that was fit for a princess, he feasted his appreciative gaze on her. She was so beautiful to him that she nearly took his breath away. He still couldn't believe that she had chosen him when she could have any man she wanted.

"I do love a woman who knows exactly what she wants and isn't afraid to say so. No shrinking violet for me. I need a woman who gives as good as she gets."

His smile softened as he eased down beside her to trail his forefinger over the peak of her breast. When she moaned softly he bent to flick his tongue against her satiny flesh and felt her shiver in response. "How am I doing so far?"

"Not bad," Maddie said breathlessly. She then reached up to pull his head toward hers—and stopped just shy of touching him.

Jonah smiled in playful amusement. This stubborn beauty was going to make him pay for his outrageous remark, but he had no qualms about seducing her into grabbing hold of him as if she never meant to let go.

He kissed her, gently at first, then intensely, savoring the addicting taste of her. When she responded he felt the fire of desire coiling inside him, and wondered if she was going to outlast him. As for Jonah, he was about finished with stubborn challenges and making points. He wanted her so badly that he was going to have to resort to begging pretty quickly.

"I love you, Maddie," he whispered as his hand glided down her hip. "With all my heart and all my soul. I can't imagine loving anyone or anything as desperately and completely as I love you."

He must have said or done something right because she came alive in his arms and hugged the stuffing out of him.

"This is never going to work," Maddie said with a ragged breath. "No matter how hard I try, I can't keep my hands off you. I obviously have no willpower where you're concerned."

Jonah raised his head and grinned into her bewitching face. "Neither do I, princess. Maybe we should make a pact that it's okay to seduce each other anytime we feel like it."

Maddie smiled impishly at him. "That might be best." She kissed the breath clean out of him and said, "I love you so much, Jonah. Come here before I go crazy!"

He came to her, eagerly, and he thanked all the powers that be that Maddie had barged into his life. He was glad he had never been able to say no to her, had never been able to let her go. He had been a man without a home, a man who had forgotten how to hope and how to dream. But Maddie had transformed him, challenged him and given his life pleasure and new purpose. She had dared to love him and he was going to guard the precious gift she had given him.

"You are my heart, princess," he told her softly and sincerely.

"And you are mine, Jonah," she whispered back to him.

It took Jonah most of the night to communicate the all-encompassing love that had burned Maddie's name and her memory on his soul. But that was all right with him, because he wasn't leaving this canyon or this woman again.

And you could write *that* down in stone because he meant it with every beat of his heart and felt it all the way to the bottom of his soul. On that thought Jonah closed his eyes and cradled Maddie possessively in his arms.

He was definitely here to stay.

* * * * *

FALL IN LOVE WITH
THESE HANDSOME HEROES
FROM HARLEQUIN HISTORICALS

On sale September 2004

THE PROPOSITION
by Kate Bridges

Sergeant Major Travis Reid
Honorable Mountie of the Northwest

WHIRLWIND WEDDING
by Debra Cowan

Jericho Blue
Texas Ranger out for outlaws

On sale October 2004

ONE STARRY CHRISTMAS
by Carolyn Davidson/Carol Finch/Carolyn Banning

Three heart-stopping heroes
for your Christmas stocking!

THE ONE MONTH MARRIAGE
by Judith Stacy

Brandon Sayer
Businessman with a mission

www.eHarlequin.com

HARLEQUIN HISTORICALS®

If you enjoyed what you just read,
then we've got an offer you can't resist!

Take 2 bestselling
love stories FREE!

Plus get a FREE surprise gift!

Clip this page and mail it to Harlequin Reader Service®

IN U.S.A.
3010 Walden Ave.
P.O. Box 1867
Buffalo, N.Y. 14240-1867

IN CANADA
P.O. Box 609
Fort Erie, Ontario
L2A 5X3

YES! Please send me 2 free Harlequin Historicals® novels and my free surprise gift. After receiving them, if I don't wish to receive anymore, I can return the shipping statement marked cancel. If I don't cancel, I will receive 6 brand-new novels every month, before they're available in stores! In the U.S.A., bill me at the bargain price of $4.69 plus 25¢ shipping and handling per book and applicable sales tax, if any*. In Canada, bill me at the bargain price of $5.24 plus 25¢ shipping and handling per book and applicable taxes**. That's the complete price and a savings of over 10% off the cover prices—what a great deal! I understand that accepting the 2 free books and gift places me under no obligation ever to buy any books. I can always return a shipment and cancel at any time. Even if I never buy another book from Harlequin, the 2 free books and gift are mine to keep forever.

246 HDN DZ7Q
349 HDN DZ7R

Name	(PLEASE PRINT)	
Address	Apt.#	
City	State/Prov.	Zip/Postal Code

* Terms and prices subject to change without notice. Sales tax applicable in N.Y.
** Canadian residents will be charged applicable provincial taxes and GST.
   All orders subject to approval. Offer limited to one per household and not valid to
   current Harlequin Historicals® subscribers.
   ® are registered trademarks owned and used by the trademark owner and or its licensee.

HIST04   ©2004 Harlequin Enterprises Limited